"I devoured *Body Master* like really good chocolate: in big, happy chomps. A tough yet sympathetic heroine locks horns with a mysterious, sexy hero—ooh, yum! Barry's skillfully structured story delivers all kinds of delicious pleasures—and zero calories. What more could a girl want?" —Angela Knight, *New York Times* bestselling author

"Sexy, intriguing, and a pure delight to read."
—Catherine Spangler, bestselling author

"This awesome book roars out of the starting gates and never looks back. Along with telling social commentary, it is chock-full of danger, adventure, and romance—a terrific keeper!"
—*Romantic Times* (4 ½ stars)

"Ms. Barry's storytelling alone makes her an author not to be missed." —*Fallen Angel Reviews*

"Simply put, *Unmasked* is one awesome book. Action, adventure, love, danger. Books just don't get better than this, and C. J. Barry proves once again why she is such a staple in this genre."
—*Romance Reviews Today*

"This is without a doubt the best otherworldly book that C. J. Barry has written thus far . . . Action-packed adrenaline-rushing adventure kept me glued to the pages of this book." —*The Best Reviews*

"Ms. Barry takes us on a wild trip through space . . . This is a must read for any fan of futuristic romances, as Ms. Barry's world-building technique is right on target." —*Romance Junkies*

BODY MASTER

C. J. BARRY

BERKLEY SENSATION, NEW YORK

THE BERKLEY PUBLISHING GROUP
Published by the Penguin Group
Penguin Group (USA) Inc.
375 Hudson Street, New York, New York 10014, USA
Penguin Group (Canada), 90 Eglinton Avenue East, Suite 700, Toronto, Ontario M4P 2Y3, Canada
(a division of Pearson Penguin Canada Inc.)
Penguin Books Ltd., 80 Strand, London WC2R 0RL, England
Penguin Group Ireland, 25 St. Stephen's Green, Dublin 2, Ireland (a division of Penguin Books Ltd.)
Penguin Group (Australia), 250 Camberwell Road, Camberwell, Victoria 3124, Australia
(a division of Pearson Australia Group Pty. Ltd.)
Penguin Books India Pvt. Ltd., 11 Community Centre, Panchsheel Park, New Delhi—110 017, India
Penguin Group (NZ), 67 Apollo Drive, Rosedale, North Shore 0632, New Zealand
(a division of Pearson New Zealand Ltd.)
Penguin Books (South Africa) (Pty.) Ltd., 24 Sturdee Avenue, Rosebank, Johannesburg 2196,
South Africa

Penguin Books Ltd., Registered Offices: 80 Strand, London WC2R 0RL, England

This book is an original publication of The Berkley Publishing Group.

This is a work of fiction. Names, characters, places, and incidents either are the product of the author's
imagination or are used fictitiously, and any resemblance to actual persons, living or dead, business es-
tablishments, events, or locales is entirely coincidental. The publisher does not have any control over and
does not assume any responsibility for author or third-party websites or their content.

Copyright © 2010 by C. J. Barry.
Excerpt from *The Body Thief* by C. J. Barry copyright © by C. J. Barry.
Cover illustration by Phil Heffernan.
Cover design by George Long.
Interior text design by Tiffany Estreicher.

All rights reserved.
No part of this book may be reproduced, scanned, or distributed in any printed or electronic form without permission. Please do not participate in or encourage piracy of copyrighted materials in violation of
the author's rights. Purchase only authorized editions.
BERKLEY® SENSATION and the "B" design are trademarks of Penguin Group (USA) Inc.

PRINTING HISTORY
Berkley Sensation trade paperback edition / August 2010

Library of Congress Cataloging-in-Publication Data

Barry, C. J.
  Body master / C. J. Barry.
     p. cm.
  ISBN 978-0-425-23455-6
  1. Shapeshifting—Fiction. 2. New York (N.Y.)—Fiction. I. Title.
  PS3602.A777549B63   2010
  813'.6—dc22   2010014027

PRINTED IN THE UNITED STATES OF AMERICA

10 9 8 7 6 5 4 3 2 1

This book is dedicated to my wonderful, creative, and talented siblings—my brother, Tom, and my sisters, Cheri and Chris. How we all became writers is a mystery that only God can explain.

ACKNOWLEDGMENTS

This book is brought to you by the best people I know. People like my terrific agent, Roberta Brown, my equally terrific editor, Kate Seaver, and the hardworking staff at Berkley Sensation. My writer friends Lani Diane Rich/Lucy March, Jennifer Crusie, Catherine Wade, and Rebecca Rohan. My beta-readers Jill Purinton and Patti Newell. All my Will Write for Wine podcast listeners, aka the Wiffers. Many unsuspecting friends and coworkers who feed me cool names and provide creative fodder. My talented family of musicians and writers—my parents, Tom and Jean Dishaw, my brother, Tom Dishaw, and sisters, Christina Walker and Cheri Farnsworth. And, of course, my husband, Ed, and beautiful children, Rachel and Ryan.

These are my people, the people who love and support me, and make me look good. My heartfelt thanks go out to each and every one of them.

CHAPTER
ONE

"Wait 'til I tell my wife we got Jack the Ripper."

Seneca looked over at her partner, Riley, sitting in the driver's side of the surveillance van.

She said, "A little premature, don't you think? We haven't even seen him yet."

Riley turned to her, the lone streetlight illuminating his balding head and cocky grin. "Never say premature to a guy, Seneca."

He tipped his half-eaten hamburger in the direction of the Harlem warehouse half a block away, shadowed in darkness and disrepair. "As soon as that Shifter comes home, we're going to waltz in there and kick his sorry ass."

She shook her head at Riley's ability to take every life and death situation and make it sound like a trip to McDonald's. Bringing down an alien shapeshifter was strictly for the pros.

"Jack might give himself up, you know. That would spoil all your fun," she told him.

Riley laughed and almost choked on his burger. "No way. Shifters never go down without a fight."

That was true. At least the mean ones. The "good" shapeshifters just hid among Americans, watching, learning, waiting. Seneca shook off the bitterness that rose in her belly and scanned the night.

The surrounding city blocks were empty except for muggers and drug addicts and XCEL agents like her and Riley. This was their job. Shapeshifter hunters got paid to be crazy. The other crazies didn't even know shapeshifters were here. And if they did, no one believed them anyway. Either way, the public was still clueless, and her undercover agency worked damned hard to keep it that way.

"I don't know, Riley," she said. "I've been sitting here for three days watching you eat your body weight in burgers, and he hasn't shown his face yet. Maybe our Roto-Rooter van's been made."

Riley answered with his mouth full. "Naw. Everyone needs their pipes cleaned out sometime, especially in this part of town. Lots of rats." He twisted in his seat. "But I hope to hell he comes home soon. I miss sleeping with my wife."

Seneca eyed him. "I noticed. You're steaming up the windows again."

He winked. "You should see me when I'm really hot. This van would spontaneously combust."

Life according to Riley: work, sex, and fast food. Seneca

laughed and sipped her coffee. "You ever wonder what you would have done with the past two years if the Shifters hadn't crash-landed in the South Dakota Badlands?"

"Probably sitting behind some desk shooting rubber bands at you all day." Then he beamed. "But look at us now. The best Shifter team that Earth has to offer—hunting down public enemy number one. Hot damn."

Hot damn, indeed. Their target, Jack the Ripper, had earned his code name by mutilating and dismembering three people in an all-night convenience store two weeks ago. Not even the money he stole had been enough to satisfy that bastard. Then he'd blended in with the general population again. And that was why she was here.

It wasn't her fault that she'd become a shapeshifter hunter. If they hadn't escaped their planet and crashed here, if they hadn't decided to steal our DNA and look like us, if they weren't hell-bent on criminal activities, she and Riley wouldn't be sitting in a van waiting to apprehend one of them.

And it *certainly* wasn't her fault that she was one of the few in the world who could see them for the monsters they were. They couldn't hide from her, and she couldn't ignore them.

"What would *you* be doing?" Riley asked her.

She smiled. "Arresting bad guys who didn't turn into blood-thirsty aliens when they got pissed off."

He gave her a disbelieving look. "Now, see, this is your problem. No life. You need a man. I happen to have a friend—"

Oh hell, here we go with the friend. "Forget it. I've met your friends, and I wouldn't be caught dead dating any of them."

"Hey, there's nothing wrong—" he started, and then his gaze

turned serious and locked on something outside. "We have action." He wadded up the rest of his burger and tossed it in the back while she grabbed the night vision binoculars.

Sure enough, a car had pulled around the corner and parked in the alley beside the warehouse. A lone male stepped out—six foot tall, two hundred pounds easy, and wearing a winter coat. He matched the general description they had.

As he walked to the back of the building, she focused on the ghostly shadow around his body that only she could see. It was shaped like a giant demon. Definitely a Shifter. Her second vision might be a curse, but she had no qualms using it to ferret out the aliens.

"What do you think?" Riley asked.

She stowed the binoculars and climbed in the back. "Close enough to say, *Stick 'em up*."

Riley smacked the steering wheel. "Hot damn! I'm getting laid tonight."

After Riley called for the cleanup crew, they pulled on tactical headgear with integrated night vision and communications, protective body armor, and custom shoulder harnesses. Seneca strapped on her thigh holsters and slipped in her two Glock 33s. A backup KA-BAR knife went into the vest along with a single-shot tranquilizer handgun, a disrupter pistol, and extra ammo.

Riley carried the same equipment as well as explosive impact grenades. They finished gearing up quickly and silently. Long, light, black trench coats went over everything. She felt the weight of her weapons as she stood up, but there was no other way. No single weapon worked on every Shifter. There were nights when she'd used almost everything she had to bring a powerful one down. Carrying AA-12 semiautomatic shotguns, they hit the pavement fully armed under cover of night.

Seneca's pulse quickened as she moved behind Riley, taking in everything—locked and boarded storefronts, the smell of sewer, and the *thrum-thrum* of the city. Two agents against one Shifter. It was a strategy that had cost a lot of lives to develop, but two agents were enough to take down the suspect while still keeping the situation contained and quiet. *If* the agents were good. She and Riley were very good.

As always, her training kicked in with the official XCEL agency mantra that was burned into her brain.

Level 1: Suspect compliance. Response—arrest. Which was a joke because they never complied.

Level 2: Suspect resistance. Response—containment and appropriate force. There was *always* resistance.

Level 3: Suspect assault. Response—all necessary force. That one was her personal favorite.

They were thirty feet from Jack's front door when gunfire erupted from a first-floor window of the warehouse and shattered the silence. Chunks of pavement sprayed around them.

Seneca dove behind a parked Honda with Riley beside her. She leaned toward him. "I think that qualifies as Level Three."

"Oh yeah," he replied. In unison, they swung up and fired back. She yelled out, "Police! You are under arrest. Come out with your hands up!"

Return fire poured through a broken window and peppered the Honda. Glass shattered and sprinkled to the ground. XCEL was going to owe someone a car.

"You know, we should just stop saying that. No one ever listens to us," Riley said. "How about we try, 'Show yourself or we'll come in there and blow your fucking brains out'? I bet that'd work."

She flipped her communications device on. "Put your money where your mouth is, Riley."

They moved behind the car with Jack watching them from the window, almost challenging them to fire. Riley took a shot with the tranquilizer, but Jack had shifted from human form to Shifter and the powerful sedative cartridge bounced off his head harmlessly.

"Shit," Riley said. "Looks like we're going to have to do this the hard way."

Seneca gave a short laugh. "It's always the hard way."

"And that's why you love it. This is like foreplay to you."

She countered. "And sometimes it's better."

"You gotta get yourself a man." Riley reloaded the tranq weapon and pulled the disrupter pistol from his holster. It was designed to deliver a potent electromagnetic charge that would temporarily disorient the Shifter's molecular pattern long enough for the tranquilizer to stick and work. Unless Jack had adapted to the disrupter, in which case, things would get really ugly.

"I'm taking the back door," Riley said. "Cover me."

Seneca laid down fire as he sprinted into the side alley. Her burst lit up the night and littered streets in shades of gray. As soon as Riley was clear, she ducked behind the car and held her fire.

Jack didn't shoot back and the city that never slept closed in on her. Car alarms jangled in the night. No sirens, which was a good sign. It meant that the XCEL cleanup crew was on-site.

They'd take care of the local authorities, the press, and anyone else asking too many questions. Her job was to take care of Jack.

Seneca listened carefully for movement, but it was all quiet inside. She scanned the building. The sensors in her duty visor didn't pick up a heat signature from Jack anymore. *Where'd he go?*

"In position," Riley whispered in her earpiece.

"Jack's on the move," she warned him.

"He's still inside. We got the exits covered. When you're ready, let me know and I'll toss in a flashbang to clear the way."

She scrambled to her feet, raced for the front door, and slammed her back against the wall. A quick check of the handle revealed it was locked.

She told Riley, "I'll need a second to blow the lock on the front door before I move in."

"Just don't shoot me again."

She narrowed her eyes. "I only did that once, and it barely nicked you, you big baby."

"Yeah, well next time you might hit a vital organ. I'd like to have a few more kids before I die."

She shook her head. Riley already had four kids. "I'm set here."

Riley said, "Three, two, one—"

There was a flash of light and a powerful concussion that blew out the front windows as Riley's grenade went off inside.

Seneca spun, shot through the knob, and kicked the door in. It crashed against the inside wall as she entered, gun ready. No sign of Jack, but she heard heavy footsteps above her.

Riley shouted in her ear. "I'm on the second floor. He's heading up the back stairs to the third."

She raced through the doorways and rooms of the warehouse. "Wait for me!"

"No, I'm good. I got him cornered," he replied, breathing hard. Gunfire exploded throughout the building.

Goddamnit, Riley, she thought. Fear pushed her faster as she took the stairs two at a time. When she hit the top step, there was a beat of silence, and then a hellish scream. She knew what had happened even as she raced toward the sound.

She cleared the doorway that opened into a cavernous room lined with boxes and crates. Her night vision turned the streetlight green through broken windowpanes and outlined a huge shapeshifter pulling his hand out of Riley's stomach as he lay on the floor. Jack lifted it to the light and inspected the dark blood.

Seneca staggered under the emotional impact of Riley's death gurgle, and then his heat signature dimmed in her visor.

Oh God, no.

The Shifter looked at her and grinned, brandishing a row of razor-sharp teeth. Fresh dread rolled over her.

Focus, Seneca. Stay focused.

He was in Primary Shifter form, deadly from his smooth, domed head to his clawed fingers to powerful, massive thighs. Black armorlike skin flexed over a muscular body. Eerie, alien gold eyes met hers. A blank, cold-blooded canvas, capable of replicating anyone.

"Next?" he hissed.

And with that, her fear was gone, snuffed out like Riley's life. Now there was only rage. She ripped off her headgear and tossed it aside. "I think it's your turn, asshole."

He spread his arms wide and took a bobbing step toward her. "Go ahead. Shoot away."

It wouldn't do any good; she knew that now. He wouldn't dare her if he hadn't adapted to bullets. He'd simply thin his molecular structure so they'd pass right through him.

On the other hand, she'd feel much better. So she hit him with the AA-12 in nonstop bursts. Jack simply stood there, and the ammo pelted the wall and windows behind him.

He threw his head back and laughed, the sound echoing through the building.

Bastard.

She glanced at the 3GL grenades strapped to Riley, twenty feet away. Too far. With her options dwindling fast, she settled on her instincts. That, and the one thing she could always count on with Shifters—their unqualified arrogance.

Jack suddenly vanished in a puff of black smoke and materialized a few feet away. Terrific, he was one of the more powerful ones. All Shifters were killing machines—lightning fast, deadly hands, thick armor skin. But one of their deadliest weapons was the ability to thin their structure to reduce friction so they could move fast—really fast. Becoming shadows. It was going to be a challenge to get her hands on him without being sliced to ribbons.

She breathed and harnessed her anger and anguish, pushing them deeply into her concentration. She'd rather die here with Riley than leave this monster alive, or worse, allow him replicate to Riley's DNA.

Her right hand flexed in anticipation and hope. *Just work one more time,* she said to herself. And so far, it had. Which was why she still used it. Luck was for suckers.

He poofed, and her second vision followed the trail he left behind. He seemed surprised as she turned to face him before he re-formed.

He said, "Aren't you gonna try to run? I'll even give you a head start."

That's more than I'll give you. "No, I'm good."

He rushed forward in a cloud of black smoke, bringing him a few feet away. She saw the hunger in his black eyes and felt the evil in his black heart. Cold air flowed around her.

"I like killin' the girls," Jack said, thoroughly enjoying his little game.

Bud, you are in for the surprise of your life. She repositioned her hands around the shotgun. "Then you should know, I'm not like other girls."

"You all taste the same to me." He lunged then, mouth open, and she jammed her gun down his throat. For a split second, he gagged, and in that second, she pressed her right hand to his chest.

Concentrate, breathe . . . "Shift!"

A burst of heat pumped through her hand, coming from a source she didn't understand and didn't question. All that mattered was what it did to Shifters. It changed them, forcing them to shift back to whoever they were last.

She wasn't kidding. She really wasn't like other girls.

The intense energy hurt, driving electricity up her arm. She pulled her hand away, stretching a ribbon of white residual energy between them until it snapped. The Shifter knocked the shotgun out of his mouth with a roar and then took a few steps back.

She held her ground, waiting. Jack's eyes widened as his

chest began to contract around where her hand had been, and he clutched his stomach and stumbled to the floor.

His body contorted grotesquely, and his joints began popping, skin rippling with twisted bones. The clawed hands sprouted rudimentary finger buds. The thick legs narrowed. His head imploded and then reshaped.

All the while, she listened to his screams with cold indifference. This was what he deserved. The same mercy he'd shown Riley and the other innocent people he'd murdered. There was no compassion in his soul, no conscience in his mind. Nothing worth saving.

She walked over to Riley and knelt to check for a pulse, even though she knew it wouldn't be there. His Kevlar vest and chest had been sliced open cleanly.

"Oh, Riley," she whispered.

A sudden sob clutched her throat, piercing her heart beneath all her armor. A hundred thoughts flooded her mind, but one was crystal clear—she'd failed him. She hung her head. *I'm sorry.*

The Shifter had stopped writhing by the time she pulled herself together. Tranquilizer gun in hand, she stood over Jack's human form, the last shape he'd used, created from stolen human DNA. He was just your average guy. Could have been her neighbor or a Wall Street broker or a husband with a wife and kids. Shifters didn't care where or how they got their "skins."

In her mind's eye, the Shifter's demon form shimmered around him like a ghost. He was still an alien, but right now he was as vulnerable as any human.

She fought the urge to use her Glock instead of a tranquilizer. She could easily blame it on self-defense. She could even justify it with Riley's death. No one would question her. No one would care if one more Shifter died.

But her orders were to bring in Shifters alive whenever possible, and she was a good agent, like Riley. She wouldn't disgrace his memory. Not today.

Today, she lifted the tranquilizer gun, aimed, and hit Jack the Ripper in the heart.

CHAPTER
TWO

Seneca knocked once and walked into her boss's office. He looked up from behind the placard that read XCEL: Extra-terrestrial Criminal Enforcement Locality, New York City Division, and motioned for her to sit down.

Director Rory MacGregor was as solid on the inside as he was on the outside. A twenty-year veteran of the politics and bullshit that went along with running a newly created, clandestine perimeter law enforcement operation like XCEL. Seneca was pretty sure he'd started with a full head of hair when he was assigned to this post last year. He was a good man, and he hated Shifters as much as she did.

"You barked?" she asked wearily, but already she could tell it was something bad. Although at this point, "bad" was relative.

MacGregor closed the file he was reviewing to give her his full attention. "I have some news you aren't going to like."

If MacGregor thought she wouldn't like it, it was beyond bad. "I had to go over and tell Riley's wife that the man she loved, the father of her four children, had been killed. Nothing can be worse than that."

His expression didn't change. "You have a new partner."

Her mouth dropped open. "Riley's body isn't even cold yet. What the hell?"

MacGregor muttered, "News travels fast."

"What, are they lined up in the wings?" she said testily.

"You weren't supposed to get him until the end of the month—"

"What? And you didn't tell me?"

MacGregor said, "Because I knew you'd react like this."

If she wasn't so pissed, she'd be speechless. "Like someone who already *had* a partner?"

He raised a hand. "It's for the good of the agency—"

That was crap. "We don't break up partners," she said. "We don't work that way. *You* don't work that way."

"I do now," he said. "You have a new partner."

She squinted as he pursed his lips until they turned white. There was more. "And?"

There was a long pause, which really worried her because MacGregor was a blunt, direct kind of guy. "And he's a Shifter."

She blinked once. She'd been up all night and all day after handing Jack over to the cryogenics boys to put on ice, taking Riley's body to the morgue, and consoling Mara. It was 4:00 P.M. now, and her sleep-deprived brain wasn't firing on all pistons. Because she *thought* she heard MacGregor say that her new partner was a Shifter.

"Come again?"

He looked at her apologetically. "It wasn't my idea. This comes from the top. A new initiative."

She shook her head, disbelief turning to dread. "This is a joke, right?"

He pursed his lips again. *Sonofabitch,* she thought. "What the hell kind of initiative puts a shapeshifter on the force that's supposed to be getting rid of them?"

MacGregor gave a big sigh. "Apparently, this one."

Well, she was wide-awake now and all she wanted to say was, *Are you fucking crazy?* Luckily, a few responsible brain cells thought better and she said, "No. We aren't doing this."

He held up his palm. "Don't even try. This is bigger than you or me."

Apparently he hadn't heard her the first time. "Okay, let me rephrase. *I'm* not doing this."

MacGregor pushed back in his chair and regarded her for a serious moment. "If you don't take him, the Committee will shut us down."

She leaned over his desk. "We go out there and face death every night. We're the only thing standing between the public and murderers who come in all shapes. How can the Committee even think about shutting us down?"

He shrugged. "Because they're paying the bills?"

She couldn't believe this was MacGregor. The man who handpicked every member of this team. The man who never left this office. The man who'd built this agency from the ground up. "Why are you buying into this crap?"

He looked at her, and she caught his frustration full bore. "I've lost twenty-seven agents in the past year. Two-thirds of my force. It's the same in the XCEL offices in Chicago, LA, Vegas, Miami . . . The Committee doesn't find that acceptable, and frankly, neither do I. I'm tired of seeing my agents come back to me in body bags."

He didn't need to quote statistics to her. Twenty-six funerals were forever burned in her memory. Soon to be twenty-seven. She knew the stakes. She also knew what would happen if they stopped trying.

"We've also captured over eighty Shifters," she reminded him.

"Sixty-two of those were in the first nine months," he pointed out. "Now they've adapted to every conventional weapon we have, and R and D can't develop new ones fast enough. And hell, we still don't have equipment to identify a Shifter on sight. One could walk in that door, and we wouldn't know it."

"We can handle this ourselves," she told him, feeling her dread grow. "All those deaths will have been for nothing if the Committee lets Shifters in here."

"You can't look at it that way," he said. "It isn't about vengeance. It's about finding a policy that works." He stood up slowly with a grunt and walked to the window overlooking Manhattan. "All we're doing now is wasting time and lives."

"That's not true," she said, her fists clenching in her lap.

"Maybe not, but something needs to change."

She rubbed her forehead where the dull headache she'd had for the past few hours was turning to thunder. "I have an idea. How about we round all the Shifters up, put them on the space shuttle, and send them back where they came from?"

MacGregor snorted. "If only it were that easy, and they were that stupid. Christ. They've managed to master to our DNA, learn our language and our customs, blend in. This is a great place to live if you can become anyone you want."

The bastards *could* be any human they wanted to, become an exact replica. She'd seen them on the streets, walking around like they belonged here. They didn't. But XCEL agents were strung out thin as it was, and she was too busy dealing with the bad ones to worry about the ones posing as model citizens.

Besides, unless she wanted everyone to know she *could* see Shifters, she'd have to keep her mouth shut. If she didn't, she'd be labeled a freak, lose her XCEL job, and her second vision would be worthless. Nothing but pure torture.

Seneca crossed her arms. "It doesn't help that we have to catch these guys and keep it all quiet, like they don't exist. We can't even go after them in the daylight, when they don't have the ability to shift."

MacGregor sat back down at his desk. "No argument from me. I'm too goddamned old to work all these nights, but the Committee thinks we'd cause too much chaos."

"God forbid their secret gets out," she muttered.

He sighed. "Don't start. The Committee also wants alternatives to freezing these guys. Something more productive."

Seneca looked at him. "Alternatives to freezing? Do they really think these criminals can be rehabilitated?"

MacGregor only shrugged, and Seneca added, "There's nothing wrong with putting them on ice after they maim and murder until we figure out what to do with them."

"Except that we've never successfully thawed one out," he pointed out.

Her turn to shrug. "Minor detail. If it were up to me, I'd put them all out of our misery."

"This is still America," MacGregor reminded her.

"Not for long."

"You don't know that." But he didn't sound entirely convinced. "Try to look at this from the point of view that we could do better. This guy is a prototype shapeshifter XCEL agent. He volunteered for this. Gave us more information about Shifters than we could ever get on our own. He's been tested, retested, studied, probed God knows where, and passed all our training with flying colors. He can ID his own kind, get into places we can't, and he can take them on head-to-head."

Like she cared. She could do those things too. "If he's so great, why does he need us?"

MacGregor gave her a telling look. "They want to see how he partners with one of our own."

Real fear replaced the dread in her bones, and that took some doing. "They want to change our partner structure? One Shifter and one human?"

"Maybe," he hedged.

Or worse. Her heart sank in understanding. "All-Shifter teams."

"Unless we can prove we're good for something," he admitted.

"Good for something? How about to keep an eye on *them*?" she shot back. He didn't say anything, and the reality of it hit her. She'd be out of the loop, and *they* would be in control. Good God, what was this world coming to?

"We can't trust them, Mac. You're giving them too much

credit. And the Committee is talking out of their collective asses. Have they ever seen a Shifter in action?"

MacGregor answered, "The majority of Shifters keep to themselves."

"It's only a matter of time before that changes. Once the Shifters feel they can take us, they will. And they can."

MacGregor shook his head. "I'm just saying, they aren't *all* bad."

"Tell that to my mutilated partner."

He rubbed his eyes. "I get it, okay? But we don't have a choice, Seneca. The Committee has spoken. *Our* job is to keep America safe from the Shifter criminal element so we don't have rioting in the streets. And that's just what you are going to do."

She slumped further in her chair. This day was pure hell.

"And another thing," he went on. "*Everyone* is watching this collaboration. Consider your ass under a microscope, because your new partner is writing the final report. Apparently, he has friends in higher places than you or me." He paused. "Be very careful."

Although they never discussed her extraordinary abilities, MacGregor knew she was different from the other agents. Only a handful of people knew exactly how different. And one of them was stretched out in the morgue.

"Do I get to write my report on him?" she asked.

He replied, "Fine by me. But I can't promise you it'll go anywhere."

Perfect. She pushed to her feet, fighting the weight of the day. "Why me?"

"That's what you get for being the best." MacGregor smiled and folded his hands on his belly. "He's waiting outside. Name's

Max Dempsey. And I'd prefer you keep his secret identity just between the two of us. No sense in causing undue friction."

She stared at him, trying to restrain herself from doing something stupid like telling her boss to shove it. All she could do was say, "You call keeping our agents informed that there's a Shifter among them 'undue friction'?"

He raised his hands. "Don't shoot the messenger. No one is supposed to know until we get the final report. The fate of this entire operation depends on you. So play nice."

"I don't have to be nice to do my job."

"Fine, just don't kill him." He handed her a folder. "Your next assignment. Code name 'Dillinger.' Confirmed Shifter. He murdered six people in a bar in lower Manhattan last week."

◆ ◆ ◆

Seneca stormed out of the office with Dillinger's folder and slammed the door behind her. The outer office area was an open suite lined with desks in the center and private offices around the perimeter. It was usually a noisy, hopping place, but as soon as she stepped out, it got real quiet. Heads poked out from every cubicle and corner.

An agent wearing a lanyard badge stood in front of her. He was well over six foot tall and solidly built under a leather jacket, white-collared shirt, and blue jeans. His hair was thick and brown, eyes a muted shade of gray, face angular, hard, and serious.

A Shifter shadow pulsed around him that no one except her or another Shifter could see.

He studied her for a moment and wisely didn't offer a hand to shake. "Agent Max Dempsey. Nice to meet you, Seneca."

Fuck you, was on the tip of her tongue, and he must have seen it in her eyes because one of his eyebrows rose marginally.

The enemy stood in the center of her sanctuary. It wasn't fair. She'd busted her ass to get here and, along the way, lost more friends than she could count. She'd put in seventy-hour weeks, become a permanent night owl, and bore scars of missions gone wrong. She hated the bastards ripping her world apart with a passion second to none. If she could give her life to get rid of every single one of them, she would.

The other agents and staff were pretending to be busy, but a few were watching with growing interest.

The fate of this entire operation depends on you.

Boy, did they pick the wrong person. But like a good little soldier, she flashed the folder and walked around him toward her office. "We have a case."

He let her pass, but she heard his footsteps as he followed. She sat behind her desk while he closed the door and took Riley's chair at the desk facing her. Her throat tightened up when she heard his chair creak.

Riley was gone. His wife had no husband, his kids had no father, and she was going to miss the hell out of him.

Now she was being betrayed by her own people. From the gutless suits who sat in their offices all day making up politically correct policy and didn't have a damn clue what was happening in the real world. They had no idea how much damage five thousand plus aliens could inflict on their people.

That was what kept her from sleep, and that was what kept her coming back here every night.

Dempsey leaned back, watching her as she shuffled through

the file. She sensed curiosity and slight amusement, which only made her want to shoot him more.

She read the report. Six dead, killed by Dillinger after he lost a pool game and shifted from a mild-mannered boozer to Primary-form shapeshifter murderer. How many of these had she read? Forty? Fifty? They all had the same ending. Innocent people died horribly.

She turned the page to find a description of both his forms—Shifter and human. One thing the agency had learned was that it took a good deal of time and energy for a shapeshifter to assume the genetic coding of a new form. So once they did, they used it a lot. The shifts were fast, and when the transformation was complete, the form was self-maintaining. Good for the Shifter; bad for everyone else.

After she gleaned what she could out of the written report, Seneca handed it to Dempsey without comment. She realized it was rude, but he had eyes. He could read it himself.

A stack of photos was next, apparently taken during the melee at Dave's Bar & Grill. She blinked when she saw them, because they almost never got photos. Usually, it required lots of legwork and investigation to identify all the Shifter forms. Weeks of work. And then it occurred to her—MacGregor had given them a gimme assignment so they'd look good. Hell. Nothing was going right today.

One photo was of Dillinger as a human, wearing a tattered flannel shirt and baggy pants and swinging a pool stick just before all hell broke loose. Scruffy beard, unkempt and unholy. The rest of the photos were of him in Primary form on the attack.

She glanced at the note attached to them. It said Dillinger

killed the photographer, who'd been using a camera phone, but the photos had survived. It was duly noted that "luckily," no one had survived long enough to tell the press.

She clenched her jaw tightly. It was getting more and more difficult to hide the fact that the aliens were here. One of these days, the government was going to have to come clean to the people of this country.

Or not. Look at Roswell.

She handed the photos off to Dempsey. As she passed them over, he didn't take them, forcing her gaze up. His eyes locked onto hers.

His voice low. "I want all this to stop as much as you do."

"Do you?" She let the photos drop on the desk between them. "And why would that be?"

He grinned, like the devil. "World peace, what else?"

You are so full of shit, she thought as she stared back.

He scanned the photos and then read the note. Disgust altered his features briefly, which she had to admit were pretty attractive. Then she wondered whose DNA he'd stolen and how. Blood? Tissue? Skin? Her thoughts spiraled downward from there.

"Do you recognize the killer?" she asked bluntly.

Dempsey's eyes cut to hers with irritation. "No. Do you?"

She smirked. "I know it's not one of my boys."

He passed the photos back. "How do you want to handle this?"

"You're asking me?"

He shrugged. "You're the senior."

Right. Until you write your report, and then I'll be tied to this desk stapling reports together for the rest of my career.

She gathered the file contents. "The normal channels are already covered. APB, informants, rewards, and all that good stuff. So since the only witnesses were murdered, I thought we'd start by flashing Dillinger's photos around some of the bars in the neighborhood tonight."

He gave a little nod. "That might stir things up."

She closed the folder and stood up. "Right. I'm going home to get a few hours' sleep. I'll meet you tonight at Dave's around eleven P.M. I want to check the crime scene first."

She reached for her coat. It was right next to one of Riley's, and her hand hesitated a fraction of a second before grabbing her own.

Dempsey was in her personal space when she turned around. He touched her wrist lightly, and she froze at the unwelcome invasion. It took every ounce of self-control she had left not to reach for her gun.

After a beat, he said, "You may not believe this, but I am sorry about your partner."

Anger and pain rose in her belly. *It's your fault.* She knew that wasn't true and it wasn't fair, but the last thing she wanted was pity from a Shifter. What did he care? Did he know Riley told the worst jokes in the world? That his youngest daughter would be graduating from kindergarten without her daddy? Had he spent the last year listening to Riley's country music? No. She wasn't going to let Riley die for nothing. And they couldn't make her forget him by giving her another partner.

"Didn't take you long to step into his shoes," she said, her voice cracking.

Dempsey stepped back and shoved his hands in his jeans pockets. "Is that the problem here?"

"Believe me, that's the least of your problems." She felt the tears behind her eyes and pushed past Dempsey before he noticed. "I'll see you at eleven."

When she reached the underground parking garage, she pulled out her cell phone and called MacGregor.

He answered on the first ring. "Yeah."

Through tears that had started to flow uncontrollably, she said, "I want to see the departmental file on Dempsey in my mail slot first thing tomorrow, whether or not the Committee approves." Then she hung up and let the tears come.

CHAPTER
THREE

Max watched her leave. His fingers still held the warmth of her skin. Her scent lingered in his mind, logged for future reference. Her sleek black hair and dark brown eyes were etched in his memory. She was tall and lean with a fire in her soul that burned everything she touched.

And did she *ever* hate him.

She wasn't afraid to let him know either. He was sure the only reason he still possessed a hand was because of her discussion with her boss. Not that Max expected anything less. He was the enemy here, always would be. His race had been responsible for countless human deaths. He was already guilty by association.

There was a knock on the door behind him.

"Come in," Max said.

Rory MacGregor entered and shut the door behind him. The

older man crossed his arms. Defensive and dominant body language for humans. No friends in the building today.

"How did your first meeting go?" MacGregor asked.

"I still have all my body parts."

MacGregor grunted. "She's been through a lot today. Give her some time to warm up to you."

Max grinned. Never going to happen. "Right."

"Got everything you need?"

"I'm fine, thank you," Max said.

MacGregor looked at his feet. "Just so you know the routine here, we start the night shift with roll call. Anyone who's not on a stakeout or undercover is expected to attend."

"Makes sense."

MacGregor's gaze rose to meet his. "We discuss the cases, administrative bullshit, and the latest technology against Shifters. What we've learned. How to stop them. How to kill them, if necessary. I know that's not the official policy, but if my agents are in a life or death situation, they have the right to protect themselves."

And Max bet that every night was a life or death situation. "I think I can handle it."

"I hope so. I'll introduce you at the next roll call."

"Of course," Max said, almost automatically. 'Of course' was his answer to everything. He'd kissed ass for so long, it was becoming second nature.

"But if it gets too much for you," MacGregor added, "feel free to skip the meetings."

Max stared at him. Was he warning him, or telling him not to attend? "I'll be there."

MacGregor's gaze met his for a few moments before the older man nodded. An awkward silence fell. Finally, he murmured a good-bye and left.

Max waited for his irritation to simmer down. It was an exercise in patience that was tempered only by his real reason for being here. He'd bucked every person in this damn agency just to get to this point. Taken more shit in the past few months than he ever had in his entire life. He should be getting used to it by now, but he always hoped that just once . . .

He sat down in a dead man's chair. Different planet, same old story. His people had never been welcomed to any planet they'd tried to settle on. Being able to replicate the native species always sparked terror in the hearts of locals. But living among them in Shifter form wasn't acceptable either. And so, planet after planet, they tried and failed. He just hoped he lived long enough to find his wife's killer before this planet turned on them too. Or at least until XCEL turned on him.

Because Max needed XCEL to find a murderer.

◆ ◆ ◆

It was dark again by the time Seneca got home and found a parking spot near the house she shared with her grandmother. For a moment, she sat in her car, wiping away tears, taking in the city she was trying to save. Streetlights glowed orange in a neat little row down the street. If only everything were so simple.

A cold New York chill breathed down her neck as she gathered her gear. Her mind was numb and her body shot. Sometimes her life felt like a never-ending nightmare.

It'd been a long, hard, shitty day all around so she was thankful when she opened the front door and smelled food. Noko walked out of the kitchen, drying her hands on a towel. She wore a long skirt and blouse that she'd sewn herself. The black, red, and turquoise geometric pattern set off flawless brown skin and soft eyes. Her grandmother was full-blood Iroquois and proud of it. Seneca was half-Iroquois, and that was all.

"There you are. I was worried," her grandmother said in her unhurried, gentle way.

Seneca silently berated herself for not calling. She dropped her stuff at the door and shrugged off her jacket. "Sorry. I didn't get a chance to check in. Had an emergency."

She gave Noko a kiss on the cheek and a quick hug on her way through. The warm kitchen barely contained the smell of beef stew. She lifted the cover on the pot and inhaled. Heaven. Or close as she was going to get to it today.

Seneca felt the stress seep out of her shoulders and reveled in the warmth. The kitchen was painted a soothing blue, set off by tall oak cabinets and wood floors. The massive center island was where meals were served, crammed with pots and pans and scraps of recipes. Soft overhead lights cast a loving glow over everything. This was a safety zone that the horrors of work hadn't penetrated.

"You are lucky it gets better the longer it cooks," Noko said, handing her a bowl that she filled to the brim. Noko sliced her a hunk of bread, and they bellied up to the center island. Noko silently watched her eat.

"You have been crying," Noko said after Seneca had wolfed down most of the stew.

Seneca looked up at her grandmother. The folds around Noko's cheeks and mouth were creased from many smiles, her eyes old and wise, missing nothing. Seneca had inherited the silky black hair, brown eyes, and smooth skin from this gene pool, but she doubted she'd live long enough to accumulate the wisdom.

"When you didn't come home last night, I thought you were with a man," Noko said with a flicker of mischief in her eyes.

Seneca set down the spoon. The words still came hard. "Riley was killed on the job last night."

Noko closed her eyes and nodded. That was it. As much emotion as her grandmother ever showed. But her silent understanding spoke louder than words. In her belief system, life was never over, the soul reborn in pure spirit of strength and goodness to watch over those they loved. Since Seneca was eight years old, Noko had patiently explained what she knew of the Iroquois way. But the old ways were for the old days. This was now, and Riley wasn't coming back in this lifetime.

Seneca rubbed her forehead where the mother of all headaches was tormenting her. "A Shifter murdered him. I couldn't get there in time." *He died. I failed. I failed again.*

She felt Noko's hand on her arm, warm and comforting. The heat of tears burned in her eyes, and she blinked a few times to push the past back to where it belonged. She couldn't fix the past. All she could do was fight for the future. "I don't know if we can stop them."

Noko made a long humming sound, and Seneca eyed her. Unwelcome words of truth usually followed the long hum, so Seneca continued. "And they gave me a new partner. A Shifter."

31

Noko's dark almond-shaped eyes blinked once. "You don't trust him."

"Of course not," Seneca said with more edge than she intended. She picked up her dishes and dumped the leftovers in the sink. "I spend every night fighting these guys, and now I'm forced to have one for a partner. I should quit."

"You were not given these gifts to waste," Noko said.

Seneca washed the bowl and put it in the strainer. "Yeah, about those gifts. It would have been nice if the Great Spirit had blessed me with laser vision or thunderbolts from my fingertips."

Noko asked, "Can the new partner help you?"

Seneca turned around and leaned against the counter. She hadn't even thought that one through. "I doubt it. If anything, it makes my job more difficult because I can't trust him. Not with my abilities or my back. Inside each of them lurks a demon waiting to attack."

Noko remained passive, nodded and hummed again. "You have a shape within you as well." She smiled tranquilly. "A white wolf. The Protector and Guide of the night. That is your totem."

Seneca shook her head. She was too tired for Native American lessons. "That's great. But I need to get some sleep. I have to go back out tonight."

"You don't believe me?" Noko said, her words stopping Seneca on her way out of the kitchen.

She turned and looked at her grandmother with a heavy sigh. "I believe that you believe, Grandmother, but don't ask me to accept it. Not here and now. Not with what I've seen."

"You see more than you know."

"Tell me about it," she muttered.

Then Noko stood and handed her a linen towel. "For your bathroom."

Seneca took it. Another finger towel. Nearly every month, Noko embroidered one with words of wisdom for her. Along the edge were the words: *One finger cannot lift a pebble.*

Seneca smiled, and her heart swelled. Noko would never give up on her. She was still here, hounding her twenty years after her parents were murdered, hoping she'd embrace her heritage and her faith.

Well, faith was for fools. There were no angels, no saviors. Just guns and blood.

Seneca waved the towel. "You think this will help me save the world?"

Noko shrugged. "Maybe the world does not want to be saved."

Seneca tossed the towel over her shoulder and gave Noko a hug. "That's because the world doesn't have any idea how much trouble it's in."

As she climbed the stairs to her bedroom, she heard Noko's hum.

◆ ◆ ◆

Max flicked on the lights in his empty apartment. Not that he needed to. His night vision was extraordinary—one of the few Shifter senses he could keep in this human form. But blending in with the indigenous population meant doing a lot of unnecessary things like turning on lights in the dark when he didn't need them. Wearing clothes in a culture that had more naked bodies on the Internet than real live people. Eating dead animals but refusing to wear their fur. This planet was more screwed up than the last one was. The longer he was here, the more amazed he was that the population hadn't already destroyed itself.

He slipped off his jacket and stood in front of the window. New York City bustled four stories down, oblivious to the number of Shifters in their midst. Although some were dangerous, most were war refugees who simply wanted to live in peace. They were the ones who lived in fear of building new lives and then having their identities discovered. The rest, well, the rest knew how to exploit a new world.

He walked into the compact kitchen to get a glass of water. Ell's necklace hung on a hook over the sink, impossible to miss. As he drank the water, he stared at it. He'd given it to her on their wedding night on a world far from here. It was the only thing she wore the rest of the night.

Then there was the night they both had fled the persecution and genocide of the Shifter race on their last planet in a ship, only to crash here and find the same crap. He remembered how excited Ell had been when the captain announced they'd found a planet, *this* planet that their dying ship could land on. She believed there was hope here for them to have an actual life, a home, and peace. Then they crash-landed and he found her murdered, and it didn't matter anymore. Every person on this planet could disappear for all he cared.

He touched the blue stone and felt only lifeless rock. It reminded him every single, crappy day why he pushed through this life. It was the only reason he put up with the likes of MacGregor and Seneca and the assholes running XCEL.

He dumped the rest of the water down the sink and set the glass back in the cupboard next to the only other one he owned. There was a quick knock on the door, and Max stilled, listening. Then he walked slowly to the door and sniffed the air. *Friend.*

He opened the door to let in his neighbor. Apollo entered and headed straight for the kitchen. "How did the first day go?"

Max followed. "It sucked."

Apollo didn't appear a bit surprised as he scoured the contents of Max's fridge. He could eat *anything*. While Max had opted for a rugged, lethal body type that would serve him well in the field, Apollo had pilfered DNA from a bodybuilder with the kind of looks Earth women were sure to fall over. Blond hair, blue eyes, square jaw, and muscular physique. Today, he was wearing a tight T-shirt and worn jeans.

Apollo pulled out a beer and popped the cap off. "More than usual, huh?"

Max took a seat at the island. "I'm working for a man who can't stand me in an office with a bunch of agents who don't know they hate me yet. My best moment was when my new female partner resisted the urge to shoot me on sight."

"A female?"

Max crossed his arms. "She'd kick your ass."

Apollo grinned. "You know how I love a challenge."

A strange possessiveness surprised Max, and he shook it off. "Not this one. I need her."

"Be careful talking like that. You might actually get yourself a woman."

Max ignored Apollo's challenge. "I had a woman. That's enough for one lifetime."

Apollo shook his head. "It's been two years, Max. I don't think Ell would agree with that. I think she'd want you to move on. In fact, I know it. She was the considerate one."

His chest tightened. Even though Ell rarely left his thoughts, he hadn't heard her name in so long, would never utter it himself. Just the sound of it hurt. "She never had to deal with humans."

Apollo shrugged. "They aren't all bad. Me? I like the women."

Max shook his head. Spoken like a man who'd never had his heart broken. "Doesn't matter anyway. This agent won't accept us. She's lost too many close friends to Shifters."

"So if she hates you so much, why did you pick her? Is she hot?"

Max rubbed his fingers where the memory of her heat was imprinted. "I just need her skills."

Apollo grinned. "We're still talking hot women here."

Max said, "Not those kinds of skills. She's the best agent XCEL has. I don't know why, but she's taken down a lot of Shifters. It's not just her weapons or the way she runs her ops. She's different from the rest of them. Better. And I need the best if I'm going to find who killed Ell."

Apollo slammed his bottle on the island and raised his hands. "Are you serious? I thought you were taking this job to finally start over again. Christ, you haven't changed at all in two years."

"My hair is longer," Max noted.

Apollo ignored him. "You dragged me off that ship and halfway across the country tracking this guy—"

"Did you have somewhere else to go?" Max asked.

"We've covered every inch of Manhattan looking for him," Apollo continued.

"Apparently not *every* inch," Max muttered.

"Wasted God knows how much time and how much money—"

Max narrowed his eyes at his best friend. "He killed Ell, remember?"

"When are you going to let this guy go?"

"When I find him and kill him."

Apollo placed both his hands on the island. "And what if you don't?"

"I will. I have help now. I have Seneca. I have XCEL—all their resources and intelligence," Max said. "The killer is still here, in this city, and sooner or later he'll show up on XCEL's radar."

Apollo leaned forward and pointed a finger at Max. "Listen to me. Ell was in the wrong place at the wrong time and ran into someone who wanted to keep her quiet permanently. Maybe it was the bastard who betrayed us back on Govan—"

"It's him. She left the mark of traitor in her own blood," Max said, feeling the anger rise despite the fact that Apollo was his best friend. "She knew we'd understand. Hell, she practically ID'd him for us."

"With what? We don't have a name. We don't have a description."

"I have his scent. That's all we need."

Apollo shook his head. "You keep saying this 'we' stuff. There is no 'we.' I'm done."

"I'm not asking for your help," Max said.

"Oh, right," Apollo said. "You have a new partner to help you out. Does she know that this guy practically wiped out our entire race by betraying us to the government? Does she know that he killed Ell because she discovered who he was? Does she know that she's next in line if you two get close to him?"

"Nope." Max had no intention of Seneca ever getting that close. The traitor was *his*. He was the only one who could find him. The only one with the traitor's scent permanently ingrained in his memory.

"You are playing with fire, my friend. If she's that good, she'll figure it out. Just imagine how pleased she's going to be when she finds out you're using her for your own nefarious needs."

"She won't," Max said. At least, not from him.

"Hey, it's your funeral." Apollo drained the beer and opened the fridge for another. "You sure you don't want one?"

Max waved him off. "I have to go back to work tonight and I don't need a reason for my partner to turn me in."

Apollo popped open a fresh beer. "Doing anything interesting?"

"Going Shifter hunting."

Apollo's eyebrows rose. "Good luck with that."

Max eased off the chair and rolled his tight shoulders. "Shifter hunting is easy. It's the friendly fire that worries me."

CHAPTER
FOUR

By 11:00 P.M. Seneca was standing in the middle of Dave's Bar & Grill. There was blood everywhere. It covered the floor and walls, was spattered across the mirrors and neon signs, and had dried in a crusty layer over the bar.

This was what it looked like when six people were slaughtered. She closed her eyes and let the ghosts whisper to her. In her mind's eye, she envisioned the fight, heard the screams, and watched the blood flow. And she saw Dillinger—slashing, roaring, and smiling. Anger welled up in her core, feeding a fire that would never die. Noko was right. She couldn't quit. Who would watch over the good people?

"Find anything?"

Wrenched from deep within herself, she jumped at the voice and spun around to find Dempsey standing behind her. She hadn't even heard him come in. In the doorway, he was part shadow, part man, and all trouble.

Noko's words came to her. *You have a shape within you as well.*

No, I don't, Seneca thought. She had a destiny that she didn't ask for, didn't want. Her grandmother could believe whatever she wanted to. The biggest concern Seneca had at the moment was keeping Dempsey from learning too much about her.

"Nothing that wasn't in the report," she said.

His eyes shone iridescent for a moment, and she caught a flash of suspicion. *Too bad, big boy.* Max Dempsey may be working for XCEL but he was on a need-to-know basis with her.

She watched him move around the room, surveying the gruesome arena until he came to the pool table in the center. He pressed a finger to the stained felt, and blood oozed up through the fabric. The memory of Jack and his bloody claw resurfaced, and her hand was on her gun before she realized it.

Dempsey swore softly, and she froze. She took a deep breath and let her hand drop, surprised by the sudden emotional overload. What was wrong with her? As much as she hated Shifters, she wouldn't kill them for no good reason . . . She stopped right there, realizing that might not be entirely true.

"Something wrong?" Dempsey was standing in front of her, a curious look on his face.

The last thing she needed was for him to suspect she was any more than a typical shapeshifter hunter. "No. I'm fine." She wasn't. Too many death scenes, too little sleep, too far from hope. "Are you picking anything up?"

His gaze lingered on her for a few moments, and then he shook his head. "I can recognize Shifters on sight, but I don't get any residual impressions. Just his scent, which is strong, and not in a good way. He smelled like he spent some time in the gutters." Then he looked at her. "How about you?"

Did he know? Impossible. "Don't look at me. I'm not a freak."

A flicker of resentment darkened his eyes at her insinuation. *A freak like you.*

He said, "I know you aren't used to working with a Shifter without shooting first, but I'd appreciate it if you'd cool the hostility act. I want this guy as much as you do, and we're both going to lose him if we don't cooperate."

"So you can write the report that's going to put us out of business?" Seneca knew she shouldn't go there, but she couldn't help herself. This was *wrong.*

Dempsey eyed her. "That's not the point of this exercise."

"Then what is the point? To prove that you are the superior species? Maybe replace us completely?"

He squinted at her. "You've put a lot of thought into this, haven't you?"

"It's my life," she muttered. "You take over here and then what? A Shifter president? A Shifter Supreme Court judge? Or better yet, just steal their DNA, kill them off, and step into their shoes."

His anger showed for the first time. "Considering how this country runs, that might not be a bad idea."

She gritted her teeth. "It might be a screwed up country, but it's *my* screwed up country. You have no right to it. You weren't invited."

He took a step toward her, bringing his shadow closer. It reached out as if to swallow her up. His voice was raspy and raw, his eyes locked on her. "We had no choice. Big difference. I don't want to be here any more than you want me here. And if *your* people spent as much time on technology as they do on building weapons to blow each other up, then we big, bad Shifters would be gone by now."

Jerk. "If your people hadn't pissed off the last planet you were on, you wouldn't have had to leave it." She knew as soon as she'd said it that she'd made a mistake.

The shadow around him pulsed brightly, a shape of a demon itching to be freed. It turned a deep, dark crimson as he moved closer to her. She fought the urge to step back and put her hand back on her gun.

"We didn't piss them off. We simply tried to live there."

She really wanted to push him over the edge. Maybe he'd do something stupid like kill her and then the Committee would know that they were wrong to trust Shifters. On the other hand, that would require that she die. It was a difficult decision, but finally she opted for righteous silence.

Then Dempsey turned his back to her, tension filling his body as he took a few deep breaths. The shadow had stilled and faded by the time he faced her again.

"I don't care what you think of me, Seneca Thomas. I don't care what you think of Shifters. And I don't care if you think it's not fair," he said, his tone under careful control. "I want this bastard, and you're going to help me get him."

❖ ❖ ❖

You're going to help me get him.

Seneca stewed as they exited yet another bar without a lead.

So much for her being in charge. It took all of fifteen minutes for that to change. Shifters. *Can't trust 'em, can't kill 'em—at least not tonight.*

No bar owners had seen Dillinger's human form in the photos or admitted to it. She told them to call her if he showed up. Her guess would be they'd give him money in hopes he'd leave. You got a lot of respect in this town for killing six people. Now if she could *tell* them that the guy could morph into a murdering monster, she'd bet they'd call in a heartbeat. But that wasn't going to happen anytime soon.

It was 3:00 A.M., and she was cold and sick of sucking smoke into her lungs. Seneca drew in a deep breath and let the frigid blast shock her brain to attention. Despite a few hours of precious sleep, she wasn't one hundred percent and she knew it. Maybe it wasn't a bad thing that they had no leads. All that could change, though, because they were headed to the pier along Battery Park for her meeting with her best informant.

She noted that Dempsey had taken "cordial" to a whole new silent level, which was fine with her. If he was waiting for an apology, he'd wait for hell to freeze over. It wasn't right that his people invade her planet.

We had no choice.

She knew that too. The official word was that his race was being exterminated and a shipload of Shifters had escaped. They'd crashed here, and their ship had exploded. Unfortunately, a few thousand had managed to escape, giving the term "illegal aliens" a whole new meaning. Even with a swift military response to the crash, the aliens had scattered to parts unknown, picking up the culture and figuring out how to replace humans with surprising

ease and skill. Most had been deemed harmless, at least by intelligence. However, she trusted her government intelligence about
as much as she trusted Dempsey.

By the time they reached the park, her toes were numb in
her boots. Bursts of vapor accompanied every breath. She looked
over the calm water at the Statue of Liberty, standing proud and
resolute.

*. . . Give me your tired, your poor . . . The wretched refuse of your
teeming shore. Send these, the homeless, tempest-tossed . . .*

Seneca huffed and wondered if Lady Liberty ever got tired of
holding that big-ass torch.

Dempsey looked around. "We're early?"

It was the longest sentence he'd spoken to her since Dave's.

"A bit. Bart's like a ghost," she told him. "If I didn't know better, I'd think he's one of you."

"How do you know he's not?"

Seneca stilled, aware of Dempsey's gaze on her and his curiosity.
Damn, she needed to be more careful. "He doesn't like Shifters."

"Then how does he get all his information?"

She shrugged. "I don't know. I don't ask. All I know is that it's
always good."

A couple walked past them, and Seneca caught the shadow.
One of them was a Shifter, the other a human. It took every
ounce of her control to not let on in front of Dempsey.

A Shifter and a human. Just something else to worry about.
Offspring. It was only a matter of time. It hadn't happened yet, as
far as she knew, but it wasn't too much of a stretch. She glanced
at Dempsey's broad shoulders, rugged face, and quiet intensity. If
he were a human, she might be more than a little interested. He

wasn't, and she knew it. But she was sure he'd met women who didn't know what he was.

"Has your species ever tried to procreate with another?" she asked, surprising herself with the bluntness of her question. Must be the lack of sleep.

Dempsey's eyes moved to hers, and she caught the iridescent glow as he turned all that intensity on her. "A little early to bring up the question of sex, partner. I figured you'd last until at least the second night."

Crap. She should have kept her mouth shut. "I assume if you have human DNA that you also have human parts, Dempsey."

He grinned suddenly, and she forgot the rest of her question for a moment until her teeth started chattering. "Forget it," she said and shivered. "Obviously, men are men regardless of what planet they come from."

"That is something I've noticed," he said and moved next to her to block the brunt of the breeze coming off the water. She sidestepped to get back into it.

"And to answer your question," he said, a smirk curling the corner of his mouth. "Yes. But every species is different. Yours doesn't appear to be compatible enough to bear children."

There was a God after all. If Shifters couldn't procreate, maybe they'd all die off in fifty or sixty years. Or maybe they were like vampires and lived forever. Or worse, like cockroaches that could survive a nuclear war. They could be here forever.

Dempsey continued, "Now sex is another story. Personally, I've never had any complaints."

She murmured, "Spare me the details." But the visual had already formed and everything.

Dempsey grinned and wisely ended discussion on the topic. The wind picked up, and Seneca ducked her head lower in her coat collar. She covertly watched Dempsey's profile as he scouted the park. He wasn't at all what she expected. She expected arrogant. Well, he was that. And cold-blooded, which he might be since the frigid weather didn't seem to affect him. And uncivilized, which he definitely wasn't.

In fact, he seemed intelligent, determined, driven, and totally into his work. He could have any job he wanted, so why was he here, trying to catch his own kind? She couldn't be the only one who gave him shit along the way, who didn't trust him. So why would he do it? Why take the flack?

World peace, my ass. She wasn't buying that for a minute. He had another reason for being here. She could feel something below the surface, something he kept under tight wraps.

"Incoming," Dempsey murmured, his gaze fixed on the sidewalk ahead. Seneca couldn't see anything in the dark and wrapped her hand around the gun in her holster under her long coat.

A few moments later, a small man approached wearing black jeans and a gray sweatshirt with the hood over his head. She released a breath of relief and shoved her hands back into her pockets. As Bart drew closer, he slowed and eyed Dempsey with suspicion.

She said, "It's okay. He's cool. New partner."

Bart nodded at Dempsey and then settled his gaze on her. She could smell the booze on him and no doubt Dempsey could too. Bart's eyes were bloodshot and a little unfocused, and his nose was bright red.

"Nice seeing you, Seneca. Sorry about Riley."

"Thanks," she said and didn't ask how he'd found out. Bart always seemed to know what was going on. She liked him, even if he did spend too much time with the bottle. He had been her main man for the past year, and he was a decent guy. More than that, she trusted the information he gave her.

She gave him the photos of Dillinger, and he bobbed his head after studying them in the dim light. "I heard of this guy. Bad dude. Likes to cut people."

"Any idea where he might be holed up?"

Bart pulled his hood down farther over his head and looked around. "Maybe. Maybe he's part of the new game in town."

She sensed his edginess. "Someone new?"

He looked at her soberly, bloodshot eyes and all. "Now I ain't been down there to check this myself, you understand."

"Down where?" Seneca asked.

He whispered, "The tunnels."

"Subway?" Dempsey asked.

Bart looked at Dempsey. "Yeah. Train tunnels too. Sewers, everywhere down there. The Shifters have taken over."

Seneca knew there were miles of underground networks crisscrossing the city. Thousands of exits and hiding places. If the Shifters were down there, they could come and go under the city practically undetected.

Bart wiped his nose on his shirtsleeve. "A new Shifter moved in. They call him Skinman, and he ain't alone, if you know what I mean. He's got friends."

"What's he doing?" she asked.

"He supplies DNA," Dempsey said next to her.

Bart eyed him. "You know? Christ, man. You gonna put me out of business?"

"Don't plan on it." Dempsey's eyes cut to hers for a moment. "I just know the type."

"Yeah, well, he's selling DNA to Shifters. So they can come up top," Bart said. "And not just for money. He's taking guns, drugs, whatever he can get."

Seneca's entire body was shaking, cold to her bones. "Where's he getting the DNA from?"

"He's cleaning out the people in the tunnels."

She closed her eyes at the realization. "The homeless."

Bart nodded a bunch of times. "Yeah."

She glanced at Dempsey, but his expression was as unreadable as his emotions. *Exactly what do you know about this?* she wondered.

Bart looked around while he continued. "Everyone's running scared. People are vanishing, and no one knows what happened to 'em. Some go missing and when they come back, they're different."

"What do you mean?" Seneca asked. "They look different?"

Bart shook his head. "No, they look the same, but they ain't the same people inside. Don't know their friends. Don't know the tunnels." He sniffed. "I think the Shifters are taking their place."

That explained how Shifters were getting into polite society. Seneca asked, "Who else knows this?"

"Nobody," Bart said. "Some people went to the cops, but no one believes 'em. They think it's drugs or booze talking."

That wasn't a bad thing, Seneca realized. XCEL had used the whole urban myth thing for all it was worth. Giant alligators under the city. It was one of the reasons they'd managed to keep the aliens a secret for this long. Their PR would put any presidential candidate to shame.

Dempsey asked, "So you think our man is one of them?"

Bart shrugged. "Could be he used Skinman to get his human form. Maybe not. I'll ask around."

"What about Skinman? Can you get a location for us?" Seneca asked.

Bart flinched. "No way."

She'd never heard Bart turn down a job, which made her want the info even more. Skinman sounded like a serious threat, and she wanted him. "I'll pay you five hundred to hook us up."

Bart's eyes widened, and then he rolled his head. "Man, you're killing me here."

"A thousand," she said.

He blew out a booze-laden breath. "I'll see what I can do. I ain't promising anything. And I ain't going down there to find out. Hate the tunnels. Nothing good ever comes outta there."

"Understood," she said. "Thanks."

Then Bart glanced around and bounced on his feet. "I need to be rolling. Been here too long already."

Seneca slipped him a couple fifties. "Be careful out there."

He tucked the money into his jacket and headed back the way he came. Seneca watched him until he blended into the night, and her stomach trembled uncontrollably. It was the perfect setup. Dark, underground, abandoned tunnels and caverns filled with their choice of homeless people to steal DNA from. Who's going to worry about a street person? They went missing all the time. Shifters steal the DNA, kill them, replicate them, and get their ticket to the surface. Dear God.

As soon as Bart was out of earshot, Seneca turned to find Dempsey watching her.

"We need to get down there," he said.

"I know." She headed past him, back to her car before she froze to death. Although, at this point, that was the least of her worries. Dempsey stepped along next to her, and she asked, "What are the chances that Dillinger got a skin from this guy?"

"Possible. The city is a tough place for a Shifter to sneak into without it."

Lovely. "You said you smelled Dillinger's scent. Could you ID him by scent if you ran into him again?"

"Yes."

That was a quick response. "Because he's a Shifter?"

Dempsey shook his head. "Wouldn't matter. I have an extremely acute sense of smell. We all do. It's one of the few senses we can use in any form."

"How acute?" she asked, looking at him.

Something flickered in his eyes as he focused on her. For a moment, she didn't think he would answer. For a moment, she forgot about her toes. He finally said, "I could pick you out of a crowd from a city block away. Blindfolded."

Her jaw dropped a little. "That's impossible."

One corner of his mouth curled as he looked straight ahead. "You use Ivory soap when you shower. Your shampoo has an aloe scent additive. You wear deodorant but no perfume. And you put on a clean shirt before coming out tonight."

She frowned at the accuracy and the unsettling intimacy. Hell, he probably knew what color her underwear were. "Lucky guess."

He grinned as he slowed at the car, and she took out her keys. He added, "Unfortunately, a city block isn't very far. I need a decent trail to follow."

Seneca unlocked the doors. "I'll take care of the trail. Just don't forget that scent."

She was in the car when she heard him say, "I never do."

CHAPTER
FIVE

Seneca stifled a yawn as she sat at her desk with Dempsey's file. She hadn't slept well today, what with the impending demise of the human race thanks to Skinman. All she could think of was thousands of variations of freshly deceased homeless people taking Manhattan. It'd be like every bad B movie come to life.

On top of that, she'd had to come in well ahead of the normal night shift, before Dempsey, in the hopes of finding something wrong with him.

Unfortunately, his file was filled with citations and certifications, and glowing performance reports. He'd scored at the top of his class in every aspect. Were all shapeshifters this good? She hoped not. Because humans would become obsolete. Or worse. She'd be reporting to Shifters.

Over my dead body.

On the personal side, he'd been granted legal status in the

United States, no doubt by higher-ups who had never seen the world she lived in. He had an apartment on the Upper West Side, drove a used Toyota, and paid his bills on time, even his taxes. A model citizen. Part of her was grudgingly relieved, part of her was suspicious of anyone who was that perfect, and the last part of her was worried for her job and her country.

Seneca slapped the file shut, hid it in her top drawer, and put her head in her hands. God, she was tired. She was sick and tired of running in place. How was she going to fix this? How was she going to convince the idiots who controlled XCEL that a Shifter did not belong in an organization designed to neutralize them? It would seem obvious, but then again, this was the government she was dealing with.

And to be fair, Shifters weren't much different than humans. And humans had managed to find plenty of reasons to turn on their own. Which led her to the more pressing question: What was Dempsey's reason for turning on his own? She'd pondered it until her head ached and still could find no good reason. She supposed she could just ask him, but chances were very good he wouldn't tell her the truth anyway. Which meant the free-floating anxiety she had been feeling for the past two days wouldn't be going away anytime soon.

There was a shuffle at the door, and she braced herself for Dempsey before looking up. Instead, it was Ken Price, almost as bad. He waltzed in without asking, all starched shirt and creased pants. Only an office manager could get away with that look around here.

He put his hands on Dempsey's desk and leaned forward until she could smell his expensive cologne, which, like his ego, rolled over her in a nauseating wave.

"I hear you've been working nonstop, girl. How about you and me go out tonight?" he said with the supreme confidence of a man who didn't know any better.

How about if the "girl" tosses your sorry ass down the trash chute? "I'm working every night this week, Price. Sorry."

"Okay, I can do breakfast," he replied with a wink. "Even better. I make a hell of an omelet."

If he didn't handle most of her paperwork, she'd tell him exactly where to go. Usually, Riley ran interference for her, but he was gone. She clenched her fist under the desk. Playing along was worth whatever it cost. Paperwork was its own private hell. So she said, "As you probably noticed, this is not a good week for me."

She sensed the change in him as he frowned. "It's that new guy, isn't it?" He pushed off the desk and stood up, his face turning crimson with resentment. "Christ, that didn't take long."

Okay, now she was mad. Through clenched teeth, she said very carefully, "It's not him. It's me. I'm busy."

"It's just one date. It's not like you have so many other options," Price said.

Now she wanted her gun. To hell with paperwork, to hell with being nice. "I said no, Price. Get a hint."

"You think you're so fucking hot," he said. "One of these days, you're number's going to be up."

She stood and pointed at the door. "Get out of my office before *your* number comes up, Price."

"Is there a problem?"

Both of them looked over to find Dempsey dominating the doorway holding two cups of coffee. He wore jeans, a T-shirt, his leather jacket, and a visibly large Glock 39 underneath it. His gaze pinned Price, and Seneca could see the office manager stiffen. She'd seen Dempsey mad at her, but not like this. This almost scared *her*.

Price twitched and then squared his shoulders. "We were talking. You interrupted us."

Dempsey's gaze flicked to hers, and she pursed her lips. His eyes narrowed at Price. "You're at my desk."

Price stumbled a little as he moved away from the desk and carefully maneuvered around Dempsey at the door. Just before he walked out, he looked at her and said, "We'll talk later."

Dempsey kicked the door closed. "Price isn't very bright, is he?"

She sat back down and mumbled, "No, but he *is* persistent."

Dempsey handed her one of the two cups he brought in, and she said, "Thank you." It was for more than the coffee, but she didn't know how to say it without looking like she couldn't handle herself with the office staff. The truth was, she sucked at the finer points of politics. Her only two methods were shutting up or shooting.

He took his seat. "Find everything you wanted in my file?"

She looked at him over the rim of her mug. "No."

One corner of his mouth rose. "You could always just ask me."

Hey, he offered. She set her coffee down and crossed her arms. "Okay. Let's start with where you got your skin?"

Dempsey leaned back in his chair. "A dead man."

His answer sent a shiver through her. "Was he dead before or after you took his skin?"

He smiled back. "Sorry to ruin your night, but I wasn't the

one who killed him. Found him dead in a ravine. Been there for a while. Gunshot to the head. Must have pissed someone off. Maybe it was you."

She replied, "A funny partner. Just what I need. He must not have looked too healthy after being dead in the open for a week."

"As long as the DNA is still viable, we can use it," he replied without blinking.

Her stomach turned. "That's disgusting." And more than a little scary. How many people were buried in grave sites around the country? At this rate, she'd never sleep.

"It's what we do. The only way we can survive. I didn't ask to be a Shifter," he said.

He sipped his coffee as if sucking the DNA from some dead guy was the most normal thing in the world. She collected her thoughts and asked the next question, "I'd hate to think there are more of you, but do you have any family I should be worried about?"

She noticed that his fingers tightened around the handle. His voice rasped. "Irrelevant. Next question."

Ooo, she'd hit a nerve, and she tucked it away for future use. "Okay, here's a good one. If we come face-to-face with Dillinger, will you be able to kill one of your own? No mention of doing that in your file."

Dempsey didn't move a muscle for a few moments, and Seneca realized she may have just crossed some strange forbidden Shifter line. Finally, he set down his cup carefully and pushed forward in his chair so their eyes met over the desks. The air around her stilled as he spoke low and slow. "Don't worry about me, partner. I'm an agent first."

He said it like he meant it, but that free-floating anxiety was firmly in place. "I just want to make sure you don't change your mind about why you're here."

"How could I forget? Finished?" he asked.

"Not yet. Why are you here?"

Dempsey's eyes narrowed. "I don't have anywhere else to go."

That was true, but not the reason. "What do Shifters want?"

His expression softened just a little. "A home."

Then you're out of luck here, she thought. Just then, MacGregor opened the door and came in. Dempsey kept his gaze on her as he sat back in his chair.

"Thanks for knocking," Seneca said, even though she was almost grateful for the interruption.

MacGregor stood with his hands on his hips. "It's my place. Got personal business? Do it somewhere else. Now what did you want to talk about?"

Seneca cast a quick glance at Dempsey, who remained silent. Didn't look like he was going to jump in and explain. Fine. "Bart says a guy named Skinman is selling DNA to Shifters underground. In the tunnels under the city."

MacGregor crossed his arms over his generous belly. "Skinman? Nice name." He looked at Dempsey. "What do you know about him?"

"It's an occupation, not a name. For Shifters, a Skinman is a necessity when you have to blend in with the locals. It's not as easy as you might think finding healthy DNA. So a Skinman sets up shop, collects DNA, and sells it," he said. "But if this Skinman is killing off the homeless population to harvest their DNA, someone is going to discover his operation sooner or later."

MacGregor let out a sigh. "I'll notify the local authorities to let us know if they find any bodies underground."

Seneca added, "And ask them to compile a list of missing homeless people. They rarely get reported, but maybe we'll get lucky."

MacGregor nodded. "How fast can they replicate, Max?"

He shrugged. "With sufficient energy, an experienced Shifter can roll over in a few days. Individual parts of the human anatomy, as quickly as a few hours."

"We have to stop this guy," Seneca said. "Like now. I think Dillinger might have gotten his DNA from Skinman. I want to go underground."

She watched as MacGregor considered it and hoped he understood how urgent this request was. She had to put Skinman out of business, because if she didn't, no one else would be able to.

"Dillinger is your first priority," he finally said. "After you bring him in, you can go after Skinman."

Those weren't the orders she wanted, and she exchanged an unhappy look with Dempsey. Then MacGregor looked at his watch and opened the door. "Roll call in thirty minutes. I'll have information by then. Don't be late."

◆ ◆ ◆

Max followed Seneca for roll call and sat next to her in the back. The small room was jammed with XCEL agents throwing things at one another and telling raunchy jokes over long tables and chairs that faced a podium at the front. He noted that Seneca was the only female in the room.

Seneca watched the other agents, silently taking everything in and probably remembering every detail. Times like this he almost liked her. "You're quiet."

"I wouldn't miss this for the world," she said and smiled.

He eyed her. "Expecting me to crack?"

She turned to him, and brown eyes met his. "I don't think you crack."

He wasn't sure if that was a compliment or something else. Probably something else. He wouldn't get any respect from her. Not yet. "So this is where you get the scoop on Shifters?"

"Anything we know is an advantage. None of us want to die."

"Same here," he said and smiled when she gave him an annoyed look.

The door at the back of the room flung open, and MacGregor stormed in. He slapped a pile of folders on the podium and swore as he tried to turn on the overhead equipment until someone came to his rescue.

"That man is going to have a heart attack someday," Dempsey murmured.

"Hey, he's mellowed," Seneca replied. "You should have seen him a year ago."

Finally, MacGregor yelled, and the dull roar settled down.

"Pay attention, people," he barked. "This could save your ass tonight."

He punched the remote and brought up a screen with a printout on it. "Our latest intel says that we now have over eight hundred Shifters in Manhattan. That's a big influx of a few hundred in the past month."

A murmur filled the room as MacGregor wrestled with the

remote to bring up the next screen, a graph that showed one XCEL agent for every ten Shifters.

"Which means, we need more men," MacGregor said. He nodded in Seneca's direction. "Or women. Or dogs. Get your friends and relatives to come in and sign up for the best god-damn job there is."

That got a chuckle out of the room.

"We believe the reason for the influx is a new source of DNA. Our homeless population. You'll all get a list and photos of folks reported missing in the past three months. If you see one of them roaming the streets, call it in."

Then the screen went black, and MacGregor swore as he tried to bring it back. Finally, he threw the remote in the corner and it broke in two. He gripped the sides of the podium. "We also got more info on their DNA structures. As you know, they can tap into any DNA source—hair, skin, blood, bones, saliva, even sperm—to build the basic structure. A good Shifter can com-pletely convert in two days. After that, they are pretty much stuck with the structure, although with some experimentation, they may be able to play with eye color, skin color, yadda, yadda."

Someone yelled out, "Does that mean they can change their dick size?" The room erupted in laughter.

MacGregor pointed to him. "Leave it to the small-dicked man in the back to ask that one." The laughter got louder.

Max crossed his arms, not laughing. He wondered what hu-mans would think if Shifters had meetings about them. *We've ascertained that the vast majority of humans are arrogant, greedy, and completely intolerant.*

"The research boys have recalibrated all your disrupters with new patterns," MacGregor continued. "They should work like a charm for a few weeks. After that, we're back to square one."

The agents clapped in response, and MacGregor raised his hand. "You're going to like this one even better. I have it on the best authority a state job can buy that you'll be getting your hot little hands on a new weapon. As you know, Shifters are sensitive to UVC light. Screws with their ability to shift and turns them inside-out, which means they can't shift in sunlight. So some pointy-headed lab coat finally figured out that we can exploit that. We're going to be the test agency for a new UVC grenade."

A roar of approval went up as Max's gut tightened.

"Well, don't get too excited," MacGregor said. "Effects will only last about fifteen seconds. The good news is that unlike our disrupter weapons, it affects every Shifter at once in an unobstructed area. It should incapacitate them long enough for you to tranquilize or take them out, whichever comes first."

A knowing chuckle went around the room.

Max let out a long breath. *Nice.*

"Can't wait to try that out," Seneca said.

He turned to find her smiling. "Remember, it only works a few seconds. And then you might be in big trouble."

She laughed.

MacGregor held up his hand. "Don't forget that Riley's funeral is tomorrow. The policy is that we aren't supposed to attend our fallen agents' funerals—"

Boos filled the room, and he waved them off. "I know it sucks. So all I'm saying is that he'll be buried tomorrow at noon in Woodland Cemetery."

Max realized that no one had mentioned it to him, not even

Seneca. Her jaw was set and she blinked furiously as she listened to MacGregor. The shock of her vulnerability wiped away his annoyance at being shunned.

Then MacGregor pointed to Max and announced, "You may have noticed the new guy. Max Dempsey. Introduce yourselves to him and try not to act like idiots doing it."

Seneca eyed him, and any vulnerability vanished. It was intriguing while it lasted. MacGregor updated them on the rest of the announcements and information. The meeting was adjourned, and Dempsey led the way out and back to their office.

Seneca followed and closed the door behind them. Dempsey ignored her as she leaned back against the door and crossed her arms. "Ready to quit yet?"

He checked the mail on his desk in all seriousness. "I've heard worse."

Seneca didn't doubt that. So what would it take to make him quit? Dempsey knew he wasn't wanted or welcomed here. In fact, if anyone found out, he'd be run out of the agency or worse. What would make a Shifter risk that? He was hiding something.

He looked up at her, his expression humorless. "MacGregor didn't mention Skinman."

"Probably waiting for some confirmation aside from our informant."

Dempsey nodded and went silent. *What is going through his head right now?* she wondered. Skinman? Dillinger? Quitting? *That* would make her entire year.

He dropped the mail and walked around the desk to come face-to-face with her. Her pulse jumped as his eyes flashed iridescent. It was never far from the surface.

"What happens to the Shifters you capture or kill?" he asked softly.

She blinked at the off-topic question. "The cleanup crew takes care of them."

"Which means what?"

She shrugged. "They bag them and take them away. I don't know what they do with the dead ones, but they put the live ones on ice. Freezing them is the only safe containment solution we have right now."

Dempsey's tone turned bitter. "But they don't have any problem developing new weapons. Jail cells must be low on the priority list."

Seneca studied him and realized that he was furious. What did he expect? "It's the best we can do."

She watched as Dempsey moved closer. His eyes were dark and unfriendly. "Then how do they know that their new weapons will work on Shifters?"

For a moment, she went blank. Then her mind kicked in. "Wait, you don't think they're using our captures for experiments or something?"

"How are they testing the weapons?" he pressed.

She put her hands on her hips. "Maybe they use rats."

"Works for human testing, why not?" Then Dempsey smiled, but it wasn't a nice smile. "Do you really think it's that hard to come up with a cell for a Shifter?"

He was trying to confuse her. "Yes, I do."

His eyes narrowed. "You'd like to think that. It'd justify your job."

She said, "It's not my decision whether or not to make cells a priority."

"No, but it is your decision to work here."

"If you Shifters weren't here, then I wouldn't be here," she snapped back.

"Do you think XCEL will stop at the bad Shifters? What about the others? The ones who want nothing more than to be left alone?"

Now he was pissing her off. "I don't know. All the Shifters I meet tend to kill and maim. Maybe deep down you're *all* bad."

His gaze held as if he was going to say something, and then he shook his head in disgust.

"My mistake," he said. "I thought you were different."

You have no idea. "I guess not." She shoved Dillinger's folder into his hands. "We're working late again."

He shoved it back. "Can't. I'm taking the night off."

She gaped at him. "You just started here."

He walked back to his desk. "Prior engagement."

"MacGregor—"

Dempsey cut in. "MacGregor knows."

Sonofabitch, he went behind her back. "Got a hot date or something?"

He grinned, and she could have sworn she heard a growl. "Or something."

For some reason, her gut tightened and her interest took a mean turn. "So you are blowing off work for date?"

Dempsey pulled on his leather jacket. "It's personal."

She waited but he didn't elaborate, and she wouldn't ask. No, she'd just stand here and fume. It would be petty to pry. She crossed her arms. Fine, she was petty. "Does your date know what you are?"

He hesitated just long enough for her to know she'd hit her mark. "Believe it or not, I have Shifter friends. Some of them don't even murder people." He fixed his sleeves. "Are you done?"

Seneca felt the heat rise in her face. "Be home by midnight."

Dempsey gave her a long, lingering look that made her want to squirm. She could only imagine his effect on other women. Thick hair, square jaw, intense eyes, and a body made for long, hot nights. How hard would it be for him to get a date? Seconds.

"Think you can stay out of trouble until tomorrow?" he asked.

She smiled. "I'm sure I'll find something to do."

"That's what worries me," he said, and then he brushed by her and left.

Seneca sat down at her desk and tossed the file on the desk. The last five minutes felt like three rounds in the ring. Working with Dempsey was exhausting.

She drummed her fingernails on her desk. So what exactly did Dempsey do in his free time? Besides dating unsuspecting women. Did he have a circle of friends? Go out to dinner? Did he have hobbies? She couldn't see him painting or playing chess or collecting stamps. Or even hanging around a gym. He'd scare all the other customers away.

And why would MacGregor be willing to give him the night off so soon after joining the agency? She could ask MacGregor but he wouldn't tell her. That man could keep a secret.

Curiosity gnawed at her until she finally got up and grabbed her coat. "Screw it."

She raced to the elevator and out into the parking garage just in time to see him pull out.

CHAPTER
SIX

Max found Carl Hannaford in a booth at the far end of the Bronx bar. The place was dark, and smelled like stale beer and urine. There was a battered pool table in the back under a bare lightbulb. Country music squawked from speakers overhead. Two men hunched over the long bar, looking like permanent fixtures. A lone, homely bartender seemed annoyed at his intrusion.

Max got a beer at the bar before sliding into the booth across from his longtime friend and the man secretly responsible for getting him into XCEL. "Your meeting places get worse every week."

Carl grinned under carefully sculpted black hair. His blue eyes pierced the dim light. A scotch on the rocks in front of him looked like it hadn't been touched. He shook Max's hand. "It's all about the atmosphere, my friend. I don't think we have to worry about anyone catching our conversation here."

"Well, next time you might want to dress down for the occasion," Max said. He noted that the bartender kept glancing at them. The man was definitely curious.

"So," Carl said. "How's it going?"

Max took a long draw from the bottle and set it down across from Carl's drink. "I have a partner who doesn't trust me as far as she can throw me. MacGregor wants me to finish my business and leave. And I'm no closer to the killer than I was when I started."

Carl laughed. "That good, huh?"

Max eyed him over his bottle. "That was my best day this week."

"And no one else knows you are a Shifter?"

"Just my partner and MacGregor. The rest of the agents don't know, but I'm betting that day comes soon enough. They have their own brotherhood. What about you? Still keeping under the radar?"

"So far." Carl nodded. "No one suspects that I'm not the real Carl Hannaford."

Good, Max thought. Then they were both safe for the time being. Carl had managed to infiltrate the government branch responsible for XCEL and helped shape policy to put Max in a position where he could find the traitor responsible for betraying the Shifters on their last planet before escaping in their ship and landing here along with them. And then murdering Ell.

"How's Apollo?" Carl asked out of the blue.

Max thought about their argument last night. "He thinks I should give up looking for Ell's killer."

"He doesn't understand. He didn't lose what you did." Carl

took a sip of his drink. "Remember the old days when you, me, and Apollo used to do this for fun?"

Max smiled. "And one of us would always end up saving Apollo from himself."

"I thought we'd be doing that forever on Govan," Carl said. "I guess it wasn't meant to be there."

It wasn't meant to be anywhere. The shapeshifter race had been refugees for the last six generations after their own home planet had become uninhabitable due to climate change. Finding a new home, a place where they could resettle in peace, had proven impossible. Govan had nearly wiped them out.

"I miss the old days, as bad as they were. My family," Carl said after swirling his drink.

He didn't have to elaborate. They had both lost their entire families. All because one Shifter had decided to help the Govan government get rid of them all—the traitor, and ultimately, Ell's murderer. Apollo just wanted to move forward and forget the past. But Max and Carl couldn't. It was that simple.

"Anything I can do to help out with the agency?" Carl asked.

"You got me this far and that was enough, thanks. I won't risk you being discovered. Besides, I'm the only one who can find him at this point." Max watched the bartender watching him. "What you *can* do is find out what happens to the Shifters that the XCEL teams capture."

"The policy is cryogenics," Carl said with a frown.

"At the rate they are developing new weapons? I don't think so. And I seriously doubt they'd put weapons in the hands of XCEL agents unless they're absolutely positive they'll work on Shifters."

Carl shook his head slowly. "It was only a matter of time before they started experimenting on Shifters."

"*Live* Shifters," Max corrected. "And one of them just might be me someday."

"I'll definitely check into that. Not that I can stop it, you realize," Carl said.

"At least I'll know what to watch out for." Max glared at the bartender until he looked away. "Amazing how much this planet is like Govan. Same small minds, same paranoia, same bullshit."

Carl shrugged. "They aren't *all* bad."

"Right," Max said. Just the ones he came into contact with. "Doesn't matter that we try to fit in. Doesn't matter that we adopt all their million rules. Doesn't matter that I know more about their history than ninety-nine percent of them. It never changes, Carl. We'll never be welcomed anywhere."

"Ell would have disagreed with you," Carl said.

Max stared at his beer bottle. "She was too soft."

"She had faith," Carl corrected.

And it killed her, Max thought.

As if reading his mind, Carl asked, "So what are your plans after you catch her killer?"

Max took a big swig and caught the scent of something else. Then he lost it in the smell of the beer. "Does it matter?"

"XCEL could still use you. He won't be the last bad Shifter."

"Probably not." Max pushed his bottle aside and inhaled, just catching a wisp of scent he recognized all too well. Ivory soap. "I have to go."

Carl frowned as Max got up and tossed a few bills on the table. "Problem?"

"Nothing I can't handle."

Carl glanced around and got to his feet. "You sure?"

Max grinned. "Oh, yes. This one is all mine."

◆ ◆ ◆

Seneca ducked into a storefront doorway after sneaking out of the bar and watched for the two men to exit. This was not what she expected. Who was the guy in the nice suit Dempsey was talking to? In a dump like that? And even worse, the suit was a Shifter. Okay, that wasn't weird, but she had expected a woman.

Personal, with a guy in a suit? Didn't make sense unless Dempsey wasn't into women. It could be possible. He never said who his date was. Or maybe it was business, which would really piss her off because she hadn't been invited to the meeting. She peered around the corner at the stairs. No sign of them yet. First thing tomorrow, she was going to see what MacGregor knew—

A hand clamped over her mouth, and she reacted with an elbow to the gut. She heard a pained *oomph*, but the hand held and her elbow hurt like hell.

"You can't do it, can you? You can't stay out of trouble."

She froze at the voice rasping in her ear. Well, crap. He wasn't kidding when he said he could pick her out in the city. How the hell was she supposed to spy on him if he always knew she was there?

Then Dempsey spun her around to face him and pinned her against the brick wall with a hand on each side of her. Even in the darkness, fire burned in his eyes. Anger simmered in his soul.

No surprise, he wasn't happy to see her.

"I was just providing backup," she said, lying through her teeth.

He chuckled low, sending a shiver down her spine. He was way too close for comfort, and she tried to slide away from him, but he wasn't having any of it, boxing her against the wall tightly.

"Is that right? You think I need a bodyguard?" he said. "Or were you jealous?"

She gave a little laugh. "Jealous? *Please.*"

"I don't need a bodyguard, and you aren't jealous. What does that leave us with?"

Busted. She never got busted. If this got out, it would ruin her kick-ass agent reputation. "Fine, I was curious about your personal life. I didn't realize you had a guy . . . friend."

His eyebrows rose. "Guy friend?"

She should shut up, just drop it. But the suspense was killing her. Why else would he take the whole night off? "You know, guy friend. Boyfriend."

She sensed the change in him almost immediately. Or was it her? Well, one of them was changing because she was feeling way too warm for New York City in December.

"Boyfriend. As in lover?" he asked as he stroked the exposed skin on the side of her throat with his thumb. One thumb. It was distracting as hell. She started to sweat under her long coat.

"There's nothing wrong with that," she said.

He grinned. Just grinned. And that damn thumb. Every stroke sent electricity down her spine. And unfortunately, it felt amazing.

"You think I'm gay," he said, and this time he moved closer.

She swallowed. That damn thumb. And what could she say to

make him stop? *Your thumb is driving me crazy?* "The suit in the bar?"

"Is a business associate," he said smoothly. She could feel the warmth of his breath, the heat of his face inches from hers, and the weight of his eyes as they watched her every move. They were gray with a little silver around the edges.

Concentrate, Seneca, you're supposed to be pissed here. "*You* were the one who said it was personal."

"If I had told you it was business, you'd have followed me."

"Don't be ridiculous. What kind of business?"

Dempsey leaned closer, and Seneca sucked in a breath as he whispered, "*My* business."

And then all she could hear was their breathing. The city seemed to fade away as their eyes locked. Bursts of vapor curled in the cold air. He smelled like beer and the night.

"And I'm not gay," he said softly.

Her body agreed wholeheartedly despite her best efforts. But he *was* a Shifter. Not to be trusted. She should move away, should do something besides fall prey to the heat.

"Why didn't you invite me along?" she managed to say, although she heard her voice crack.

"Why didn't you invite me to Riley's funeral?" he said and pressed his thumb firmly into her skin. She inhaled sharply at the pressure.

"I didn't think—"

He moved even closer, his face nearly touching hers.

"I didn't think you'd want to go," she finished.

"You were wrong."

Suddenly, her vision changed and he began to disappear into

a strange darkness. She heard herself gasp as his Shifter shadow rose up, enveloped her, blocking out all sound, smell, and sights. And then she felt something unfold in her mind, a flash of a scene that wasn't hers, voices, sounds. She tried to block it out, but it was like it was inside her. Panic swamped her.

"Stop it," she hissed, and struggled to free herself.

Reality crashed through as Dempsey abruptly let her go and stepped back, breaking the connection. Seneca's heart was racing as she stumbled out of the doorway and out onto the sidewalk. The night sky shimmered above, and she inhaled cold air as she walked, trying to sort through a flood of questions. What was he doing to her? Or was it her? Did her abilities make her more vulnerable to Shifter thoughts? Oh God. She didn't need or deserve that.

Dempsey cut in front of her, stopping her in her tracks. "What just happened?"

"Nothing," she snapped. *Nothing I want to talk about with you. Or anyone.*

"You're shook up. Something happened."

That was a mistake. All of it, whatever it was. She brushed her hair out of her face with a trembling hand. "I'm fine. Just leave me alone." She tried to pass by him, but he stopped her by snagging her arm. She winced at the touch and shook free. She was not about to have another schizophrenic episode with him.

"Why did you really follow me here, Seneca?"

She wouldn't meet his eyes, looking away to the safety of the city. "I didn't trust you, although that shouldn't surprise you."

"It doesn't."

She looked at him then. His eyes flashed incandescent for a brief moment, and she remembered why she didn't trust him. *You don't belong here.*

"I don't give a damn what you and your Shifter friend do together. Whether or not you are gay. What you do in your spare time. You're right. It's none of my business."

He narrowed his eyes. "What did you say?"

She sighed. "I said, you're right—"

"No," he interrupted. "Before that. How do you know he's a Shifter? I didn't tell you that."

Seneca felt her stomach drop. Oh, damn. "Lucky guess."

Dempsey studied her. "I don't think so. You knew he was a Shifter. How?"

She blew out a breath. One stupid slip. Two days ago her world was normal. Well, at least as normal as it could be. How could everything fall apart so fast? Who in the great cosmos did she piss off?

Dempsey asked, "Can you *see* Shifters?"

Perfect. Just perfect. Well, Riley had known and MacGregor sort of knew. What was one more? "A little."

Dempsey shook his head. "You either do or you don't."

"So I do," she snapped. "So what?"

For a moment, he just stared at her. "That explains a lot."

She frowned. "Like what?"

"Like why you're the best agent XCEL has."

"No, I'm just extremely good," she said.

He asked, "Are there others like you?"

"In XCEL, are you kidding?"

"Anywhere," he persisted.

"There is no one like me," she said, through clenched teeth.

"I noticed," Dempsey said. "Did Riley know this?"

"Yes. But no one else knows," she said. "And I'd like to keep it that way."

His eyes narrowed. "Of course. Wouldn't want the whole world to ostracize you."

It occurred to her that he'd been around humans too long. He knew exactly what would happen to her if the other XCEL agents found out.

"Are we done here?" she asked. "Because I've had all the excitement I can handle for one night."

He stepped aside to last her pass.

"I'll see you tomorrow," she said, and escaped to her car at the end of the block.

◆ ◆ ◆

Max pounded the heavy bag for all he was worth, nearly knocking Apollo off his feet. The sound echoed across the quiet boxing hall in the middle of the afternoon.

"Venting much?" Apollo asked as he held the bag in place.

"You have no idea," Max answered and landed another brutal punch that jolted his entire body. He was covered with sweat and hadn't even begun to shake the lingering remnants of last night.

"How's your partner?" Apollo asked, and grimaced when Max nailed the bag again.

"Just great."

"Well, she must be something because I haven't seen you this worked up since, well, never."

Max hit the bag hard, sending pain up his arm. Seneca was at the funeral that she hadn't invited him to right now. She had told Riley about her Shifter sight, but she hadn't planned to tell him. And she followed him because she didn't trust *him*? Granted, his expectations of humans were pretty damn low, but she was supposed to be his partner. Apparently, it was in name only.

"Unless . . . You two hook up last night?" Apollo said with a grin.

Max eyed him. He really didn't need the reminder of Seneca's scent, Seneca's skin, Seneca's warmth ingrained in his brain and body any more than it was. "No, I haven't slept with her. I seriously doubt she'd have me."

"You never know until you try."

Right. He unleashed a reckless volley on the bag, his arms burning. "And tell me how many women you would have slept with if you'd told them what you were?"

Apollo grinned. "More than you."

Max grunted. "You can't fool Seneca." He jammed his glove into the bag, feeling the reverberation through his bones. "She can see Shifters."

Apollo nearly lost his grip on the heavy bag. "You're shittin' me? She told you that?"

Eventually, and only after I caught her. Which explained why she was such a good agent on paper. Couple that with the fact that she hated Shifters, and she was perfect for XCEL. He clenched his teeth and gave the bag a merciless uppercut. "She picked out Carl."

"Hell," Apollo said, his eyes widening. "Did she make the connection between him and the government?"

Pound, pound, pound. "Not yet, but it's only a matter of time. She's smart."

"Among other things. This bag can't take much more," Apollo said with a laugh.

Apollo had a death wish today. Max dropped his gloves, feeling as drained as he was going to get. "I've got bigger things to deal with. We have a Skinman in town."

Apollo let go of the heavy bag and shook out his arms. "I'm surprised it took this long for one to surface. Do you know where he set up shop?"

"Underground. He's harvesting the homeless."

"Now, there's some good, healthy DNA for you," Apollo said. "I'm assuming you think he's the traitor slash murderer?"

Max held out one glove for Apollo to unlace. "I'll let you know when I visit him."

"You and what army? You know he'll have protection."

Skinmen were the only Shifters who could afford bodyguards. The rest were on their own. "Luckily, Seneca is all fired up to keep him from soiling the pristine human race. So not only will I have to take out him and all his friends; I'll have to keep her alive."

Apollo pulled off the glove he'd just unlaced. "Wow, keeping the hot babe safe. Sounds like you kinda like her."

"I still have one glove on, bud," Max said.

Apollo laughed. "If you need help, you know where to find me."

Max unlaced the other one himself. "I thought you didn't want to get involved?"

He shrugged. "Who else can I box against? These guys are all soft."

Max shook his head. Apollo might act like the universe revolved around him, but Max knew better. Surviving genocide had a way of binding people together. He pulled off his other glove, slung his towel over his shoulders, and headed for the lockers. "I'll call you if I need you."

Apollo walked next to him. "You won't call me."

"I might." Or not. Max had decided long ago that he'd die to avenge Ell's murder, but he wouldn't take anyone with him—not Apollo, not Carl. The Shifter race was doomed to die out anyway. He'd just beat the rush.

They stopped at their respective lockers to change out of their workout clothes.

Apollo asked, "Have you told Seneca about all this yet?"

Max pulled off his soaked shirt. "No, and I don't plan to. It doesn't involve her."

"Except the part that this is her planet and these are her people and you both work for the same agency. Other than that, she's out of the loop."

"I can't trust her with this information," Max said. Especially since she wasn't trusting him with any of hers. This was turning into a hell of a partnership.

Apollo shook his head. "I don't know, man. This could get ugly."

"Everything's ugly. Or hadn't you noticed?"

"You know what I mean."

Yes, he knew what Apollo meant, which was exactly why Max was better off with nothing left to lose.

Apollo hiked his gym bag over his shoulder. "I'm serious. You need me, you call me. We had a deal. No matter how crazy I think you are."

Max smiled and slammed the locker shut. The deal was made between Carl, Max, and Apollo when they escaped a burning ship. Day or night, they were there to cover for one another. He hated to be the one to break the pact, but he was going to.

"Of course," he said and slapped Apollo on the back.

CHAPTER
SEVEN

Seneca stood outside Max's apartment door for a full minute before knocking. As much as she didn't want to intrude into his personal life ... Eh, scratch that. She did, but after last night, she was going to be a lot more careful about it. For her own sake, she had decided to stay at least three feet away from Max Dempsey at all times. Except that he was her partner, which complicated things a bit.

She knocked again, harder this time. "Come on, Dempsey. I don't have all day."

At that moment, the door swung open and her brain cells kind of all froze at once from the shock of Dempsey with a towel around his hips, held up by one hand. The rest of him was wet and really nicely humanoid. Wide shoulders, deep chest, narrow hips and ... She suddenly realized that she was working her way down, and he knew it.

"I could have been the Avon lady," she said, dragging her eyes back to his.

"The Avon lady doesn't smell anything like you," he replied, his expression smug.

A fine time for her mouth to go dry. She licked her lips. "Bart gave us a location on Dillinger. I tried to call, but you didn't answer your cell phone or home phone."

His eyes never left hers, but his mouth was curving. "Shower."

"I can see that," she said, her voice cracking. *Smooth.* "You're wet." *Oh, just shut up, Seneca.*

Dempsey broke into an all-male smile, and she silently cursed herself. "I brought the van. We need to set up a stakeout. Bring your jammies."

He didn't move. For a moment, she wasn't sure if she'd actually spoken over the pounding of her heart. Finally, he nodded. "Come on in."

He opened the door for her, and she tried not to look like she was taking in every detail of his place.

"I'll be ready in a few minutes," he said as he disappeared through a doorway at one end of the apartment.

She scanned the sparse furnishings. No sign of company, but just in case. "I hope I didn't interrupt any . . . one," she called out.

From the other room, he replied, "You didn't."

Good. Not that she cared.

She walked around the furnishings and peered through the open doorway where he'd gone. Over the corner of a bed, she caught his reflection in a mirror as he opened his closet. All she could see were bare back, shoulders, and thick biceps before she stopped herself and shook her head.

What was the matter with her? Ever since last night, she'd been on edge. Maybe that little turd Price was right. She needed a date. Just not with him.

She turned her attention to Dempsey's apartment. A brown sofa, two matching chairs, one lamp, and a coffee table took up most of the living room. A small kitchen occupied the other end and an island formed the dining area. The walls were white and bare. Clean and simple and sterile.

Then she frowned. A little too sterile. No personal touches. No throw pillows or pictures or artwork. It felt . . . temporary. A lot like a hotel room, in fact. She wandered into the kitchen and opened the fridge to find milk, bread, and beer.

"Men," she murmured and closed the door. An unexpected flash of color drew her to a long silver necklace with a brilliant blue stone that hung from a hook over the kitchen sink.

Seneca touched the stone, surprised by its brilliance and light weight. It wasn't lapis or azurite or any other blue stone she'd ever seen. She rubbed her thumb across the smooth surface and felt the stone give a little under the pressure. Amazing. The chain was a simple design but innately delicate—for a woman. So whose was it and why was it the only decoration in Dempsey's place?

"Ready?"

She jumped at Dempsey's sharp tone, nearly knocking the necklace from its hook, and spun around to find him standing directly behind her. She didn't need any special abilities to sense the irritation that radiated from him. Why? Because she was in his kitchen?

"Don't your people have a saying about curiosity killing something?" he said, his voice flat.

"Cats," she replied with a careless wave. "Doesn't apply to me."

Dempsey grabbed his coat. "Nothing seems to apply to you, Seneca."

She winced at the terse response. What button had she just pushed? She gave the necklace a final glance; answers would have to wait for another day. Then she followed him out of the apartment. He locked the door behind them and turned to face her, his face a little too close and his voice a little too polite.

"Let's go, partner," he said and cruised past her.

Seneca blew out a breath as she watched him retreat. Great. She'd pissed him off, and she didn't even know how. Dempsey was more human than she'd imagined. He definitely had issues, and she wasn't looking forward to the next eight to ten hours trapped in a van with them.

✦ ✦ ✦

Seneca checked a new message on her phone. "We can move at any time. The prep crew just finished clearing the building residents and most of the neighbors."

Max scanned the dark, quiet street. They were parked half a block from a three-story building east of Conover Avenue in Red Hook. Dillinger was inside in the third-floor, left-side apartment.

Max asked, "How do they get them out?"

Seneca picked up the night vision binoculars from the van dashboard and pointed them at the apartment building. "Probably told them there was a gas leak. Should keep everyone away for a few hours."

Max shook his head. What they went through to protect their secrets. "Do you think your government will ever come clean and make this public so we don't need to sneak around?"

"Not unless they have to."

"Do you agree with that?"

"No."

Maybe there was hope for her yet. "How was the funeral?"

"Far away. We aren't supposed to attend. Violates our security, but—"

"He was your partner."

"Yes." She lowered the binoculars to look at him. "You could have attended too."

He shook his head. "I didn't need to be there." He didn't want to tell her that he was too busy working her out of his system. "You're sure Dillinger is still in there?"

She nodded, and looked through the binoculars. "All the exits are being watched by other agents. So when our boy's lights go off, we can get moving."

"We could move now. He can see in the dark anyway," Max reminded her.

"Yes, but I always prefer to rouse them from a sound sleep before I shoot them."

"You aren't like most women, Seneca," Max said, laughing despite himself.

She smiled under the binoculars. "And don't forget it."

Like he could if he wanted. Max adjusted his position in the driver's seat for the fifteenth time in the past six hours. Despite the hard workout, he still had a lot of pent-up energy. Sitting next to Seneca wasn't helping the situation. Seeing her with Ell's necklace . . . He was surprised by how fast he'd reacted. He had to learn to control himself, or Seneca was going to suspect he wasn't really here for the good of mankind.

And to that end, he turned his concentration to capturing a bad Shifter—his first chance to prove to Seneca and the rest of XCEL that he was worth something. Sometime in the past twenty-four hours, he'd decided the only way he could gain their trust was to prove his value and dedication. Right up until he didn't need XCEL anymore.

The building schematics had been e-mailed to them, and Max paged through the notes on his phone. The building had six units, one set of stairs inside, with a fire escape down the back. A narrow alley lined the left side of the building, and it butted up to another apartment on the right side. No basement. No roof access from the inside. All the floors and apartments had identical layouts.

"No movement inside Dillinger's apartment, but I can see the flicker of the TV against the walls." Seneca lowered the binoculars and rolled her neck. "I hope this doesn't take long. I hate taking down a Shifter when I'm tired."

He glanced at her. She didn't look tired. Her hair was long and loose over the full-body black armor suit she wore. It hugged every curve like it was custom-made for her body alone. He wondered who got the lucky fitting job.

He shifted again and said, "By the way, I flashed his photo across most of lower Manhattan last night after you left. No one recognized him."

Seneca pursed her lips. "I covered the east side. Nothing."

Max stared at her. "You know, this whole partner thing would be a lot more productive if we actually worked together."

Her mouth dropped open. "Hey, I thought you had the night off."

"And I thought you were going back to the office," he said.

Seneca shook her head, her silky hair shimmering. "This is never going to work."

She sounded serious, and that worried him. He needed XCEL and her to find Ell's killer. "I think we need to do some trust-building exercises," he suggested, trying to lighten the mood.

She looked at him and raised an eyebrow. "If you think I'm going to fall backward and let you catch me, forget it."

He had a better idea. "Ask me a question."

Seneca stared at him. "Any question?"

"Anything, and I'll answer it truthfully."

She licked her lips, which was a gesture she had that he was really starting to like.

"Who did the necklace belong to?" she asked.

Any question but that one. However, he couldn't back down. He was trying to build trust here. He took a deep breath and stared out the window. "My wife."

"Wife?" Seneca sounded like she was choking.

"She was killed," he added. "When we crashed." That part was a lie, but Seneca would never know.

"I'm sorry," she said. The sincerity of her expression surprised him once again. "Did you have any children together?"

"No. She was a native, not a Shifter," he replied. "They weren't a compatible species."

"She wasn't from your home planet?" Seneca asked.

He gave a short laugh. "We haven't had a home planet in

three hundred years. Even if we did, there aren't enough of us left to save the race."

"That's a shame. For all of you." She held his gaze for a few moments and then lifted the binoculars once more.

Max leaned back in his seat and stared at her. Sometimes, he couldn't figure her out at all. Was that sympathy? Couldn't have been. Not from Seneca. She could never, would never understand what it meant to have no home. No safe place. Plus she killed Shifters for a living. That said it all.

"Lights out," Seneca announced suddenly and tossed the binoculars on the dashboard. She grinned at Max. "Ready or not, here we come."

CHAPTER
EIGHT

They worked silently in the back of the van, checking and double-checking gear. Dempsey seemed to know what he was doing, which made Seneca feel slightly better. But first time out with a new partner was always a crapshoot, and who knew how Dempsey was going to react?

"I'm ready," he told her.

She looked at his short-sleeved T-shirt, pants, and shoes. Okay, she knew he didn't need armor or night vision or the plethora of weapons like she did, but still. "What happens to those clothes if you shift?"

He pulled on the communications headgear. It was for her benefit, not his. Shifters could literally hear a pin drop. "All organic materials. I can integrate them."

"Good to know," she said, momentarily distracted by how that miracle could happen. She scanned his height and breadth.

He was a big man, and there was a lot of material to integrate. So, where did it go? Inside, or did the molecules get absorbed and reused? And then—

She realized he was watching her study his body.

"I can see the wheels turning," he said, grinning.

She rolled her eyes. "Please, I've seen plenty of naked Shifters. However, clothing doesn't seem to fare particularly well in the transformation."

"No such problem here." Then he leaned toward her as he shoved his Glock in the small of his back. "Were you worried?"

She wrinkled her nose. "You all look the same to me."

He smiled like he knew better. Then he grabbed the disrupter pistol and jumped out the back van doors. "I'm lead."

The hell, she thought as she followed him. "You do realize that I wouldn't be here if I couldn't hold my own."

"I know," he said and shut the doors behind her. "But this way, if it all goes to hell, you can blame it on me."

Now he was confusing her. What happened to the whole Shifter prototype agent initiative? On the other hand, why was she arguing about it? "Have it your way."

They hiked it to the building, down the side alley, and toward the rear entrance. The prep crew had made sure they'd get inside with no problems. It was always nice when Seneca had the time to plan and do things right. Prep crew cleared the way. Backup and cleanup crews were at the ready. They used the best equipment known to man. All this for one shapeshifter. If the taxpayers only knew where their money was going.

For his part, Dempsey was all business, moving ahead of her noiselessly and cleanly, weapon drawn. She followed his silent signals to the back door. The city hum faded to the background as she focused her senses on every detail of the building. The location of the fire escape and garbage cans, the smell of rotting food, the reflection of lights on puddles in the alley.

Seneca readied the AA-12 shotgun loaded with monster slugs, and suddenly she missed Riley. She knew what he would do, how he'd react in every situation. She'd trusted him implicitly. Now she had to start all over again. She whispered to Dempsey into her comm, "Have you ever done this before?"

Dempsey smiled, his teeth white in her night vision goggles. "Plenty of times."

She groaned. "You are so full of crap."

He chuckled in her earpiece. "Ready?"

Seneca nodded and turned the door handle slowly. It swung open, and Dempsey slipped inside. She followed close behind and down the hallway dotted with stingy ceiling lights. Dempsey slowed and she noted the next doorway had a beam of light streaming from under it.

The thought of someone still in the building chilled her to the bones. They didn't need witnesses, or worse, victims. Did the prep crew miss someone? Dempsey motioned for her to wait as he moved along the wall to the door. He inhaled deeply a few times, and then she heard him say, "Empty."

She let out a breath, feeling far more anxious than she'd realized.

They cleared the first floor, second floor, and stairs to the third-floor landing in a few minutes. They moved in unison into position on either side of Dillinger's door.

Dempsey showed her three fingers to start the countdown.

Seneca gripped the rifle and exhaled to calm herself.

Two fingers.

It'd be fine. Dempsey was one of them. He should know how to stop them.

One.

Dempsey stepped out and kicked the door in with a single deafening blow. Then he was inside, and she was right behind him into a narrow foyer, then an open living room.

One moment Dempsey was in front of her, and the next, he was sailing through the air and crashing against the wall, leaving her face-to-face with the biggest Shifter she'd ever laid eyes on. Through her green night vision, his skin was mottled, his head domed, and his eyes glowing.

All seven feet of him swung around to face her. She glanced at Dempsey out cold on the floor. Looked like it was going to be the hard way again.

"Police," she said. "You're under arrest. Don't suppose you'd like to give yourself up?"

His mouth split into what she assumed to be a Shifter smile with a whole lot of teeth.

Guess not.

She fired the rifle, and the slug ripped through his stomach before bouncing off the wall behind him. He simply stood there and smiled.

Oh, *perfect.*

He rushed her in a puff of black dust, reappeared beside her, and swatted the rifle, breaking it in two. She dove beneath his clawed hand in the split second that he was out of position. His hand narrowly missed taking off her head, instead ripping off her night vision and headgear. She ducked behind a big recliner and drew her Glock as Dillinger's slow, deep rumble rang in her ears. Her cheek was bleeding from the blow, and her eyes were having difficulty focusing.

"Dempsey, get your ass up!" she yelled. Then she peered over the top of the chair to see where Dillinger was, just in case he'd decided to bolt. The window illuminated his black figure standing in the middle of the room. No such luck.

"You are so pathetic," he said, walking toward her. "Slow, stupid, arrogant human. You don't even know that you're extinct, do you?"

"Hey, at least no one is kicking me off my own planet!" she snapped back, and then realized that might not be the best way to win him over.

With a loud growl, he grabbed the recliner and tossed it aside like a toy. Trapped in the corner, Seneca unloaded her Glock at his head, knowing full well she didn't have a chance of stopping him unless she could get her hands on him.

He swiped at the gun, and she grabbed for his arm but missed as it came back and connected with her head. She slammed against the wall and felt herself slipping into darkness. Desperate, she reached for some part of his body to force-shift.

But he suddenly disappeared out of reach. She tumbled forward and shook her head to clear it. The room faded in and out for a moment before she realized what she was seeing.

In front of her two Shifters were locked in combat. One was Dillinger, and the other was . . . She glanced over where Dempsey had been. The only thing left was a blood smear.

He was about the same size as Dillinger, but his skin was a

lighter gray, his body more muscular, powerful and sinuous. And he fought like a wild animal. Alien bodies collided, merged, re-formed, and slashed. Black dust filled the room and blood spattered across the ceiling and walls.

Every slash, every blow was filled with murderous intent. This battle would be to the death. She watched the horrific action, feeling detached and helpless as they collided with walls and furniture. Every impact Dempsey took seemed to pierce her skull.

She crawled on the floor looking for a weapon. She knew she was outclassed, outweighed, and out of her element here, but she had to do something. If Dempsey lost, Dillinger would finish her off and walk away to kill another day. That was not going to happen on her watch. She spotted the disrupter pistol ten feet away.

Dillinger landed a solid right, and Dempsey grunted and slammed against the wall beside her. He spared her a quick growl that sounded like, "Get outside!" before attacking again.

Get outside? Did he just order her out? Well, screw that. Who the hell did he think he was? She was the senior member here. So instead, she made a dash for the disrupter. Just as she grabbed it, she heard glass breaking and spun around to find a hole in the apartment where the window had been. Both Shifters were gone.

She ran over and looked down. They were in the narrow alley, lying motionless on the pavement. She holstered the disrupter and pulled out the tranquilizer gun. The barrel had been flattened, and the cartridge was leaking. She tossed it aside and checked her spare tranquilizer darts. All were busted except for one. It was cracked and half empty. Not enough to hold down a Shifter, but enough for a human. She hit the floor running.

By the time she got down three flights and outside, Dillinger was stirring. She skidded to her knees beside him and put her hand on his chest. *Concentrate.* "Shift!"

He let out a long wail as his body began to contort. She gave Dempsey a quick look. He was still in Shifter form, which meant he was either too injured to shift back or unconscious. She should check but Dillinger was taking his sweet time shifting back to human form, and she wasn't leaving him until she knew for certain that he was down for the count. She said to Dempsey, "You alive over there?"

No reply, and she was surprised to realize how worried that made her.

Minutes passed before Dillinger fully shifted to a thirty-something white male. She jabbed the tranq dart into his chest and watched until the vial emptied.

Then all the energy seemed to seep out of her body. Her arms and legs hurt like hell, and the side of her head throbbed. She got up and made her way to Dempsey, who was moving slowly and had shifted back to human.

She dropped to her knees next to him and pulled a cell phone from her suit. She speed-dialed the troops and told them the package was ready for pickup. She was ordering an ambulance for Dempsey when he grabbed her arm and said, "Don't."

"What?" she asked.

His eyes were closed. "No ambulance. No doctors."

"You need to be looked at, Dempsey."

He opened his eyes. "They can't help me. Your medicine doesn't work the same for us."

She realized he was probably right. XCEL knew nothing

about Shifters health-wise. They were just going to be put on ice anyway. "Cancel the EMTs," she said and hung up.

Then Dempsey rolled to his side with great effort.

"What do you need?" she said.

"You really don't want to know," he replied, sounding distracted. He seemed to be concentrating on his breathing. She glanced up thirty feet to the hole in the apartment. That was why he'd told her to get outside. He was expecting to push Dillinger out. Dillinger wasn't.

"Try me," she said.

He rubbed his neck. "I could use a cold drink."

Seneca helped him to his feet as the cleanup crew arrived. They could take it from here, and luckily, they never asked questions. "That makes two of us."

◆ ◆ ◆

From the shadows, Max watched Seneca deal with the guys in black suits. An ominous-looking truck had pulled into the alley, blocking most of it. Dillinger was neutralized and being loaded into a steel container.

And Seneca Thomas could make Shifters shift against their will.

In all the places he'd been and all the people he'd seen, he'd never met anyone who could do that. Was she unique or were there others with that ability? How had she discovered her power? Did she know about it before she joined XCEL? Did *they* know? He had a lot of questions, but he doubted he'd ever get answers from her.

Seneca glanced at him with a flicker of concern and then

turned around to talk to another uniform. He'd had the opportunity to see her in action, and she was good, even without the added special skills. Between being able to spot them and being able to make them shift, she was a born Shifter hunter.

The lid was closed over Dillinger, and Seneca walked back toward Max. She handed him a bottled water. "Sorry, the best I could do."

He took it and nodded toward her bloody cheek. "Thanks. Are you okay?"

She gave a short laugh. "I've had worse. You?"

"All healed," he said and took a drink from the bottle. "Did you ask them where they take the bodies?"

Seneca nodded her head. "They wouldn't tell me."

She'd asked? He was surprised, which, considering everything he'd just witnessed, was quite a feat. He turned to her. "I saw how you made Dillinger shift. I'd like to know how you did it."

She didn't look at him. "I don't know what you're talking about."

He could see the tension in her shoulders. She knew exactly what he was talking about. "You put your hand on him and said, 'Shift.' And he did. Care to explain that?"

"Not really," she said, her gaze fixed on the cleanup crew.

Max leaned back against the brick wall. "I know what I saw."

She finally looked at him, her expression guarded. "It's personal."

This was why he preferred to work alone. Partners were a royal pain. "Or I could talk to MacGregor and all the other agents to see what they know about it."

Seneca glared at him for what seemed an eternity. "Yes, I can force-shift or shift-force or whatever you want to call it. I can, but don't ask me how. End of discussion."

Like it was no big deal. Maybe not to her. To a Shifter who had to work very closely with her, it was a bit worrisome. "Are there others who can do that?"

"I have no idea," she said. "It's not like there's a club for freaks like me."

"Can you force a Shifter from human form back to Shifter form?"

She crossed her arms over her chest. "I haven't found a Shifter willing to let me try. Are you volunteering?"

"I'll pass. Dillinger didn't look too comfortable."

"He got what he deserved," she said, and she meant it.

"Do we all deserve that?" he asked.

Seneca hesitated a moment, just long enough for him to realize that she had to actually think about it.

"No. You don't," she said. "Unless, of course, you tell anyone what I can do."

Ah, so that was it. "Riley knew this."

"Yes, he did. Deal with it." Then she slapped her palms together. "Well, that was fun. I think I'll go somewhere to be alone now."

Dempsey snagged her by the arm just as she turned to leave. He could see the anger and determination in her eyes, but he didn't care.

"You aren't a freak. And neither am I," he said softly. "We are what we are."

"You had a whole world of people like you," she whispered back, her voice breaking. "There's no one here like me."

Her eyes were starting to water, her hands clenched into fists. He understood exactly how she felt. "I know. I'm sorry."

It was all he could think of to say. For a few moments, they didn't move. Then he released Seneca and stepped back.

"We need to get back to the van," she said and started walking away. "By the way. Good job tonight."

Max smiled in the dark.

◆ ◆ ◆

Hager took a sip of the twenty-year-old cabernet sauvignon he was sharing with the man he'd recently put into the Skinman role for Shifters in New York City. The former Skinman had become lazy and uncooperative, and Hager decided that replacing him was necessary in order to move his plan along. George, the new Skinman, was a Shifter who Hager had worked with on Govan, and a business man first and foremost. His motives were clear— money. Hager liked that. It made it easy to manipulate him.

Hager said to him, "You can understand my concern. I need to be sure you can supply me with enough virgin DNA. I don't want duplicates. I don't want anything artificially altered. I want pure, unadulterated DNA."

Skinman grimaced as he tried the wine again. Hager knew he didn't like it, didn't understand the point of a fine wine, the symbolism of an alien savoring the fruits of human labor. Pity. Opportunities were meant to be taken.

"No problem," he said. "I got enough for you and your boys. You just keep the protection and the money coming."

"Of course," Hager said and set his glass down on the granite table that stretched between them. Dim light from the overhead bulbs caught the cut-crystal wineglass and reflected tiny prisms across the cool cellar. Dusty bottles stacked in careful order lined the walls. The floors of the old cellar wore the passage of time.

Hager loved old things. The things that no one else seemed to want. Shifters didn't often live long enough to watch their possessions get old. He planned to.

"Can't do a damn thing without money on this crappy planet," Skinman grumbled. He pointed a boney finger at Hager. "You don't have money on this world, you got nothing. No life, no women, no respect."

Hager picked up his glass and swirled the wine, watching it dance red and maroon in the light. "There are more important things in life than sex and respect. You should have learned that by now."

Skinman gave a grunt. "These worlds, they're all the same. All uptight and totally screwed up. They're just too stupid to know it."

Stupid, yes, but this country was tenacious in relinquishing its civility. Govan had been simpler, its military government more than willing to engage in large-scale violence. A genocide there hardly made the headlines. Here, he'd need to be far more careful if he wanted to gain the level of power and prestige he was accustomed to. This was going to require a more methodical, calculated, and subversive attack. One that the people of the country wouldn't notice until it was too late.

"Now, that's no way to talk about our hosts," Hager said, lifting his glass. "To the Americans."

"May they live long enough to make me rich and happy," Skinman said and drained his wineglass.

Such a waste, Hager thought. Both of mind and body. He savored a small sip, let it glide along his tongue and all the taste buds courtesy of human DNA. An amazing sense, really.

"Unfortunately, not all of them are stupid," Skinman said.

Hager lifted an eyebrow. "Is there a problem?"

Skinman pushed to his feet and started pacing the length of the wide underground tunnel, alternately blocking out the ceiling lights. His long black hair and goatee meshed with the black custom shirt, tailored pants and high-end shoes—all very expensive. But expensive clothes didn't make a man. Power made a man.

Skinman finally stopped in front of Hager. "I got word that XCEL has a Shifter."

Hager narrowed his eyes. "As an agent? Are you certain?"

Skinman nodded his head a few times. "He was spotted in an XCEL operation last night. He and a female partner took down a Shifter in short order."

XCEL. The one feeble attempt of this country's government to combat Shifters. They'd managed to pick off a few rogue Shifters but posed no real threat to his fledgling organization. Still, they were a nuisance. At some point, he'd need to address them. He'd hoped it would be later, when his all-Shifter army was at full strength. He may not have that long, after all.

"He could be a problem," Skinman said. "He can see us."

A problem, yes, but fascinating as well. Cooperating with the enemy. Hager couldn't remember anything like that happening on Govan. Well, except for him of course.

"Name?"

"Max Dempsey."

Hager didn't recognize it. He didn't expect to. Shifters adopted whatever names fit in with their current environment. "Address?"

"Not yet, but I can get it," Skinman said. "You want him killed?"

Hager shook his head. "Unnecessary."

Skinman sputtered. "But he can ID us. He's working for an agency that hunts us down. Why not?"

Hager smiled. "XCEL is not a threat to us. But we wouldn't want them to rally any additional troops, would we?"

Skinman's disappointment was palpable. "You used to be more fun, Hager."

Hager swirled his wine in thought. He found it hard to believe XCEL would approve of a Shifter working among them. He'd been here long enough to understand exactly what their reaction would be. "Do they realize there is a Shifter in their midst?"

Skinman shrugged his shoulders. "I don't know. I don't care. I just don't want to run into him."

"I told you I'd protect you." Hager pushed out of his chair to shake the man's hand. "Keep your head down. I do not want to have to find another Skinman."

Skinman said, "Well, neither do I. Tell me when you are ready to roll. I wanna be there to see this city brought to its knees."

"You'll be the first to know. And remember, I need thirty orders by this Friday," Hager said. "And send in Puck on your way out."

Skinman left with a "Will do."

Hager sat back down in the leather chair and pondered his next steps. The XCEL Shifter needed to be neutralized and perhaps even recruited. That would be quite a coup, having a former XCEL agent in his ranks. He needed a few more good recruits, Shifters who were serious about making this world their home.

He'd already filled the borough lord positions with allies he knew he could trust. They formed the inner circle of his organization and were busy recruiting new Shifters for the next phase of his plan. That new army would give him the power and numbers to take down the established organized crime families and then move into their positions. One by one, block by block, borough by borough, this city would be his.

Hager traded his wineglass for his mobile device. Updates and information from his sources streamed down the tiny screen, keeping him in touch with every corner of this city and beyond.

Puck scurried in. For some reason that Hager would never understand, he wore the skin of an old Irishman and refused to change.

"What's up?" Puck said, coming to a quick stop in front of Hager.

He put down the device. Technology was too insecure, and he'd been burned before. Some things were better handled the old-fashioned way. "I need the location of the local XCEL office, and the entire list of agents working for them. Get my best tracker on it."

Puck nodded furiously. "Tracker, got it."

"That'll be all."

With that, Puck scurried away.

Hager picked up his wineglass, pleased with his current position. Once the Shifter was exposed, XCEL would be steeped in disorder and a whole new set of opportunities would present themselves.

He tipped the glass to his mouth and let the remainder of the exquisite liquid slide down his throat. A very good year indeed. He was sure the human owner who'd sacrificed his life, his house, and his wine cellar to Hager would have agreed.

CHAPTER
NINE

Max knew there was a problem the minute he walked into the office for the evening shift. The entire floor was quiet, voices subdued, tension high. The hair on the back of his neck prickled, an instinctive human sign that indicated something was very wrong. He'd found it quite useful.

As he crossed the suite, Price stepped in front of him. "Max Dempsey, what a surprise."

Max narrowed his gaze. "I work here, Price."

Then Conklin blocked his way when he tried to enter his office. Conklin was a good agent, always the first one to volunteer for cases. The life of the party. But today, the agent stared him down. "But you aren't one of us, are you, Dempsey?"

Max had almost liked Conklin, until now. He scanned the office as agents began to converge around him. Every eye, every glare was on him. He had known when he started that this day would come. So who'd given him up? Seneca? He couldn't believe that. She was too much about the job. MacGregor? No, he wouldn't want to deal with it.

Conklin shoved him in the chest as the other agents backed him up. "Not going to deny it, are you, you bastard?"

Max planted his feet and stood his ground. "You don't want to start this."

Conklin laughed. "Are you gonna turn into a big bad Shifter? Go ahead. We know how to handle those."

Max clenched his fists. He really didn't want to hurt these guys, didn't want trouble. But no matter what he did, trouble always seemed to find him.

Conklin shoved him again. "Go ahead, shift."

"That's enough, Conklin."

Everyone turned to the suite door where Seneca stood. Her intense gaze scanned the room before settling on Max. Without another word, she walked up and stood next to him. Every fiber of his being seemed to align with her.

Conklin looked at her in absolute disbelief. "Do you know what he is?"

She replied calmly, "Yes. I do. Leave it alone."

Max noticed that she didn't flinch. *His partner*. Who'd have thought?

"You expect us to leave it alone?" Conklin said. "*He's* the reason we're dying. Or haven't you noticed all the funerals lately?"

Her voice remained level, but there was a dangerous edge to it. "Don't be a moron. There are good and bad Shifters, just like there are good and bad humans."

She tried to push past him to their office, but Conklin stepped in her way and said, "Yeah, but they don't rip you to shreds with their bare hands."

Max's hands were clenched so hard, they hurt. If Conklin so much as touched her . . .

Seneca crossed her arms. "Well, you proved me wrong, Conklin. You are a moron. Since you seem to know everything, did you also know he helped take down our number one killer last night?"

"I could have done that," Conklin said.

"No. You couldn't have." She looked over the rest of the faces. "None of you would have been able to handle that one. You may not like it, but we need Dempsey."

Conklin turned red. "You're screwing him, aren't you?"

Max felt the last bit of self-control snap. He was just about to slug Conklin when Seneca hauled off and punched the man right in the face. He fell into a few of the guys, and they launched him back at her. Then Max was between them. Enough was enough.

He grabbed and twisted the collar of Conklin's shirt like a garrote. It was only because he had an audience that he stopped himself from tightening it too much.

"Don't," he said softly, a growl echoing his single word, sounding more alien than human. The men around them took a step back. He smelled fear for the first time. Not a particularly good way to charm the coworkers. He released Conklin with a bit of a push.

Conklin was sputtering through the blood running down his lip. "You bastard—"

MacGregor's door swung open, and he bellowed, "What the hell's going on out here?"

Conklin glared at Max. "Nothing."

"Nothing, my ass," MacGregor roared as he headed for them.

"We had a situation," Seneca said, shaking her hand. "You might call it undue friction."

"Shit," MacGregor grumbled and planted himself in front of Conklin. "You got a problem with the team I assembled?"

"No, sir," Conklin said and wiped his lip on his sleeve.

"Good. That's one less thing you gotta worry about. Now get your ass out there and do your damn job."

Conklin grumbled and wandered off. The rest of the team dispersed quietly.

MacGregor turned to Max and Seneca and frowned. "My office. *Now.*"

Seneca gave Max a weary look as she walked past him. They all filed into MacGregor's office and closed the door. He sat heavily in his beat-up chair. "I'm sorry that happened, Max. If I find the leak, I'll plug it."

Max said, "It was going to come out sooner or later."

MacGregor shook his head. "Well, I got a problem somewhere." Then he turned to Seneca. "And you, no more punching other agents. You're undermining all my goddamned team-building efforts."

She looked indignant. "How do you know it was me?"

He rolled his eyes. "Don't bullshit me. I know he probably deserved it—"

"He did," she said.

"But don't do it again. He got the hint," MacGregor finished.

She waved her hand. "Okay, okay."

Seneca gave Max a quick smile, and the rampant confusion in

his mind settled. Why had she defended him? Why? Good and bad Shifters? Where did that come from?

MacGregor opened a file on his desk. "Now that the foreplay is over, I hear you got Dillinger last night. How did it go?"

"Seneca did most of the work," Max said at the same time Seneca said, "Dempsey kicked his ass."

MacGregor looked from one to the other. "Nice to see you worked out your differences. Too bad you aren't working any cases for a while."

"You promised us Skinman," Seneca said, shaking her head.

MacGregor lifted his gaze. "Yesterday. I promised that yesterday, *before* the leak. Now I have to deal with that."

"This is my fault, not Seneca's," Max said.

"You guys got something going on that I don't know about?" MacGregor asked, frowning deeply.

Seneca gave a groan of frustration and leaned forward. "Look. Skinman is a major threat. Every day we wait, he kills more people. He has to be stopped."

MacGregor closed the folder. "He's also underground, which means it'll be harder than hell to provide you with backup." He spared Max a quick glance. "Especially now."

"We don't need backup," Seneca said. "We can handle it."

MacGregor pointed a pudgy finger at each of them in turn. "No Skinman. And that's a direct order. Not until I figure out where our leak is. This could be serious. The Committee will have my ass in a sling if their plan is put in jeopardy. And until further notice, you are both taking some well-deserved time off."

Seneca was on her feet in an instant. "What?"

"I realize that a life outside this agency is a foreign concept to you," MacGregor said as he settled back in his chair. "But you will take it, and you will not come into this office until I give you the all clear. Is that understood?"

Max eyed Seneca as she crossed her arms and pursed her lips. "Yes."

"I'm so glad we had this little talk," MacGregor said. "And don't leave town. I still need you. You two are the best agents I have. You don't come back, you leave me with the likes of Conklin."

◆ ◆ ◆

"I'd like to know why everyone thinks we're screwing," Seneca muttered as she shut their office door after Dempsey.

"Interesting, that," he said.

And disturbing. Was it something she'd done? Or the simple fact that they were a male-female team? Maybe she'd put a stop to it by hitting Conklin. Her hand still hurt, but it was well worth it. He'd be okay and now everyone would drop the whole screwing thing.

Besides, in the grand scheme of things, Dempsey as a Shifter in their midst was a bigger issue. She'd been surprised at Dempsey's restraint, which was obviously better than hers. Then again, she'd known that. He had to have supreme self-control in order to work here and with her. It wasn't like she'd made it easy for him.

But now she had "time off" to think about it. She hadn't taken more than one day off at a time since joining the agency. What was she supposed to do with more than that? Get a mani-pedi?

She pulled out her briefcase with a huff of disgust and started loading case files into it. Might as well do some homework while she was exiled to normal life.

Dempsey sat in the chair across from her and crossed his arms over his chest. "Is that the Skinman file?"

She looked at him. He wore a pale, faded chambray shirt under a brown leather jacket and nicely fitted jeans. Dark eyes gazed back at her, the edges crinkled in amusement. A sexy smile tugged at his lips. It suddenly occurred to her why everyone thought she was sleeping with him.

"Of course not. That would be going against a direct order," she said and slid the Skinman file into the case.

"That's true," he said with a nod. "Plus it'd be unwise to go after a man like that without XCEL support. Especially since you are essentially one of us now."

That stopped her midpack as she recalled the looks of betrayal she'd gotten from the other agents. MacGregor could yell all he wanted, but he couldn't make that prejudice go away. He couldn't force them to change their mind-set. She was no longer one of them. She was an outcast, just like Dempsey.

"They'll come around," she said with a shrug.

"No, they won't," Dempsey said. After a few beats, he added, "I'm sorry."

She closed the latch on her briefcase. "I don't need anyone to save me, Dempsey."

"What about dinner? Do you need that?" he asked smoothly.

Her pulse jumped. "A date? That's not going to help my rep."

Dempsey said, "I have to eat too. And I have wine."

She hesitated. Food and wine sounded *very* good. Still . . .

"And maybe we can discuss how we plan to spend our time off." He stood up and walked to her, reaching for her briefcase. "I'll carry that out for you."

She eyed him. "You realize this contains incriminating evidence that could get you fired."

"I know." His expression was serious. "I don't expect any problems."

She gave him a little smile as she passed over the briefcase.

◆ ◆ ◆

Max smelled the intruders before he reached his apartment door. Talk about a rotten way to ruin an otherwise promising evening.

He held a hand up to Seneca behind him and drew his gun. Silently, she placed the bag of groceries and briefcase on the floor and pulled out her weapon. He moved along the wall to the open door and noticed the busted lock. No movement inside. No sounds.

He turned and mouthed, "Wait here," to Seneca. She looked at him like he was crazy and shook her head.

He mouthed, "Shifters."

She mouthed back, "So?"

Christ, the woman was relentless. Giving up, he shouldered the door open and stepped inside, gun first. The kitchen light was on, and it took only a moment to confirm that the place was empty.

And trashed.

Couch and chair stuffing were strewn across the floor along with pieces of lamps and other furnishings. His laptop was in pieces along the wall. The television had an end table leg rammed through it. The kitchen cabinet doors were ripped off, the contents tossed out, and the countertop damaged. He entered his bedroom. Clothes and bedding lay in heaps. The mattress had been ripped to shreds. The bathroom sink was cracked, and water squirted from the busted showerhead.

And every room had the word "traitor" spray painted on the walls.

"It's clear," he said as he joined Seneca in the main room.

Seneca holstered her gun and took in the destruction. "Must have been a hell of a party. You think it was Shifters?"

He walked over to the kitchen and noticed Ell's necklace lying in the sink. He picked it up and slid it into his jeans pocket. "Positive."

"Seems quite a coincidence that you were just outed at work today too," she said.

Yes, it did. Someone knew he was a Shifter working for XCEL. He mentally cataloged the three individual Shifter scents that covered his apartment. Then he turned and moved quickly through the wreckage into his bedroom. The closet door hung on by one hinge and his clothes had been flung from their hangers. He reached under the clothes and found the duffle bag. Seneca had followed him into the bedroom and stood behind him. Carefully, he slid his hand into the false bottom of the duffle. The package was still there. He breathed a sigh of relief and sealed the false bottom. Then he pulled the duffle out and set it on the bed. It was going with him this time.

Seneca said, "You can't stay here. It's not safe."

No kidding. He stood up to face her and promptly froze in

his tracks. It was dark in his bedroom—she couldn't see him very well but his vision was perfect, and there was something different in the way she looked at him. Ever since last night, she'd become more approachable, like the Do Not Touch sign had been turned off. As precarious as that felt, it sent a charge through his body that dominated the destruction and the betrayal around him.

"I'll get a hotel room. Just need to pack some clothes."

At least that was what he'd planned to do, but at the moment, he couldn't take his eyes off hers. They were beautiful and clear, without condemnation, without judgment. Almost, with kindness. He hadn't seen that look in so long.

"Doesn't this bother you?" she asked quietly.

"They were just things."

"What about the invasion of privacy?"

Her hair looked silky in the dark, her skin smooth, her voice sexy. His thoughts were heading way out of line. "Nothing I can do about it. However, if they know about me, they might know about you."

She raised her chin in challenge, but her voice softened. "I doubt it. I'm not a traitor to them."

Traitor. They had called *him* a traitor. It was poetic perhaps, but not in a good way. He stepped up to Seneca until he was close enough that she filled his vision. Close enough that her scent overwhelmed the smell of intruders.

"This could prove dangerous to you," he whispered.

She smiled darkly. "I live for danger."

He moved closer to her warmth, despite all the reasons why he shouldn't. "I'm as dangerous as it gets, Seneca. Make no mistake."

Her eyes widened slightly, her breath quickening. He was close enough that she could see him now, in the darkness. He watched her lips part a little, an invitation she didn't even realize she was giving him. Heat poured over him, blood pounded in his veins, desire unfurled in his belly. Just one touch . . .

"Max, you in here?"

The stranger's shout jolted Seneca to the core and drained the heat that had been building in her bones. She pulled her gun, only to feel Dempsey's hand on hers. He whispered, "He's a friend."

And then his heat was gone as he headed to meet whoever it was. An odd disappointment lingered in his wake. What was wrong with her? She didn't act like this with *human* men.

And he was an alien, for God's sake. She should be running for her life. His race was probably used to cavorting with other aliens, but this was all new to her. Unfortunately, her libido didn't seem to care what he was. In human form, he was all male, all sexy, and all her signals were flashing go.

"I need a date." She holstered the gun before walking into the living room.

Dempsey was talking to a Shifter in human form—tall, blond, handsome, and built like a Mack truck. His eyebrows rose when he laid eyes on her. She sensed an easy camaraderie between the two men, a past. An old friend.

Dempsey motioned to her. "Apollo, meet Seneca. My partner."

Apollo gave her a devastating smile as she shook his hand. "Nice to finally meet. I've heard a lot about you."

Seneca said, "Really?" Then she looked at Dempsey, who was glaring at his friend. "What have you heard?"

Apollo grinned. "Let's just say, it's all true." Then he turned to Dempsey. "I was gone all day, didn't see or hear a thing."

"Probably just as well you weren't here," Dempsey said, his tone dry.

Seneca watched him pick up a shredded pillow and toss it aside. How could this *not* bother him? He treated it like any other day. Maybe it was. Maybe they were all this bad. A pang of compassion came and went. She really had to stop doing that. It was no way for a Shifter hunter to act.

"Were they after something or did they just want to leave you a message?" Apollo asked. "My guess would be traitor."

The brief look that passed between them mystified Seneca. What was that about?

"I'd ask you to bunk with me, but I like my place. Just the way it is," Apollo said. "No offense."

Dempsey half smiled. "None taken. I'll stay at a hotel. I want to keep this quiet for a while."

Apollo nodded. "I can see why. You may not be getting your deposit back. Call me later."

Then he turned to her, lifted her hand, and kissed it. "Very nice meeting you, Seneca. I hope to see you again."

"Good-bye, Apollo," Dempsey said.

Apollo winked at her. He left, forcing the busted door closed behind him.

Dempsey headed back to the dark bedroom. Seneca opted to stay put in the living room. It was a little too warm in his bedroom. She licked her dry lips. "So, does *he* think we're screwing too?"

"No," came the reply from the other room.

Quick response. "Why not?"

"He didn't smell you on me. We aren't lovers."

Well, how about that? The only people who knew they weren't sleeping together were the Shifters. That just wasn't fair.

Her cell phone rang. It was Bart. She answered, "Thomas here."

"I got you a location," Bart said.

"Thirty minutes, the Central Park meeting place?" she asked as Dempsey stepped out of his bedroom with a duffle bag.

"Got it," and he hung up.

She said to Dempsey, "Bart has Skinman's location."

"Good. I have a plan to get close to him."

She pocketed the cell phone. "Am I included in this plan?"

Dempsey said, "You are *definitely* part of the plan."

The way he said it sent a shiver down her spine. She would never have to worry about being cold around him. "Can't wait to hear it."

He smiled. It wasn't a lady killer like Apollo's. It was slow and riveting. "You'll love it. It's full of danger."

"*That's* your plan?"

Max ducked his head against the wind and let Seneca work through the disbelief before replying. Central Park lay silent and somewhat primal at midnight. A half-moon was etched with branches above. The wind rattled the dead leaves that escaped the few inches of snow, and whistled through the stand of trees where they waited for Bart.

Seneca lowered her voice. "Lovers. That's the plan you came up with?"

"No, the plan is we *pose* as lovers. I need a new skin because we want to have a wonderful life together. But we can't because I've done some bad things and need a new identity." He looked at her. "I thought you'd like the part where you changed my evil ways."

"Oh, believe me, I adore that part," she replied. "I'm a little concerned, however, about the part where we prove to the other Shifters that we're lovers. Can't we just be good friends?"

He was finding it hard to concentrate every time she said "lovers." "If we were only friends, I wouldn't need you along to choose the new face and body that you plan to spend the rest of your life with."

She processed that for a few seconds, shifting her weight from one foot to the other anxiously. Who would have thought that Seneca Thomas was afraid of anything? Was it the Shifter factor or just commitment in general? Finally, she wrinkled her nose. "If I find out you're lying about this whole smell thing, Dempsey, you are a dead man."

"Don't I know it." He also knew what was going through her mind. How, exactly, were they going to prove to other Shifters that they were lovers? He didn't offer, and she didn't ask again, but the possibilities would keep him up tonight. And that hadn't happened in a long time, not since Ell . . .

He stopped, surprised that the pain he usually felt at the thought of her didn't manifest. Part of him was disappointed. He never wanted to forget anything about her. The other part of him was too busy concentrating on Seneca's every move. The way her hair spun in the breeze, the way she moved closer to him to block out the cold wind. Max turned a little so she was better sheltered.

She whispered, "I know why I'm here, but why are you defying orders to do this? You could blow the whole prototype Shifter agent experiment if you get caught. All for one guy?"

Max paused before answering. How could he tell her that he was on the trail of a Shifter who murdered his wife? That he was only using Seneca and XCEL to find that man? That was what he should do, but the part of him that trusted no one to help him or even give a damn about him refused to budge.

"Skinmen are notorious for killing the locals to stock their inventories. If you let him continue, the body count will rise, and someone's going to notice."

She gave him a concerned side-glance. "How many Skinmen are there?"

"On Govan, there was usually one per city. I don't know here. This city is pretty big."

Seneca asked, "Then what's to stop more of them from moving in?"

Max gazed down at her. "How much of a message we send with this one."

"Ah," she said, understanding dawning. "And since we are on our own time here—"

"We don't have to follow the rules," he finished for her. "There is only one way this will end, Seneca. We need to take them out permanently. Are you okay with that?"

She blew out a breath that evaporated in the breeze. "We may not have much of a choice. Can't call in backup, can't call in the cleanup crew. Still . . ."

He couldn't let her vacillate. Shifters would die. She should be happy about that. "Everyone in Skinman's posse is harvesting humans, and any one of them is willing to step into his shoes. This will not end unless we end it."

She nodded a few times, her gaze far away. "I know."

Then he squinted at her. "I didn't think it'd be so hard to convince you to kill Shifters."

Seneca eyed him. "Only some of them."

Warmth shot through him, despite the cold. She was his partner. She was with him. She trusted him. It was as good as he was going to get. Now, if only Skinman and Ell's killer were one and the same man, his life would be perfect.

"No one outside XCEL is supposed to know where we live," Seneca said after a few silent moments. "Our identities, our covers, are highly secure. Families protected. So how did they find your place?"

"I don't know." He'd been careful, especially with XCEL. "They could have followed my scent."

"They could have followed any of our scents," she said. "I'll have to tell MacGregor our covers have been compromised. Warn the others."

"Maybe we'll get on their good side for that," Dempsey replied.

Seneca laughed, a deep, throaty laugh. "Your optimism is sweet."

He leaned into her slightly, into the warmth. "Nothing about me is sweet."

Her eyes met his as their breaths merged in the cold. For a moment, he was back in his bedroom. Or maybe he was just wishing. "Bart is here."

Seneca's eyes widened, and she turned her head to the small man approaching, swearing as he stomped through the trees.

When he finally got close, he said, "We gotta find better places to meet. I ain't a damn Boy Scout."

Max shook his bare hand. "Sorry, man."

He sniffed and nodded to Seneca. "You got the money?"

She smiled. "All business tonight, Bart?"

"I'm freezing my balls off," he said and took the wad of bills Seneca handed him. Bart gave her a rumpled piece of paper from his pocket.

"Sure you don't want to come with us?" she said, stuffing the note in her pocket without checking it.

"No way," Bart sputtered. "This guy has protection. I was lucky to get a location and stay in one piece. You ain't gettin' me that close again."

Seneca nodded. "Anything else going on?"

He looked at Max. "Your boy here's been made."

Seneca cast Max a quick glance. "We know."

"Yeah, lots of buzz on the streets since you got Dillinger. I know you guys are used to it, but you might wanna warn Noko."

Max noticed how Seneca stilled. *Who is Noko?*

"Is there a contract on us?" Seneca asked.

"Naw. Not yet anyway. Just talk," Bart replied. "But you know how things can escalate, 'specially if you go after a big target like this guy."

Seneca had turned serious. "Thanks for the warning."

Bart looked uneasy for a moment. "I ain't shittin' you. I know I take your money, but I hate to see somethin' happen to you."

Seneca smiled. "You either. You going to lay low for a while?"

Bart nodded. "Plan to. Gotta go."

He was out onto the path before Max asked, "Who's Noko?"

"My grandmother," Seneca said, her eyes staying on Bart. "She lives with me."

Damn. Dempsey hadn't planned on that. He was the only one who was supposed to be affected. Seneca pulled out her cell phone. "I'll call and warn her."

"Will that be enough?" he asked.

She turned to look at him as the phone dialed. "You've never met my grandmother."

◆ ◆ ◆

Noko met her at the door, with a shotgun.

Seneca stepped inside, checked to see if anyone was outside who could see a gun-wielding grandmother, and then closed the door behind her.

"I'm glad you took me seriously," she said and kissed Noko on the cheek. "But they probably won't be coming through the front door. Any leftovers in the fridge? I'm starving."

Noko followed her into the kitchen. "Pork chops and scalloped potatoes. Be ready in ten minutes."

"Perfect," Seneca said, dropping her bag and shrugging off her coat. "I'm going to take a shower and try to warm up."

Noko hung the shotgun on the gun rack on the wall. "Cold tonight."

"I noticed." It had been a cold, long night. She was looking forward to a hot shower, good food, and six solid hours of sleep. She took a step toward the stairs, and Noko asked, "Do you like him?"

Seneca stopped and turned to her grandmother. "*Like* is a little strong. More along the lines of mutual tolerance."

Noko smiled, and Seneca could tell she wasn't buying it.

"You trust him?"

Seneca sighed. "Mostly. But he's hiding something. I can feel it."

"Give him time. You are more alike than you think." Noko had a way of cutting to the chase, no matter how hard Seneca tried to divert her.

Seneca headed upstairs but decided to skip the shower and took the second flight of stairs that led to the brownstone's rooftop patio. On the way outside, she snagged her telescopic binoculars. At 4:00 A.M., night was firmly in place and her breath blew white in the darkness.

She stood in the middle of the small patio and lifted the binoculars to the stars. The sky was crisp and clear, but in the city, only the strong stars shone through. For long moments, she moved from one celestial body to another.

A song rose in her mind. "Star light, star bright . . ."

How many times had she sung those words?

Made the same wish? *Come and take me away from here.*

And waited.

She lowered the binoculars and marveled at the great expanse of the sky. Out there somewhere, she'd always known there were others. She'd felt that even as a child, growing up in northern New York State where the stars blanketed the heavens. She used to sneak out into the backyard at night and wish for cosmic strangers to come down and take her away to a place where there was no pain and no death. Where she could forget the past, leave it behind like a child's toy.

With the aliens.

"Be careful what you wish for," she whispered, her words disappearing into the night.

✦ ✦ ✦

Max heard Seneca murmur, "This is madness," as she walked behind him through the trees and brush to the location Bart had given them. It was after 1:00 A.M. and Saw Mill Park lay peaceful and still, even in the heart of Yonkers. Max breathed in, following the heavy scent of Shifters that had blazed a trail that only he could trace. A trail to Skinman.

Here, deep in the park, nature had found a single foothold, doggedly protecting its secrets with vegetation and stone. Max liked the feeling, the room to breathe in a city that was cramped with too many people. If he were to settle down, it would be in an open place like this. Not that that was going to happen. In fact, settling down was a dream he was certain he'd never live to see.

"What if they recognize your scent? What if they recognize us as XCEL?" Seneca asked for the third time.

He smiled. The first time she asked, he figured she was worried about her own safety. The second time, he figured it was about XCEL. But she hadn't liked his assurances to either of those, and it finally dawned on him that she might just be worried about him.

"Then we'll have to fight our way to Skinman."

"Look, I know you are good and all, but there may be a lot of Shifters down there," she persisted.

He walked through low-lying brush and random trash that covered the ground. "Just stay close to me."

"So you think they'll just let us waltz in, and no one is going to check me for weapons?"

"Trust me."

"Crazy-ass plan," she muttered under her breath, and he almost laughed. It wouldn't be a crazy-ass plan if it were hers, but for some reason, she seemed nervous not being in charge of the operation.

A new scent stopped him and he lifted his hand to halt Seneca. Ahead the brush thickened and traversed a vine-entangled stone embankment that led up to a bridge. It appeared to be a solid wall, but to a man with his sense of smell, in there somewhere was a doorway to the underground.

Seneca followed him silently through the vegetation and along the wall, where a wedge of broken blocks created a hidden opening. They squeezed through the narrow gap. Inside, it was pitch-black. A place only a Shifter could navigate. A low arched access tunnel stretched downward into the earth. Moss covered the stonework and dead leaves carpeted the floor.

He didn't sense any Shifters in the immediate vicinity, but he knew sentinels would be waiting at some point. Skinman would have a few levels of defense.

"Can you see anything?" Max asked Seneca, who was right next to him, keeping close.

"All I can see is your shadow."

He frowned at her. "What shadow?"

She was looking around him in a wide circle, her pupils enlarged as her eyes tried to adjust to the loss of light. "Every Shifter has a shadow, even in human form. I can't see in the dark, but I can see Shifter shadows in the dark."

He hadn't thought how Shifters might look to humans who could see them. "Any details?"

"Head, arms, legs, torso. Just your basic shadow. Color varies from white to black."

"Amazing," he said.

"Oh yeah," she murmured.

"Can you pick me out from other Shifters?"

Her face lifted to his, and she smirked. "Worried I might shoot you by mistake?"

"It crossed my mind. You did say we all looked the same to you."

Her head tilted a little as she studied him. "You're . . . unique."

He smiled at that. To a man who lived his life wearing someone else's body and identity, unique sounded pretty good. Seneca might not be able to see him in detail, but he could see her perfectly. No headgear, nothing to give them away as XCEL agents to Skinman or his cronies. She'd opted for no protective gear under her Gore-Tex jacket, just a thin T-shirt and jeans. The only weapons she carried were hidden in the lining of the jacket.

Right now, she was cool and calm to the danger facing her. Ready to do whatever it took to make things right. He'd never met anyone like her, and he felt his heart leap in his chest. It was then he knew he was in trouble. Here he was on the brink of what might be the last day of his life, and he'd finally found someone worth living for.

He closed his eyes and struggled between hope and reality. The hope was that he could find the killer today, survive, and be free. Free for what, was another story, but free just the same. The reality was that he'd die and so could Seneca.

"You know that we may not come out of this tunnel," he said softly.

"Speak for yourself, Dempsey. Plus you owe me food and wine. You aren't getting out of those so easy."

She might sound fearless, but underneath there was more.

A woman, a kind, compassionate soul. Something special that she didn't let many people see. Max touched her hand. Seneca blinked as he stepped into the void between them. In the silence, he could hear her breathing quicken.

"It's time," he whispered, surprised by the huskiness of his own voice.

"Time for what?" she asked, frowning and backing up until she hit the wall. It occurred to him that she wasn't scared of battle, but she was terrified of an intimate touch. He wondered who'd done that to her.

Max leaned under the curve of the ceiling and placed his hands on the wall to support himself. Then he brushed his lips against hers. "For our cover."

She inhaled a shuddering breath and swallowed. "Is this really necessary? Can't we just shake hands or—"

He captured her mouth midsentence, discovering her unique taste. She moved her lips against his, tentative at first and quickly bolder, revealing a hunger he never would have guessed was there. He growled a little, unable to stop the mad rush of energy that rose from his belly. She opened her mouth to his, wholeheartedly giving him access. Their lips merged, tongues deep, and Max soon lost his mind.

He pressed the length of his body against hers, confined by the low ceilings, wedged his knee between her legs, and felt his erection growing by the minute. All the frustrations, all the self-control unleashed at once. His growl echoed in his ears, Seneca filled his senses, and for a moment, everything else was forgotten. Her desire flooded through his blood. *She wanted him.*

It was only when Seneca moaned and bit his lower lip that he remembered where they were and why. Only then did the mission's call echo loud enough for him to hear it. He broke off the kiss and buried his face against her neck and hair. Both of them were breathing hard. Seneca trembled against him, and he cursed himself for distracting her to that degree. He needed her to be fully aware, fully battle ready. It would be the only way they'd survive.

He pulled himself together, while every moment aching to go back. And every moment remembering Ell's body, battered and stretched out across the deck of the ship. The scent of her killer strong. The symbol for "traitor" she'd left written in her own blood for Max to find.

Then he pushed off the wall and quickly checked the tunnel. Christ. What was wrong with him? Had he completely forgotten why he was here? One kiss. It sure didn't take much to sidetrack him. Seneca wanted him. That would do it.

She licked her lips and took a deep breath, turning serious once again. Out of reach, at least for the time being. "Okay. I guess that handles the cover?"

Max agreed. "Should do it. Last chance for you to bail."

"Don't even, Dempsey." She patted her jacket where her guns were concealed.

"Let me do the talking," he added.

She wrinkled her nose. "I know, I know. I'm just the distraction."

"And you do it very well," he said, and he meant it. He was totally distracted.

He watched her smile. "I know."

He shook his head. Fearless. "If I raise my right hand, shoot any shadow that moves except me."

"Then don't get in my way."

CHAPTER
ELEVEN

S he was still trembling as she followed on Dempsey's heels. *"Cover," my ass,* she thought. Kissing Dempsey had totally screwed up her concentration, and part of her wondered if he'd done it on purpose just to get even for treating him like crap. Now she was shaking like a leaf from her reaction to one kiss. Sexual energy zinged through her body. Her lips may never recover. If she shot him, he'd have no one to blame but himself.

It worried her that she was getting used to the strange cocoon that enveloped her every time they touched. Aside from the passion and sexual overdrive, she was convinced the sights and sounds she tapped into were coming from deep within him. They seemed to be drawing her in, toward something that she couldn't quite grasp. Did he realize that? Could he see inside her as well? If so, he wasn't admitting anything. Regardless, she didn't want to be there, and it wouldn't happen again. It couldn't. He was an alien and he was her partner, and her hormones were going to have to deal with that.

It was a damn shame too, because Dempsey's rock-hard body harnessed some serious raw heat, and she was like a moth to the flame. When she became entangled with him, when the flame got too hot, she wasn't even considering the risk of getting burned. And that could prove to be the scariest thing she faced tonight.

Her fingers brushed a clump of moss on the tunnel wall as her hand trailed along the slick stone behind Dempsey. She was completely blind. Any minute now, she could crack her head against a stalactite or something equally bad. Like a shapeshifter. Seneca was beginning to understand why it took a Shifter to catch a Shifter. She and Riley would never have been able to get this far.

Dempsey slowed to a stop, and she tried to focus on something, anything, without success. He stood still for a few moments, and then led her to the left. They must have come to another turn. No human could sneak in here without a flashlight or night vision. She hated this, hated letting him run the show. Step after silent step, she followed in air so black she couldn't tell up from down. The only thing grounding her was Dempsey's shadow.

Then he stopped dead. She looked around him in the narrow tunnel and saw two Shifter shadows up ahead. Then she heard the ratchetting of guns and a voice rose in the passageway. "Identify yourselves."

Dempsey said, "Need to do business with Skinman."

"Who's the human with you?"

"My girlfriend."

Seneca watched the shadows approach, filling the width of

the tunnel, and put her hand against the disrupter concealed inside her jacket. If they found it, all bets would be off.

"You got an appointment?"

Seneca studied them. Were they in Shifter or human form? She couldn't tell in the dark.

Dempsey answered, "No."

The shadows moved to block the way. "No appointment, no business."

"Look, if you can't help me, I'll just have to find another Skinman," Dempsey countered. "I'm sure there's enough business in this town for more than one."

The two shadows began talking in whispers. Seneca had her hand in her jacket when one Shifter finally answered. "I'll take you down. *After* we check you out."

A Shifter moved forward, and she could see him frisk Dempsey's shadow. Then he moved toward her.

Dempsey stepped between them. Wait. Was he *protecting* her? Hell. This cover sucked.

He said, "Hey, she's not unbreakable, and I don't appreciate anyone touching my girl."

My girl? She was going to kill him if they survived this.

"Orders. No one gets through without being cleared."

She felt the air move as both Shifters closed in, but Dempsey didn't relinquish her. He growled, "If she looks like a threat to you guys, then you must not be very good."

Seneca tried to look as innocent as possible, and realized she didn't know how to. Tension hung in the air. All she could hear was breathing and the hum of a challenge. Adrenaline pumped through her veins.

"Have it your way, but if they kill you, don't come crying to me," the Shifter said.

Seneca gave a silent exhale of relief. They were still alive. Although, the night was young.

Dempsey found her hand and took the lead. One of the Shifters followed them, calling out directions. They navigated the tunnels and she tried to count footsteps along the way. Random air movement and smells indicated there were probably side tunnels.

They veered to the right, and Seneca heard the rush of water. Meager light framed the end of the tunnel. Light at last. Moisture settled on her face and hands. The access tunnel opened to a walkway along an underground water canal. Overhead, a few ancient, orange light fixtures burned with their last breath. In front of her, a strong current of water cascaded by, ten feet wide and moving fast.

For the first time, she got a look at the other Shifter. He was in Primary form, charcoal black from his domed head to his broad feet. He carried a massive, deadly looking rifle that hadn't shown up in his shadow form.

Dempsey stood beside her in human form. He hadn't shifted yet, and that was probably to keep the others off guard. They followed the narrow walkway that ran along the edge of the water conduit, passing a whirlpool created from a break in the canal. Another fifty feet and she could hear sounds and voices ahead. A doorway appeared. Behind it, Shifters.

Showtime.

◆ ◆ ◆

Max sized up Skinman's office in the first few seconds. No windows, a hallway in the back and a door to the right. There were four Shifters in the bunker—all in human form, two to Max's left, one to his right, and one in the middle sitting in a wide chair. All four had distinct scents, and to his immediate disappointment, none of them was Ell's killer or the Shifters who'd trashed his apartment.

The three goons jumped forward at the same time and pulled their weapons.

"What the hell, Kab," one of them said to the Shifter who'd escorted Max and Seneca. He had brown hair, blue eyes, was unshaven and nasty-looking, with the gun. "You don't bring down customers unless they have an appointment."

"Bite me, asshole. Let's see you stand up in that stinking tunnel all night," the Shifter said and ducked out.

Max would have two Shifters to deal with on the way out, which was better than he expected. He looked past Brownie to the man seated quietly in the big chair. He had long black hair and dark eyes. A black goatee looked out of place against his pallid face.

Max addressed him. "I'm here for a new skin. I hear you're the best."

Brownie pointed the gun at Max's chest. "You talk to me first."

Max eyed him. "I don't deal with the hired help."

"Fuck you—" Brownie said as he lunged toward Max. One quick sidestep sent him sprawling and told Max everything he needed to know to take him down. Frankly, Max was more worried about the quiet bald guy hanging back. The other one was young with spiked hair and multiple piercings. He looked easy, although those weird ones could be unpredictable.

"That's enough," Skinman said, standing up. The three minions stepped aside as he approached Max and shook his hand. Firm handshake, but not a fighter. Things were looking up.

"Who sent you?" he asked Max.

"Levinson. Friend of mine. He says he got a skin off you." It was a partial lie. Max had never met Levinson, but Bart had given them the name.

Skinman studied him and Max hoped he bought it, or this was as far as they'd get. Taking on four shifters in close quarters would be suicide, even for him. He needed to split them up. Hopefully, Seneca had figured that out too.

"I don't usually accept walk-ins," Skinman finally said, his gaze falling on Seneca. "But I'll make an exception this one time."

A strange possessiveness gripped Max. It had started in the tunnel and now threatened to rage out of control. Besides, Seneca would kill him if he got too protective of her. He tried to draw Skinman's attention. "I'm looking for new skin. This one has some baggage associated with it."

Skinman grinned and spoke to Seneca directly. "Is that right?"

She smiled demurely, a look Max had never seen and would never forget. Her voice was slow and sexy. "That's right, sugar. And this time, I get to choose what I want."

Skinman crossed his arms and asked Seneca, "You know how this works?"

"All I want to do is pick out his new look. You boys deal with the details." She latched onto Max's arm and her jacket opened enough for Max to see that she wasn't wearing a bra. He resisted the urge to cover her up.

"I work in cash or trade," Skinman said, staring at her breasts. "Which are you interested in?"

"Cold hard cash," she replied with a sly smile.

"That's a shame," he replied.

Max was seconds away from knocking the lecherous look off Skinman's face when he said, "Follow me." Then he turned and ushered them through the open doorway in the back of the room. Seneca slipped her hand in Max's and played the good girl. Her transformation was nothing short of a miracle. She could be a Shifter if she wanted to.

Brownie and the pierced kid followed them into the back room with guns drawn, while the quiet one stayed in the main office area. The bunker was made of concrete and was probably damned thick. Skinman pushed the heavy steel door at the end of the corridor open, entered, and flicked on a light.

Cold air hit them in the face, and Max heard Seneca's gasp. The interior room was lined with shelves and shelving units. Every shelf was packed with jars and containers—bits and pieces of human remains.

Skinman spread his hands out wide. "The finest inventory you will find anywhere on this planet."

For a moment neither of them moved, and then Seneca said, "Dear God. Where did you get all these—these people from?"

"The morgue," Skinman replied smoothly. "No humans were harmed."

Bullshit, Max thought.

For her part, Seneca kept her cool and gave a disgusted grimace. "Well, I'm not buying anything based on a foot."

Apparently, Skinman found that funny and laughed. He said,

"You'll find a picture of the body on every container. With all the parts you're looking for. What are your specifications?"

Max surveyed the containers. There were a lot of bodies here so photos would definitely help identify the victims. Then he realized that Seneca was talking about him.

"I'm looking for someone with his height and build. I like them big," she said, emphasizing the "big" part.

Max eyed her as she sized him up. "Maybe a bit more muscle," she added. "Darker hair, blue eyes, big hands, bigger feet. Perhaps a better sense of humor. And, of course, he needs amazing stamina."

He might have objected if he weren't just about to tear this place apart. "Give the lady whatever she wants."

Skinman motioned to the far corner of the room. "I think I have exactly what you're looking for. Let's start over here."

Seneca and Skinman walked past the first shelving unit, and the pierced kid followed her with a gunpoint. When she turned the corner, Seneca glanced over her shoulder and gave Max a pointed look.

That was when he moved on Brownie.

TWELVE

t took every bit of self-control Seneca had to not kill Skinman on the spot, the sonofabitch. She'd never seen so many remains in one place in her life. There must be hundreds of people in those jars and containers. A leg here, an eye there. It was morbid, but not as morbid as the photos of each dead body stretched out on the floor. And the bastard had the gall to be proud of his slaughter.

"You've got enough DNA here to build an army," she said, offhandedly.

He smiled smugly. "I do."

He could too, and who would prevent him? Dempsey was right. This had to end now.

Skinman stopped in front of a shelf with four large containers. Each sported the photo of a young, perfect, twenty-something corpse. "I think this specimen will do."

Specimen. Like the dead man had been nothing more than a piece of DNA. A hunk of meat. Her anger grew, but she needed to play nice long enough to give Dempsey a chance to take out the other Shifter.

"Not bad," she said, forcing a smile. "Was he healthy? I don't want someone who's died of some gross disease."

Skinman shook his head. "Perfectly healthy. Pristine, virgin DNA."

"Then how did he die?"

"Gunshot," Skinman deadpanned.

And that much was probably true. The victim had been murdered in the prime of his life to fill an inventory slot. "How much does he cost?"

"For you?" Skinman said, stroking his chin. "Twenty thousand."

"Dollars?" she asked, genuinely shocked. "That's a little steep. What's to stop me and my fiancé from finding some dead guy on the streets?"

Skinman squinted at her. "I have a guarantee."

It gets better. "What kind of guarantee?"

He grinned. "If you don't like the final product, I'll replace it."

Lovely. "I don't know—"

"Hey, I like my customers happy. Otherwise, I don't get more clients."

She sighed. "You have a deal."

Then his grin turned ugly, and his voice became a snarl. "And if you ever breathe a word of this to anyone, we'll find you and kill you. And your family, your pets, your neighbors, and I'll pin your lover for everything."

She gasped. "What?"

He raised his hands. "I'm just protecting my business."

And she was really going to enjoy putting him out of business. "I'll never tell a soul. I promise."

He nodded to the kid with the pierced face. "Carry the container."

Seneca's pulse quickened. The kid would have to holster his gun to carry the container. He'd be defenseless, except for the part where he was a Shifter.

The kid did just that. He led the way with Seneca behind him and Skinman behind her. She calculated the steps, the open space between the rows of shelves, and figured Dempsey had already dealt with the other Shifter and was waiting for them. He could handle the kid. Skinman was hers. She reached into her coat and slid the disrupter out of its hiding place.

They turned the corner and a big, gray Shifter hand caught the kid in the face, sending him flying into the wall. Seneca swung around and elbowed Skinman in the face as hard as she could. He gave a yell and covered his face, even as he began to shift. He knocked jars and containers out of the way as he quickly morphed into Primary Shifter form.

By the time she had the disrupter pistol pointed at him, he'd shifted into the smallest, scrawniest Shifter she'd ever seen and had disappeared around a shelving unit before she could get a drop on him.

She cast a quick glance at Dempsey, who ran past her, massive and solid. He yelled at her, "I'll take Skinman. *Don't* go after the one in the office alone. Wait for me."

Seneca watched him turn the corner in disbelief. She hated

when he ordered her around, and she headed in the other direction. The kid with all the piercings was slumped on the floor, dead. She found the other Shifter stabbed and lifeless at the entrance of the cooler. Dempsey wasn't kidding around. He didn't plan to leave any survivors, and now she understood why. How many more of these coolers were there? She shuddered to think. But maybe if they took this one down, it would send a message to any wannabe Skinmen in this town. Don't screw with XCEL.

Then the lights went out.

Busted, she thought. Did the guy in front kill the lights or someone else? She was taking no chances. She reached for the prototype UVC grenade with her free hand. She hadn't had a chance to test it. In fact, she wasn't even authorized to have it without proper training, but that didn't stop her from stealing it from the XCEL weapons room. She peeked around the cooler doorway into the hall leading to the front office area. It was completely black as well. No shadows, but the Shifter was waiting for them. There was only one way out of here, and he knew it.

She had a flashlight in her pocket but she couldn't use it, couldn't risk it giving her location away. She'd have to rely on her ability to see his shadow. She dragged her shoulder against the wall as she walked the corridor, counting steps. She'd ticked off forty-two on the way in, and right now, they felt like an eternity. At the same time, she kept her gaze and her gun focused on the end of the hallway. When she got to thirty-five steps, she slowed and pressed against the wall. No sounds, no movement in Skinman's office.

Just maybe, the Shifter had skipped out and she wouldn't have to kill anyone. She took a careful look around the corner. The room was illuminated only by a stream of light from the canal.

Then she caught a flash in the room, a ghost behind a chair. She flicked open the safety on the grenade and rallied her concentration. All her senses rose, noting every nuance, every sound, every moment. Time slowed. Her body hummed and synchronized.

In a fluid second, she pressed the grenade trigger, started a mental count, and tossed the grenade into the room. There was a blue flash and she entered the room, disrupter leading the way.

One.

Crap, there were a pair of Shifters—one on each side of the room.

Two.

She fired at the closest target to her left as his shadow floundered under the effect of the grenade, and hit him in the center of his body mass. He dropped.

Three.

She spun right, where the second target was stumbling toward her.

Four.

She shot at his torso, but it didn't seem to slow him down.

Five.

His arms flailed at her clumsily, almost blindly, in the aftermath of the UVC blast.

Six . . . She ducked out of the way of his blows, hopped up on the edge of the desk, and rolled over the top of it.

Eight.

The Shifter turned toward her faster, recovering with amazing speed. Damn, they were good.

Ten.

She grabbed the chair and flung it over the top of the desk at him. She launched herself after the chair, smashing it into him. He stumbled backward to the floor, the chair landing on top of him. She hit the concrete floor hard beside him, jamming her shoulder. Ignoring the jolt of pain that shot down her arm, she reached out, grabbed a piece of Shifter, and said, "Shift."

Energy pulsed through her body and hand. The Shifter let out a shrill yell and took a whack at her. He caught her in the temple, sending pinpricks of light across her eyes. She spun out of reach, and he curled up like a baby. His cries echoed off the walls as she sat back, gathering her senses.

All the noise was sure to draw more Shifters. She pushed to her feet and reached the first Shifter, who was still disoriented, and force-shifted him before he came to. Then she heard thumping footsteps from the side door just before it opened. Couldn't be Dempsey; he hadn't come down the hallway yet, so as soon as the shadow appeared, she fired the disrupter.

The charge struck a Shifter in human form, creating a dark spot on his upper torso, and he staggered slightly as he stopped to stare at her but he didn't fall.

"I knew I should have brought the Glocks," she muttered and ran for the canal, the only lit place she had. He followed, nearly catching her before she rounded the doorway into the water tunnel. She ran for her life, but she had no idea where she was going. The tunnels were out of the question, and she couldn't see how far the canal walkway ran.

Then she noticed the break in the concrete and remembered the whirlpool. She stopped and turned to face the Shifter as he lurched toward her, a little woozy from the disrupter. That was when she saw the gun in his hand.

"I'm unarmed," she said, tossing the disrupter on the walkway between them.

"I'm not," he said, slurring his speech. He leaned against the wall, waving the weapon at her. "Sucks to be you."

"A big boy like you afraid of one woman?" she said, truly disgusted. "What a coward."

He frowned. "I'd rather be a live coward than a dead human any day."

She lifted her chin. "Fight me like a man. Or maybe you aren't a man. Can never tell with you freaks."

"This freak can kill you either way," he said and shoved his gun in his waistband. He lunged at her, and she ducked low, dropped her shoulder, and took him out at the knees. Her sore shoulder buckled under his weight. One of his feet caught her in the head, nearly knocking her into the rushing water with him.

She scrambled to the safety of the wall and watched him splash in the water as he was pulled deep into the center of the whirlpool. And then he vanished.

"Let's see how fast you can turn in to a fish, asshole," she said and checked the underground tunnel. Thankfully, she didn't see any more Shifters around because, frankly, she was beat. Her shoulder hurt like hell, her hands were battered and bleeding, and she had a headache that would kill a horse.

"I told him it was a crazy-ass plan. Did he listen? *No*." She hauled herself up and retrieved the disrupter before heading to the cooler to back up her partner. Dempsey owed her a damn fine bottle of wine.

◆ ◆ ◆

Max chased Skinman through the racks of body parts. The bastard was small but fast. Obviously, he was used to running from a fight. He poofed behind another rack, and Max swore as he tried to keep one eye on the door for Skinman's guards. Plus if Skinman made it out of the cooler, Max would have a hell of a time tracking him through the maze of tunnels.

To top it all off, Seneca was nowhere to be seen, which meant she'd gone after the quiet guy up front by herself. She was going to be the death of him yet.

A few more minutes of hide and seek, and Max had had it. He raced to the last rack, braced himself against it, and pushed. It rocked, hung for a moment in the air, and then toppled over, taking the next rack with it. The racks crashed, one after another, sending jars, glass, fluid, tissue, and containers falling in a deafening racket. It wasn't quiet, but it was effective.

There was a scream as the last rack smashed into the far wall. Max made his way around the rubble, following Skinman's groans. He found him wedged between two racks, pinned by shelves and covered with human remains.

Skinman clawed at the debris, trying to free himself. "You're him. Dempsey."

Max pulled one shelf off the stack piled on top of the Shifter so he could get to him. "Yes, and we wouldn't be here if you weren't so sloppy. Any other Skinmen in the city?"

"Look, man. I'm just trying to survive, same as you."

"We aren't the same," Max growled. "Are there any others?"

Skinman didn't answer; he was too busy shifting back to his smaller human form. Probably trying to wriggle out from under the rubble. Fat chance. Max waited until Skinman finished his shift before reaching in to grab Skinman by his skinny human neck.

Skinman gagged, his eyes widening as Max ripped him out of the mangled pile of metal and glass. Blood dripped from the man's arms, chest, and hands as Max lifted him high in the air. Max squeezed Skinman's neck, feeling the tendons and bones give under the man's weight. "Where did you get the bodies? Homeless?"

Skinman choked and tried to nod his head.

"From the tunnels?"

Another nod.

"And you didn't think anyone would notice?"

A squeak came out of the Skinman. *Moron.*

"Did your men trash my place?"

Confusion on his face answered that question. Max pulled Skinman close. "Who did?"

And that was when Max smelled it, with the full range of his Shifter abilities—the faint odor of Ell's murderer on Skinman's shirt. For a moment, he froze as old memories washed over him. Ell's body bathed in blood, the sign she'd drawn, and the grief that left only pure, red rage behind.

His hand tightened around Skinman's neck, his voice raw with emotion. "Who is he? Who killed my wife?"

Skinman's hands flailed as he shook his head in terror and confusion. Max forced himself to loosen his grip and shoved Skinman back against the broken leg of a rack. Skinman yelped as Max pushed his spine into the pole.

"Who have you talked today? Besides these guys?"

Skinman looked at him. "No one. Just you."

Max put a little more pressure on. "You talked to someone. Tell me who he is."

Then Skinman's eye widened. *He knew.* "I can't. He'll kill me."

"No," Max said, his teeth gritted with the effort to control himself. "*I'm* going to kill you. It can be slow and painful or quick and merciful. The choice is yours."

Skinman started to whimper. "Please."

Max pressed hard enough for bones to crack. Skinman screamed, "Hager! Name's Hager!"

Relief flowed through Max, a heavy weight lifted that he hadn't realized he'd been carrying. He had a name. It might not be the right name, but it was something. He'd given up so much just for that.

Skinman cried, "Don't kill me."

"You signed your own death certificate when you murdered all these innocent people," Max said, and then he heard Seneca.

"Dempsey, look out!"

✦ ✦ ✦

In the slender beam of her flashlight, everything moved in slow motion, a little like when Riley was killed. The Shifter who'd gotten past her while she was dealing with the others charged Dempsey, jumping onto his back and driving him into Skinman. There was a chorus of screams before Dempsey raised up on his legs, throwing the attacking Shifter off him.

When he turned around, Seneca gasped at the deep, bloody gash in his torso. Behind him, Skinman was impaled on a jagged metal post, staring wide-eyed at the ceiling. Despite the fatal-looking wound, Dempsey moved fast, grappling with the attacker and slamming him against the wall. He attacked again, and blood spattered in every direction with each meaty collision.

Dempsey absorbed several blows to the face and body, and she saw his knees buckle. He couldn't take much more. She raised the disrupter, studying the attacker's twists and turns. Time slowed, she could hear her own breathing, and she fired. The payload struck the attacker in the back, and he faltered long enough to give Dempsey the opening he needed. He formed his hand into a blade and drove it into the Shifter's belly. The attacker crumpled, a low groan filling the room, and he dropped to the floor.

Dempsey staggered on his feet, and Seneca holstered both the gun and the flashlight to help him. Plunged in the dark once again, all six feet of him slumped against her. She wrapped her arm around his back to give him support.

"How bad is it?" she asked him, hoping for the best.

It took a moment for him to answer. When he did, she could hear the agony in his voice. "Had worse."

"You can't lie for shit," she said as her mind began to run through how they were going to get out of there alive. "Is he dead?"

"Yes."

And Skinman was definitely down for the count. That cleared this room. Now all she had to worry about were the guards standing between them and salvation. "Good. I think our work here is done. Can you walk?"

"Yeah."

With the disrupter in one hand and her other arm around him, she moved forward with all her might. Dempsey was damned big, and every step was hard work for both of them. What would she do when another Shifter got in their way? How would she fight?

When they made it out of the office and onto the ledge along the canal, she saw the full extent of Dempsey's injuries in the light. He was trailing a ribbon of blood behind them from the deep belly wound. Worse than that, his shadow, which usually hugged his Primary form tightly, kept wandering from him in random patterns. He was in bad shape.

"Would it be better if you changed to human form?" she asked, trying not to sound as panicky as she was becoming.

He shook his head. "We heal faster in Primary form."

"That's good, because I'm going to need your nose and eyes to lead us the hell out of here," she said as he stumbled, sending them both into the rock wall. She gave an *oomph* and winced at the brunt of his weight. Then he rolled off her and leaned his back against the canal wall to rest. His hand covered the wound, and she was hesitant to move it in case he was somehow stopping the bleeding.

"You need a doctor," she said.

He shook his head. "No doctor."

"You can't fix this," she said, feeling the helplessness rising in her voice. "You guys have Skinmen, what about doctors?"

Dempsey's eyes were closed. "Don't know any."

She raised her hands in frustration. "You do this job, you risk your life every day, and you don't have a doctor?"

He opened one eye and looked at her. "So shoot me."

Hell. She rubbed her forehead. She was exhausted—mentally and physically—and if he passed out right now, she'd never be able to get him to the surface. "I swear to God, from now on, I do the planning. Your plans suck."

He gave her a weak smile, and she exhaled. "Come on, hero."

They stumbled along, forming a strange team as Dempsey gave the directions through the black maze of tunnels and Seneca carried the gun.

After what seemed an eternity, they turned a corner, and Seneca halted. A single Shifter stood dead ahead. Dempsey wasn't talking much anymore, and she'd figured he was internalizing his pain and unable to battle. Which left her on her own.

She dragged him forward, gun at the ready. The shadow zoomed toward them at alarming speed.

"Stop right there," she yelled, raising the disrupter. "Or I'll shoot you where you stand."

When he didn't stop, she shoved Dempsey to the side, aimed, and shot the Shifter. He spun backward, but stayed on his feet. The disrupter was fucking useless. She'd have better luck hitting Shifters in the head with it.

"That's one," she said, bluffing. "The next one will kill you. I'm in no mood for games. So you let us pass, and I let you live."

"Or I could shoot you both," he replied.

These Shifters weren't all stupid. She opted for a dose of reality. "Well, you *could* but Skinman is dead, and you aren't getting paid to die anymore."

"Says you."

"Just use your nose. Smell anything familiar?"

It only took a few seconds for him to detect Skinman's heavy scent and blood. "He's dead?"

"Unless you guys can walk around with a steel rod through

your belly. So I can kill you and you die for nothing. Or you let us pass and do something else with your life."

There was no answer, and the shadow didn't move. Close enough; she'd already wasted enough time. She shouldered Dempsey again, and he gave a pained groan pain as they squeezed past the Shifter. After they'd passed him, Seneca turned. He was gone.

There was a sliver of light straight ahead, and Seneca saw the glow of the moonlight beyond it. "Almost there, Dempsey."

He was breathing hard and loud as he pulled her to stop. "Need to shift. Can't be seen."

His head was down, his teeth gritted in agony. She asked, "Can you do that in your condition?"

"I'll try. If not, you have to shift me."

Sudden panic set in, and she shook her head vehemently. "No way. You've seen what happens when I do that. It hurts."

He raised his face to the ceiling, crazy with pain. "Won't have a choice."

"Forget it. Stay in Shifter form."

"Too risky."

"Well, I'm not force-shifting you," she said, and she meant it. He needed all his strength to mend himself. "We just need to get you to the car—"

Dempsey pushed himself away from her and stood unsteadily. Before she could stop him, he shifted, and the tunnel echoed with his anguished growl.

CHAPTER
THIRTEEN

Seneca wrestled her half-dead partner into the car without anyone seeing them. She slid into the driver's seat and fought the crippling exhaustion that swept over her. Her night was just beginning. Dempsey had managed to shift to his human form on his own, but just as she feared, it took everything out of him.

His breathing was shallow, his coloring bad, the gaping wound in his gut had already soaked through his clothes, and she was covered in his blood. If he were a normal human, he'd be finished. With shapeshifters, who knew? She laid her throbbing head on the steering wheel to think. She had basic first aid training, but she certainly wasn't a medic. She bit her lower lip and finally decided she had exactly one option.

She turned the ignition and headed for home. As she drove, she morbidly realized that if Dempsey died, most of her troubles would be over. She would have proven that he was no better at capturing Shifters than human agents were. No report would be filed. The Committee would abandon their prototype Shifter plan.

She stopped in traffic and looked at Dempsey. And if he died, XCEL would be in more trouble than they could handle. And that was the damn truth.

The light turned, and she jammed the gas pedal.

◆ ◆ ◆

Noko was waiting for her when she pulled up front. They hustled Dempsey into the house and got him into the second-floor guest bedroom with major effort. If he didn't have any broken bones before, he probably did now.

They rolled him onto the bed. There were clean towels and sheets at the foot of the bed, and a pan of water and bandages on the nightstand. But Seneca was beginning to doubt any of it would help.

As he lay in bed, Seneca watched the shadow of his Primary form hovering around him, weak and disorganized. It didn't look right, and she was worried it meant something really bad for a Shifter.

What happened if he couldn't hold his form together? Was it like breathing, where it just kind of took care of itself? Or would he simply fall apart at a molecular level? Would human medicine work on him? She knew shapeshifters used human DNA to form themselves a human body, but where Shifter ended and human began was unknown. If he survived this, she was going to make him give her a crash course in Shifter anatomy.

"Did he say anything before he lost consciousness?" Noko asked her as she used scissors to carefully cut away his shirt to check his wounds.

"Nothing. All I know is that he doesn't have a Shifter doctor. I'm not sure there are any," she said. "He sustained his injuries in Primary form, impaled on a steel pole. Then he used a lot of energy to shift himself to human." She took a deep breath because her voice was shaking. "I told him to stay in Shifter form. He could help heal himself."

"He didn't want to jeopardize you or your mission," Noko said matter-of-factly.

"I know." Seneca was going to kick his ass for it too.

Noko checked his eyes. "Finish undressing him. Clean his wounds as well as you can. I need to make some tea." Then she stood up and walked out.

Seneca looked after her. *Undress him? By herself?* She looked down at Dempsey. He outweighed her by at least fifty pounds. It was a miracle she'd gotten him this far at all. She took a deep breath. If he could shift himself when he was half-dead, she could do this.

It took her ten minutes to cut, tug, and remove his clothes. After, she sat on the side of bed and surveyed the damage. Aside from the stomach wound, he was covered in bruises and abrasions. And that was just outside. He was sure to have internal injuries that were far more serious.

The blood, flesh, and gore turned her stomach. Not that she hadn't seen it all before, but not . . . This was personal. She stopped herself. No, Dempsey was her partner and he needed her. Seneca shoved aside her emotions and detached herself from the task at hand like she'd been trained to do.

She dipped the towel in the tub of warm water to gently remove the blood. She patted disinfectant over the cuts and pressed clean towels to the bigger wounds and bruises. There was a pile of bloody discarded towels by the time she finished. She pulled a sheet over him, but to her dismay, his shadow still wavered uncontrollably.

She sat beside him and brushed hair from his face. *Damn you, Dempsey.* She didn't want to bury another partner. Didn't want to bury *him.* She laid her hand flat on his sternum and closed her eyes. His skin felt much too warm. Through her palm, she felt his heartbeat, his lungs fill and empty, and something else . . . She squeezed her eyes together as the familiar connection began to form. There was pain and struggle deep inside, as if he was being torn apart in some internal battle only he waged.

Her first instinct was to pull away, leave him to do battle alone, but she couldn't. Then he stirred and clumsily threw his hand over hers, pinning it. She looked into his face, but he didn't seem to be waking. Her hand burned between his grip and his chest. She felt energy pass between them, sensed the desperation within him.

As the connection strengthened, the bedroom slowly faded away into the distance—the same way it had in the doorway when he'd caught her spying. She felt darkness overtake her and fought the urge to escape. He needed her.

Sounds and voices came first, and she was drawn toward them. The darkness was replaced by a blurry scene that sharpened slowly into steel walls and floors. A low-pitched rumble resonated through her body; a hum filled her ears. She was kneeling on the floor in a darkened, still room.

Lying on the floor before her was a woman. Not a Shifter but not quite human either. Slender build, distinctly feminine features, long hair. She was facedown, but her head was turned and her eyes opened. Blood had flowed from her throat and pooled around her head. Her face had been beaten badly, and a necklace was wrapped tightly around her neck, embedded in a deep wound.

Seneca followed the woman's dead eyes to her outstretched hand. One of her fingers rested at the edge of a symbol drawn in blood—a circle with a line through it. What did it mean?

And then pain ripped through her. Unbearable grief, intense anger, abject failure flooded every nerve ending. Seneca found herself trapped in emotional overload. *Stop!* she cried and lurched back, breaking the connection. She fell hard, jarring her body and mind. Her thoughts reeled and the room spun as she struggled to recover bits of reality and pieces of herself. Time ticked by before she finally shook the last remnants of images that did not belong to her.

When she opened her eyes, she was lying on the bedroom floor looking up. *What just happened?* She struggled to sit up, light-headed and wobbly, and checked on Dempsey. He looked exactly the same.

She sat back on the floor and rubbed her eyes. The vision was clear and felt as real as the carpet under her. She'd been with him, been in his mind, and experienced what he had. But where? It could have been the Shifter ship, that would make sense. And the woman had to be his wife. The necklace matched the one in his apartment. Seneca was sure of it.

He'd lied. His wife didn't die in the crash. She'd been murdered, strangled with the necklace. Who would want to kill his wife? So many questions, and so much pain. She looked at Dempsey and saw his memories. Memories that were now hers. It complicated things.

Noko walked in carrying a tray, and her eyebrows rose when she saw her. Seneca couldn't even begin to explain and stated the obvious. "I fell off the bed."

Noko hummed. She placed the tray next to the bed and opened the bedroom closet. From it, she retrieved a two-foot-tall wooden mask and set it on top of the dresser at the end of the bed. Seneca had never seen it before. She would have remembered. One half of the crudely carved face was painted red and the other black. Long, black coarse hair hung down each side.

Seneca pulled herself to her feet. "What's with the mask?"

"It will help to bring his two halves together," Noko said simply.

Seneca eyed it. Yeah, and it would creep her out to no end.

Noko handed her a cup of tea. "This will help you heal."

She glanced in the mirror. The right side of her face was bruised, and the rest was scratched and smeared with dried blood. Her T-shirt was bloody, torn at the shoulder, and her skin scraped underneath. It'd been a hell of a night.

Seneca sipped her tea while Noko took a seat on the edge of the bed, facing Dempsey. Noko placed her palms over his eyes, her fingers on his scalp. Seneca heard her murmur soft words, and the teacup froze halfway to her mouth when the skin under Noko's hands began to glow green. Dempsey's shadow wavered and stilled as if listening. Then it turned to a pale shade of green.

What the hell? Seneca shook her head. That was impossible. On the other hand, she could force Shifters to shift. Anything was possible.

Noko moved her hands to Dempsey's torso and her fingers stretched over the wound. She murmured softly again and the wound glowed brightly with an unseen power. It spread out across his human form all the way to his Shifter shadow. The struggle subsided, soothed at last, as his shadow tightened around him like a thick glove.

Somewhere in the back of Seneca's mind, an old memory surfaced of her mother touching her knee where Seneca had cut it. A green glow with healing warmth. And then just as quickly, the memory was gone.

Noko lifted her hands and looked at Seneca. "He needs rest. We will give him some tea when he awakes."

Seneca put the cup down, completely confused, especially since Noko wasn't the slightest bit affected by any of this. "Wait, *wait*. What did you just do to him?"

Noko's eyes shone with wisdom. "I will tell you when you believe."

"What does believing have to do with *that*?" she asked, pointing to the green cocoon surrounding him. "He's green."

"It is healing power."

Seneca sighed. Noko wasn't going to tell her. "Okay, whatever. Is he going to stay that way? People will notice."

"He will return to normal when the healing is done," Noko said. "Take a shower now. Tend to your wounds. I will wait here until you get back. You must stay with him tonight."

Seneca closed her eyes for a moment. "Why?"

"If he becomes restless or his form begins to separate, come get me," Noko replied, her tone firm.

Seneca sighed. Noko had great patience, but when she made up her mind, that was that.

"Fine." Seneca set down her tea and walked past the creepy mask to the bathroom. She stripped and took an extra-long hot shower that threatened to put her to sleep for twelve hours. She checked her body in the mirror. She was a mess, but nothing major. Bumps, bruises, scrapes, and a sore shoulder. Sadly, the usual.

As soon as she'd changed into a soft T-shirt and shorts, she returned to Noko and noticed that Dempsey seemed to look better. Noko stood and walked out of the room without a word, leaving Seneca alone with a glowing green human shapeshifter and the reservations that came with him. Like where she was going to sleep. There were no chairs, her body hurt all over, and she could vouch that the floor was not at all comfy.

Screw it. She grabbed a spare blanket and threw it over him. If she didn't touch him, she should be safe from whatever lurked in his mind. Whatever happened, happened to him, not her. She had her own nightmarish past to deal with.

Then she got another blanket for herself and crawled into bed next to him. His body heat wrapped around her in seconds, and the promise of sleep overshadowed the hellish last few hours.

She looked at the mask staring back at her in all its creepiness, and closed her eyes.

You can't scare me. I see shapeshifters.

FOURTEEN

Max came to with a rush, followed by pain, heat, and hunger. His skin was burning, every muscle ached, and his head pounded with each heartbeat. He tried not to move and simply concentrated on holding the excruciating combination at bay. When he finally opened his eyes, the first thing he saw was a ceiling fixture that wasn't his and a room he didn't recognize. Light shone from outside a single door and there was a strange-looking red and black mask on a dresser beside it.

Faced with the unknown, he went on the defensive, drawing a fresh wave of hurt when he tried to move. Then he felt a warm body next to his, saw the long silky black hair and bare neck. He exhaled and calmed his racing heart.

He let Seneca's unique scent fill his mind. Her soft bottom pressing against his thigh took care of the rest of him. He relaxed, knowing he was safe because Seneca was here. He breathed deeply and noted that her scent filled the room. This had to be her house, and she'd brought him here after . . .

The battle. The shifting— Had he done it himself or had she forced him? He couldn't recall, but he did remember the look of horror on her face and her refusal when he'd asked her to do it. He remembered how it made him feel . . . good. Like she cared. Because one thing he'd learned about Seneca Thomas was that she didn't pull any punches.

He had a name too. Hager, the killer of his wife. Max let the victory sink in. He'd searched for two years for that man. Now he actually had a chance to stop Ell's murderer and rid all Shifters of the traitor who had betrayed them to the Govan government. It occurred to Max that that second reason had never been a consideration before last night. He wasn't sure where it came from, but suddenly, everything was clear. Ell hadn't left the symbol of the traitor in her blood so that Max could avenge her death. She'd left it so he could stop the traitor who'd helped Govan destroy the Shifter race. She wanted him and his race to survive here.

Max felt the lull of peace for the first time in years. As if he'd been set free from an invisible prison. Anger melted away, leaving determination. Hager wouldn't get a chance to betray his people again.

Then Seneca sighed softly and pressed the length of her back to him, and all thought vanished. Max's body reacted with alarming speed. Hunger swamped him, dredging up a yearning he thought he'd buried long ago. Against all better judgment, he turned on his side toward her. Her warmth penetrated his skin and bones, offering both comfort and discomfort.

He ignored the sexual edge his body hovered on and wrapped

one arm around her—slowly, carefully. Just for a moment, he wanted to hold her, without any strings or any baggage or anyone standing between them. She nuzzled him, and he closed his eyes to savor it all.

This is wrong, his mind warned.

He brushed off the warning and concentrated on how good she felt. He'd had more than one sexual encounter with human women. But Seneca was different—dangerous and sexy and totally, *totally* off-limits. Which was why his lips brushed against her hair. It was as silky as it looked.

His free hand slid up and against Seneca's belly. Soft but firm. At that moment, everything was okay. No past, no future to think about. He let his fingertips trace the fabric over her skin. Human touch, it was an amazing thing. More sensitive than his people's and highly prized on this world. He could see why. The human body was the perfect vessel for tactile pleasure and worth every effort it took to replicate it.

His fingers slipped off her shirt and onto bare skin. He inhaled sharply at the rush of blood to his erection. He wanted her, all right, but there was no way she'd want him. Or was there? She'd kissed him in the tunnel, been right there with him when he went too far. She hadn't backed down then and . . . that was when he felt Seneca's body stiffen.

"*Men.*"

He winced at Seneca's humorless whisper. Well, it was fun while it lasted. And then Seneca pushed away from him. He groaned as reality returned along with every ache and pain he'd earned.

Seneca stood next to the bed, hands on her hips, her face

flushed with anger. "Are you kidding me? You were impaled, nearly bled to death on the way here, and . . ." She picked up a pillow and threw it at him. "You have the energy to do that? Are you trying to kill yourself?"

He knocked the pillow out of the air and attempted to sit up but stopped when his head started spinning. He was not ready for this. "I was still out of it."

She crossed her arms. "Oh, really. Amazing dexterity for someone who's out of it."

He grimaced at the pain in his belly and collapsed back on the bed. "Okay. I thought you were someone else."

It didn't work, because then she went from upset to quiet. Real quiet. He braced himself.

"And I thought you were dead," she said, her gaze burning into his.

He waited for his thoughts to settle down before answering, sensing that this was important to her. "I warned you this might happen. It's part of the job."

She rubbed her arms. "You don't have to tell me what the job is. I buried one partner this week. I don't feel like burying another. People will start thinking I'm bad luck."

It was a lie, a cop-out to how she was really feeling. And it made him smile. Not too much. He didn't want her to shoot him. "Did anyone see me in Primary form?"

"No," Seneca replied. "Which reminds me, we need to talk about your anatomy . . ."

"My anatomy?" he said and smiled.

Her eyes narrowed dangerously. "And how we fix it when we need to."

Too bad. "What did MacGregor say?"

"You think I told him?" She threw her hands up in the air and started pacing the small room. "When would I have had an opportunity? When I was dragging your ass out of that hellhole? Or when I was dragging your ass to my bedroom—"

"This is your bedroom?" he asked, feeling his smile growing.

She stopped pacing and glared at him. "My house. They're all my bedrooms. No, I didn't call MacGregor."

Huh. "There are a lot of victims down there. Although, chances are good the scavengers have already moved in."

Seneca bit her lip. "If XCEL gets involved, they're going to know it was us. It's not like I had a chance to pick up our toys before we left."

He couldn't take his eyes off her. Long legs, round ass, strong shoulders. She looked amazing in this light. "We can handle MacGregor."

She took a deep breath, pushing her breasts against her T-shirt. He was feeling better by the minute.

"Right," she said, her voice sounding suddenly weary. Then he realized that her face was bruised and slightly swollen, her arms and legs covered with marks. Those were his fault.

He, on the other hand, was feeling far healthier than he should, considering the number of injuries he'd sustained. He looked at his stomach. The skin was red and raw, but the wound had closed up. That was fast, too fast for a human or even a Shifter. Strange recollections surfaced. There was an older woman, a soft voice. No one he knew. He looked at Seneca. "Was your grandmother here?"

Her eyes widened with something that looked like panic. "You remember her?"

"I remember something."

Seneca licked her lips. "She treated you for a little while. I'm not sure what she did."

Interesting. "I'll have to thank her."

"Well, she may not be available next time, so we're going to find you a Shifter doctor."

He raised his eyebrows at her firm tone. "Worried about me?"

To his surprise, there was no witty comeback. Instead, Seneca's gaze dropped to the floor. "I'm tired of funerals, Max. I mean it."

She looked up, and he saw the pain in her wary eyes. He knew that pain—it was loss and grief. She knew what it was to lose someone close, someone you couldn't live without. The understanding, the connection stunned him.

"I'm sorry," he finally said.

"So am I," she said. Before Max could ask her what she meant, she swept a hand toward the bed. "This never happened. We work together, and that's it. It has to be. Otherwise, it gets too . . . complicated."

"Okay," he said, watching her. She'd just shut him out again.

"Noko will bring you some tea shortly. Drink it. It tastes like sewer, but it'll help." Then she walked out.

◆ ◆ ◆

Hager scrolled through the pictures of what was left of Skinman's lair sent to his BlackBerry. "Are you sure it was Dempsey?"

Puck nodded several times. "I smelled 'im myself. And his partner, the lovely Seneca Thomas."

Those two were becoming more than a nuisance. "Were you able to salvage any of the DNA from the cooler?"

"Some. Don't know if it be virgin, though," Puck answered. "Only Skinman knew that. Gonna take some time to replace 'im."

Yes, it would. And until then they'd be stuck here underground. XCEL had won and put his plan behind. It would take weeks to get a new Skinman set up, especially after word of this massacre got out. And even longer to build a new inventory. He didn't have that kind of time.

Recruits were getting harder to find, too complacent in their new world. Too lazy to fight. Unless . . . Unless he gave them a *reason* to fight.

Hager pocketed the device and steepled his fingers. A reason to fight, that had always been the Shifters' weakness. They would blend in if allowed, but if someone came after them, they'd fight for the lives they'd built.

As for the DNA, if he brought the battle to XCEL, he'd have all the DNA he needed—from XCEL agents. In fact, he'd get much better, higher-quality specimens. It would take care of two problems at once, and his plan could actually accelerate.

It always amazed him how he could take a bad situation and turn it to his advantage. It was a gift, really. And this time, it would give him everything he wanted.

"What do you want to do?" Puck asked, sounding bored.

"Send the photos to the borough lords for their recruiting. Plus our friends, our business partners, every Shifter we know."

Puck looked shell-shocked. "Why would we want to do that? It's bad publicity, ain't it?"

Hager replied, "Tell them this is what XCEL has in store for us unless we stand up for ourselves."

"You think that'll work?" Puck asked.

"Oh, yes." He'd make sure of it.

◆ ◆ ◆

Noko was alone in the kitchen when Seneca finished her 5:00 A.M. run. She had hoped it would help her work through the past twenty-four hours, but it hadn't. Her body was buzzing with un-requited energy. It didn't help that the object of her desire had been sleeping in the next room for the past day. Thus, the 5:00 A.M. wake-up call.

She filled a tall glass with water and leaned back against the counter to drink it. She needed sleep. She needed sex. She needed something that would stop the whirlwind of thoughts and ques-tions and memories that swirled around in her head nonstop. Maybe she was the one who needed the half-black, half-red mask. It'd go with her newly formed split personality. The one where she actually enjoyed how it felt to wake up next to Dempsey. And the other where she envisioned tossing roses on his grave.

The good news was that he'd touched her, and they hadn't connected. Interesting, that. Perhaps it was because she'd fin-ished the scene. The memory of his dead wife, his pain and grief, lingered in every cell in Seneca's body. They shared that moment.

"He is an Eagle," Noko said, seated at the island with her hands clasped.

Seneca's mind returned to the here and now. *Of course he is.* "That's nice. How is he?"

"He drank some tea and ate a little. He slept all day and all night. He grows stronger."

Seneca grunted. He was doing better than her.

"He asked about the mask."

She almost chocked on water. "Are you surprised?"

"He is not afraid of it."

Seneca eyed her. "I'm not either."

Noko smiled. "I know."

Nothing surprised Noko. She just took life as it came and accepted it. Good or bad, pretty or ugly. It didn't matter. It just *was*.

"His heart is good," Noko said.

Seneca drained her glass and put it in the sink. "Yes, I see it. I get it. He's a good man. Or alien or whatever. He's brave and selfless and kind to small animals."

Noko was grinning at her when she turned around. "You like him."

Seneca rolled her eyes. "I barely know him. Besides, he's my partner and that's all it can be. I can't do my job if I'm trying to protect him or thinking about him in a—" She stumbled through the words. "Another way." Then she sighed. "You know what I mean."

Noko nodded. "You may not have a choice. Love does not ask permission."

Oh God, *love*. She hadn't even dealt with sex yet. Love wasn't even on the table. "That's true. But luckily, I'm not destined for love in this life. I'm destined to save the world, remember?"

Noko just looked at her and smiled. Her words went unsaid, but Seneca could still hear them. *The world doesn't need to be saved.*

"This world is not ready for aliens, Grandmother."

"They will be discovered," Noko said. "How will you handle that when it happens?"

"I don't know," Seneca said. It was the truth. Someday, all hell would break loose and the Shifters would be made public. Until recently, she was certain what she would do and who she would align with when that happened—humans. The rightful inhabitants of this planet.

But now . . .

She looked at the stairs going up to the second floor. Now when it happened, she had no idea how she'd handle it or even whose side she'd choose.

She said to Noko, "I need you to show me how to heal Max."

Her grandmother's eyebrows rose. "Max?"

Seneca frowned. "Yes, Max. Who else?"

Noko smiled. "You already know how."

Seneca blinked. "I don't have green hands."

Noko walked up to her and took both of Seneca's hands in hers. They were warm and soft. "It only works if you believe."

"In other words, Max is doomed," she said.

Noko patted her hands. "When the time is right, you will figure it out."

"Well, hopefully, he won't die waiting," Seneca muttered.

CHAPTER
FIFTEEN

It was nearly dawn when Max dressed, feeling almost human as he descended the stairs in search of food. He was hungry, more so than he could ever remember being before. He followed the smell of food to the kitchen where the woman he'd met as Noko was making scrambled eggs in a pan on the stove.

"Sit," she said without looking up, her voice soft and soothing. Old, wise, patient. It wasn't something he was used to. There weren't a lot of old Shifters around.

He pulled up a seat and noticed that Seneca was nowhere to be seen. Her scent lingered, which meant she wasn't far. She hadn't visited him again since that first night. His own fault. It was a wonder she hadn't killed him in his sleep for the sorry excuses he'd made. He should have been honest with her, but it wasn't exactly easy to say that he wanted to sink his entire body and soul into her soft flesh.

No, not if he ever wanted to do just that.

Noko set a plate of eggs and sausage in front of him, and he didn't wait for an invite. After eating two helpings, he pushed back from the counter. "That was excellent, Noko. Thank you."

She smiled at him as she cleared the dishes, and he felt a strange peace. She was special, like Seneca, but in a different way, in an old way that went to her bones—quiet strength and power.

"Where's Seneca?" he asked.

"On the roof," Noko replied. "She goes there when she wants to leave this world behind."

Leave this world behind? Seneca? He pegged her for being firmly grounded to this place. "Is it so bad here? Or just recently?"

Noko sat at the counter across from him. That was when he noticed that her eyes were like Seneca's—brown and almond-shaped.

"When she was a child, she watched her parents die. A burglar entered their house and shot them both. Seneca hid and was unharmed, but she saw it all. No one knew until later that night when I came by. She sat on the stairs looking at their bodies until I found her."

Max closed his eyes for a moment. Her seriousness, her anger at him because she thought he was dead, her mention of the funerals. It was more than just working for XCEL, and it explained a lot about her. Why did he think that he was the only one who'd suffered in life?

He looked at Noko. "Why are you telling me this?"

"Because Seneca needs you. Her totem is the White Wolf, tracking and hunting on the ground. Surviving with her claws and her instincts. You are the Eagle, high above, seeing all. You know where the Wolf is and where the Wolf's enemies are. You know what the Wolf needs to survive."

Max shook his head. "I'm not who you think I am—"

"She will not survive without you," Noko added calmly over his objections. "Your people will not find peace without you."

He stared at the older woman, so still and sure in her convictions. How did she know so much about him? "I'm no one's savior."

"You have a purpose here," Noko said. "Listen carefully, and you will find it."

◆ ◆ ◆

Seneca heard him open the door to the rooftop patio and pursed her lips. *Thank you, Noko.*

She felt her long coat being draped over her shoulders.

"Cold morning," Dempsey said, and her heart jumped when she lowered the binoculars and turned to him. He looked good. Healed, healthy, and virile. And she was going out today and buying a vibrator and big pack of batteries. "Thanks."

Dempsey moved next to her and looked up where the morning was primed to take the sky. "I didn't know you had an interest in space."

"Can't see the stars worth a damn in the city," she answered. "I don't know why I bother."

He said, "You can always use your imagination."

"That's okay. I'm pretty sure I already know. Besides, life is what it is. Imagining it different doesn't change it."

Dempsey asked, "You never dream about the future?"

She focused the binoculars on a smudged patch of stars far from this little world and its big problems. "Dreams only come true if you make them. Which makes them goals."

"Okay, what are your goals, then?"

He was healed *and* nosy this morning. "Not to kill my partner."

"I like that one."

Smart ass. She looked at him. "Your turn. Do you dream, Dempsey?"

He didn't answer for a moment, and she smiled. *Gotcha.*

"I did once," he finally said, and Seneca realized he was serious.

"What happened?" she asked, even though she already knew. His wife.

Dempsey cast her a somber look. "Someone took it away from me."

Seneca wanted to tell him that she understood. She'd been there, in his head; she'd seen what happened. But she couldn't bring herself to breach something so personal and painful. No one should have to be forced to relive the past. It was already heavy enough to carry day after day.

"No new dreams, then?" she asked.

He looked back to the sky. "Like you said, doesn't change reality."

She pursed her lips, regretting her words. Who was she to kill his hopes? If he did indeed have any. "So what's it like out there in the great cosmos?"

He scanned the sky. "About the same as here."

"Jeez, Dempsey, you sure know how to kill a girl's fantasy."

"I'm sorry about your parents."

The sudden change of subject stunned her. *Noko.* She murmured, "Thank you."

"Did they ever find who did it?"

Seneca was going to have a talk with her grandmother. "No."

"Even worse."

Although he seemed sincere, she didn't want to be having this conversation. "Can we talk about something more cheery? Like global warming?"

Dempsey grinned. "Here's something that will make you happy. I'm going back to the hotel."

"Why?" she asked, surprised by the disappointment in her voice.

"I've imposed long enough, and I'm healed," he replied and then he turned his silver eyes on her. "Besides, if I stay here much longer, I can't promise I'll be a good boy."

He said it softly and so matter-of-factly that it sent a shiver all over her body.

"I know you drew the line at partners," he continued, his eyes riveting her in place. "But we both know it's just a line."

She felt her mouth drop open. "Don't beat around the bush, Dempsey. Why don't you tell me what you really think?"

The smile that stretched slowly across his face spoke volumes of whispers and kisses and wild, reckless sex. The kiss in the tunnel came back to her in all its glory. She already knew what it would be like with Dempsey—perfect.

A phone rang somewhere in the background of the new fantasy that was occupying the majority of her brain cells.

Dempsey's lips moved. "I think that's yours."

"What's mine?" she said without thinking, and then shook her head. Her pocket was ringing. She retrieved her cell phone and answered, "Yes?"

"Don't say my name. Are you alone?"

It was Bart. Seneca glanced at Dempsey. "Yeah, what's up?"

"Meet me in twenty minutes at our spot near Ryders Alley. Alone. *No* partner." He sounded hurried and sober. Both bad signs.

"I'm fine, thanks for checking in." Then she hung up. Shit. Bart sounded shaken. What the hell was up with that? Why meet him alone?

All the doubts about Dempsey that she'd been burying under sexual desires resurfaced. He'd killed his own, done everything for XCEL, but deep down, was he really one of them? Or had Bart uncovered something so bad that he wouldn't trust Dempsey with it?

She closed the cell phone. "That was MacGregor."

Dempsey was watching her a little too intently. "We're going to have to talk to him."

"I know. Just not yet." She shoved her hands in her pockets. "I'm freezing. I should go back inside."

He nodded. "I'll be at the hotel if you need me."

Seneca smiled. She hated lying to him. "Enjoy your time off."

His eyes narrowed with suspicion. Or maybe she was just paranoid.

"You too," he said.

◆ ◆ ◆

"What's wrong?" Seneca asked even before Bart got close. He hunkered down into himself, looking jumpy and strung out as his eyes darted back and forth between each end of the open alleyway they used for their meetings. Early morning didn't diminish the smell of garbage. The high walls on either side created a narrow gauntlet that she wasn't entirely comfortable with. The rat traps lined up on the cobblestone didn't help either.

"A whole lot," Bart answered.

"Why didn't you want Dempsey here?" she asked, lowering her voice.

Bart leaned close, his breath rotten, and he didn't look like he'd slept in two days. "'Cause he's one of them and I don't trust any of them right now."

Seneca frowned. "What is it, Bart?"

He sniffed. "It's bad. Real bad. You gotta get out of town."

Bart was either high or really scared. "Just tell me what's going on."

He checked the alley again. "There's a contract out on you, on all XCEL agents. Big enough to interest a lot of nasty folks. The shifty kind, if you know what I mean."

"Who signed the contract?" she asked.

"A big scary-ass Shifter name of Hager. Word is he's recruiting Shifters, and you all are part of initiation dues—dead or alive."

He was talking so fast that Seneca had to work to keep up with him. "Recruiting Shifters for what?"

Bart continued, ignoring her question as he talked faster. "Hager has them all riled, 'cause of the Skinman killing. They're comin' out of the fucking woodwork to join."

Oh crap. What had she and Dempsey done?

He added, "They're pissed. Tell me Skinman wasn't you."

She closed her eyes. "Can't."

"*Fuck*," he said with feeling. "You started a war. That's a real bad thing 'cause the word is Hager's building a goddamned Shifter army under this city."

That explained the recruits and Skinman's big inventory. Considering Skinman was in XCEL's sights already, he would have been taken down eventually. That was what she tried to tell herself, but guilt was still winning. "An army for what reason?"

"Don't know. Don't wanna know. I'm too close as it is." He looked scared shitless. "And Dempsey, he's public enemy number one right now in the Shifter world."

Damn. Now she really felt like crap for not telling him about Bart's call.

"And so are you," Bart added. "They know about you, where you live, what you smell like. Do you know how much money Hager's offerin' for your heads? Someone's gonna turn you over. It's just a matter of time. You stay here in the city, you're dead."

Noko wasn't going to be happy when Seneca ordered her to leave.

"Do you know where Hager is holed up?" she asked.

"No," Bart said. "I don't want no part of this."

"Well, if you happen to find out, call me." Then Seneca tried to slip Bart some fifties, but he backed up, refusing it.

"I don't want your money either. Or your scent," he said, looking at her like she had the plague. "I'm done. Serious. We're done. Sorry."

❖ ❖ ❖

178

Max stood around the corner of the alley and spied on Seneca talking to Bart. And he wasn't invited.

She'd lied to him. The question was why? What did he have to do to prove himself to her? He thought they had passed the trust level and were moving along nicely toward sex. Apparently not.

He dialed his cell phone and it rang four times, five, and finally a pick up.

"Six A.M., Max. You know what time that is? Time to *not* be calling me."

He smirked at Apollo's unhappy voice. "Rise and shine."

"I have better things to be doing than talking to you."

Ah, Apollo wasn't alone. "Anyone I know?"

Apollo said, "Will you get to the point already?"

"I found the murderer. And the traitor."

That got his friend's attention. There was a shuffling and some mumbling on the other end, and then Apollo came back all serious. "Are you sure? Where?"

"Didn't actually locate him yet, but I found his scent on Skinman. He did business with him recently. His name is Hager."

Max peered around the corner. Seneca was frowning. Must be bad news. He wondered if she was going to bother to share it with him.

Apollo talked in his ear. "Hager. Not familiar with the name. Must be a new one. Want me to ask around?"

Bart looked really nervous. "Whoever Hager is, he's plenty feared. Be careful who you ask."

"Got it. What are you going to do?"

Bart suddenly backed up from Seneca, his hands raised. *Did he just refuse her money?* Then Bart turned and walked quickly in Max's direction. He flattened into a doorway and watched the informant scurry by.

Max said into the phone, "I'm tracking down a lead right now."

Then he hung up and followed Bart.

CHAPTER SIXTEEN

Noko didn't seem too upset about relocating and for that, Seneca was glad and a bit curious. If Noko didn't fight it, then she knew something Seneca didn't. Not that Noko would tell her. Oh, no. She'd make Seneca learn it the hard way. These life lessons were hell.

Seneca packed the suitcase hastily. It wasn't supposed to happen this way. XCEL was supposed to protect their agents and their identities, going as far as creating whole new careers for them, providing aliases, the works.

"Is one suitcase going to be enough?" she asked Noko for the third time.

Her grandmother moved in her unhurried way, carefully folding a dress. "One is plenty. You worry too much."

That was the understatement of the year. If anything, they should be flat-out running for their lives. "We started a war,

Grandmother. The Shifters are gunning for us and our families. I think that's worth worrying about."

Noko placed the dress in the suitcase and patted it down. "These things have a way of working themselves out."

Seneca rubbed her forehead. It was like talking to a wall. "This won't solve itself. It'll come down to who survives."

Noko hummed and pulled another dress out of her closet. "There is always hope. Faith. Some people live by that."

And die by that, Seneca thought. She wasn't about to take that chance. "Maybe you're right and it'll all be fine. But just humor me for now. I need to know you're somewhere safe."

Seneca checked her watch. It was afternoon, and Dempsey still hadn't returned her calls. Damn him. She needed to tell him what Bart said, but she hated to leave a message on his cell in case it fell into the wrong hands. She tried not to think along those lines, but she couldn't help it. Dempsey was a major target.

"Uncle Joe and Aunt Lavina know when to pick you up at the Plattsburgh train station, right?" she said to Noko.

"Yes."

"And you'll be okay alone on the train?"

Noko tucked a sweater into the suitcase. "Yes."

"And you know you can't tell anyone about the aliens," Seneca added.

"No aliens," Noko repeated, and Seneca was beginning to think her grandmother was toying with her.

Her grandmother nodded. "I'm packed."

Seneca closed and locked the suitcase. "I'll take this. I'll meet you downstairs."

Noko left, and Seneca took a final cursory walkthrough of

the bedroom to make sure she hadn't forgotten anything. Then she lifted the suitcase and noticed an old book that had been lying underneath. Seneca picked up the book and opened it. It was a journal full of her grandmother's handwritten pages. Native American stories, quotes, and her own family history. Had she meant to include in the suitcase or leave it for Seneca to find? She stood holding the book for a few moments before sliding it into the front pocket of Noko's suitcase.

❖ ❖ ❖

Seneca parked her car in the agency parking garage and took the elevator up. She'd tried to call Dempsey again, but he still didn't pick up. He wasn't at his hotel room. She'd finally broken radio silence and sent him text messages, telling him the current situation and about Hager. He could be dead already. And to top it all off, she now had the pleasure of telling MacGregor the whole ugly story.

She sensed tension the minute she walked into the office. The suite was quiet, voices subdued, and it looked as though they were running on a skeleton crew. In fact, just the administrative staff was there. Where were the agents?

She walked up to Price's desk and asked, "Busy night?"

He looked up from his desk with a frown. "About time you showed up. Didn't you get the page to come in?"

"I was otherwise occupied," she replied, ignoring his attitude. "What's going on?"

"Conklin disappeared last night."

She narrowed her eyes at Price. "I didn't do it. Maybe he pissed off someone else."

He pointed his pencil to MacGregor's door. "Tell it to the big guy. He's been a bear all day."

Like that was unusual, but there was an intangible feeling of dread that she couldn't shake. She went directly to MacGregor's office, knocked once, and pushed the door open. For a moment, she couldn't breathe as she stared at him. This was bad.

"Get in here and close the door," MacGregor barked.

She closed the door behind her, locked it silently, and took a seat across from his desk. "I hear Conklin disappeared last night."

MacGregor said, "That's right. I've got all available men out looking for him."

Seneca leaned forward on the desk with one arm and covertly unholstered her gun with the other. "Everyone's out? Isn't that a little unusual?"

"Tough shit. My call. You and your partner should be out there too," he growled, stabbing a finger at her. "Where is he?"

"You told us not to come in, remember?"

"Vacation's over," he replied. "Tell Max I want him in here pronto."

"I thought you wanted us out looking for Conklin?"

MacGregor turned red. "Look, don't mess with me. I'm the boss here. You do what I say."

"You used to be such a nice guy," Seneca said. "Right before you became a shapeshifter."

Then she raised her Glock and shot a startled MacGregor at point-blank range in the head. Blood and brain matter exploded. His head dropped backward, eyes open, and the Shifter shadow wobbled.

The office staff were banging on the door by the time she reached his dead body and force-shifted him from human to Shifter. He convulsed violently and fell out of the chair. She watched his body darken and morph.

So, she *could* change a human back to Shifter, even dead. That answered that. The only question left was: Where was the real MacGregor?

Just as the imposter finished shifting, the agents broke down the door and piled in.

"Are you crazy?" Price yelled at her.

She stepped around the desk and holstered her weapon. "He's been replaced by a Shifter. Bring all our agents in. Call an emergency meeting."

"Crap," Price said, staring at the dead Shifter in disbelief. Then he pushed out of the room.

She said to the others, "Someone try to get ahold of MacGregor."

The deputy, Witley, nodded and scooted out. The rest of them stood there in shock, and they hadn't even heard the worst of it yet.

Thirty minutes later, the role call room was filled with every agent, except Dempsey. Seneca was trying not to worry about him, which wasn't difficult considering all the other things she was worrying about. The good news was there were no Shifters in the group of agents, which meant they'd only replicated MacGregor so far.

She'd given everything she knew to Witley. He was in charge now. She stood in the room behind him as he took the podium.

"Okay, listen up," Witley started. "This is going to be short and sweet. MacGregor was replaced by a Shifter. We checked, and he isn't home and we can't reach him. Consider MacGregor and Conklin missing."

A yell came from the back. "How do we know more of us haven't been replaced?"

"Well, that's a good question," Witley said, and cast her a glance. "Dempsey can ID them. We'll have him come in—"

Witley's voice was drowned in accusations and hollering. Seneca knew no one trusted Dempsey, especially now. The room was in uproar, agents looking suspiciously at one another. XCEL was unraveling before Seneca's eyes. She knew only one way to pull her agency back together, and that was to sacrifice herself.

She stepped up to the podium and spoke above the voices. "*I* would be able to tell."

The room quieted in seconds, everyone staring at her.

She raised her chin. "I can see Shifters. That's how I knew MacGregor was one of them."

It went eerily silent in the room. Some agents frowned at her like she was insane, some glared at her like she was a freak, and the rest were in shock. Pretty much what she expected. It was also the end. The end of her career. Her friends. Her job. This was turning into a really shitty day.

"Good enough for me," Witley said as if stuff like this happened every day. Then he returned to the podium. "Next item—"

"Is she one of them?" came a shout, accompanied by nodding heads.

Witley replied, sounding more than a little like MacGregor. "She's not. If she were, a Shifter would be giving you orders right now. End of discussion."

No one made a peep.

"Good," he said. "Now, there's a contract out for all XCEL agents. We are initiation fees for a new underground Shifter organization led by a man named Hager. XCEL is under attack; each one of you is a target."

"Like we weren't before?" someone asked.

"Not like this," he said. "What do you think happened to Conklin and MacGregor? Any one of you could be next. Get your families somewhere safe, and get your combat gear ready."

There was a lot of grumbling.

"And then what?" someone asked.

"Then we fight," Witley said. "If Hager wants us, he'll come to us. We hit the streets in teams. If you are under attack, you contact HQ for backup. Everyone covers everyone. The offices will be moved shortly. All communications go through Price."

Price spoke up from the front row. "You can't make those calls without Committee approval."

Witley gave him a hard look. "The Committee can kiss my ass. They knew this could happen. Or maybe they've forgotten that we're on the front line."

Seneca grinned at Price's reddened face.

Then Witley said, "That's it. Go."

Seneca left the room and gathered her weapons. Noko was out of the city, XCEL had been alerted, and she'd probably be fired. That left Dempsey. She hiked her duty bag over her shoulder and headed down to her car to try his hotel room again. She walked out of the elevator doors on the garage level and confronted two very large shapeshifters in human form. The doors closed behind her before she could jump back in.

The pair converged on her—both big, burly, and, in the darkness, free to shift at will. And her with all her weapons in the bag except for the Glock in her shoulder holster.

The first one grinned. "Seneca Thomas. Fancy meeting you here."

She gripped the bag with her left hand. "Don't tell me, let me guess. You want my autograph."

His grin split into an ominous smile. "Nope. Just you, babe."

Seneca pulled out the Glock and leveled it at them. Before she could shoot, both Shifters changed. She fired a full round into them in turn, and then slowly lowered her weapon. It was useless.

They were all black, their features barely distinguishable against the dark garage background. Then she realized the lights were out except for right in front of the elevator.

"You're coming with us," one of them said.

She holstered the weapon so they couldn't use it against her. Shifters were physically superior to her, but mentally? That was another story. She smiled and bluffed for her life. "I'm to be your blood-in, huh? So which one of you gets the credit? Because I'm thinking Hager isn't going to let you both in for lil' old me."

They each looked at the other. Seneca wasn't sure if it was from the fact that she'd identified Hager or because they didn't have an answer to her question. She shifted to one hip and opted for the latter. "Ah, that hasn't been discussed yet?"

One of them turned to her. "We'll decide after we kill you."

That didn't turn out as well as she'd planned. Dead would be bad. Alive and in front of Hager might also be bad, but it occurred to her that it might also be the only way she'd be able to get inside his organization. Time to play the bait card. She tapped her foot. "No, I'm thinking Hager wants me alive."

A Shifter took a step toward her with the other one on his heels. "Maybe he did say alive, but he didn't say in what kind of shape."

Hell, that wouldn't do either. She needed to come up with better plans. Now her options were death, near-death, or escape. Easy choice.

Seneca concentrated her vision on them, waiting for their shadows to give away their next move. She raised her chin. "Go for it, asshole."

A shadow reached for her. At the last second she twisted and lunged right as the Shifter's hand jammed into her gear bag. She slipped the bag off and sprinted for the nearest fire alarm. She almost made it too. Then a big hand smacked her on the side of the head, slamming her into a nearby car. Her knees gave out, but an arm caught her around the neck and yanked her off her feet.

Her head spun as Shifter skin tightened around her throat. The Shifter whispered in her ear, "Do that again, and I will kill you."

She couldn't think, couldn't breathe, couldn't inhale. Her fingers dug into his arm, trying to loosen his steely grip that was suffocating her. No chance of that happening. Then he turned them both around to face the other Shifter, who was grinning. She tried to concentrate on force-shifting her captor. Unfortunately, her rattled, oxygen-deprived brain wasn't functioning enough to comply.

Shift, she thought. *Shift!*

But nothing happened, and the garage started to fade to black.

No one is going to save us.

Her hands lost all strength and dropped to her side. She was six again, hiding behind a door, watching her parents die.

There is no Great Spirit, no heroes.

Her body shuddered and shut down.

No one came. No one.

Her final thoughts floated away from her. *I'm dying. I'm dying, and I'll never see Max again.*

Black crowded out everything else. Suddenly, she had the sensation of being shoved hard and freed. She landed flat on her back on the concrete floor, dazed and gasping for air. Around her, there was yelling and crashing and fighting, but she couldn't move. She told her body to sit up, knowing she had to defend herself.

Seneca opened her eyes and watched three Shifters battle across the garage. Their shadows merged, slashed, and separated. Her muscles finally lurched, moving awkwardly and out of sync. Coughing, she rolled on her side, struggling to get up as the floor tilted.

She finally managed to sit up, swaying unevenly. One Shifter was down on the ground. The other two slammed against the cars and walls. Car alarms were blaring, wrecking havoc with her brain and disorienting her senses even more.

Have to get up, she kept thinking. *Have to fight.* But her body just wouldn't do it. She put her head in her hands. After a few moments, the fighting stopped. With dread, she opened her eyes. The last Shifter would either finish her off or take her alive to Hager. And then she'd be dead. No one would save her.

She saw Shifter feet walking toward her and slowly looked up to accept her fate. Her heart leapt in her chest as the Shifter morphed with every step closer, his human face and body and clothes changing.

Dempsey.

CHAPTER
SEVENTEEN

S
he was alive. It was all that mattered. He didn't care that she'd lied to him and met Bart without him All he cared about was the unguarded look of joy and wonder on her face as she gazed at him.

"It's you," she rasped.

Her words melted something inside him. She wasn't looking around, only at him when she said it. He knelt down in front of her as she rocked slowly, her face pale and her eyes glassy. She was in rough shape, possibly concussed.

"Good thing or you'd be in trouble," he said softly.

Seneca tried to laugh and coughed. "Already am."

"Anything broken?"

When she shook her head, he helped her to her feet, and then swept her up into his arms. Without objection, she relaxed into him as he carried her to his car and laid her in the backseat.

Max called the office and told them to get a cleanup crew in the basement garage pronto. It gave him something to do besides thinking about Seneca's condition. The Shifters had targeted her, which meant he couldn't bring her to a hospital or to her house. Which was fine, because he wouldn't be letting Seneca out of his sight again. His heart couldn't take it.

Twenty minutes later, he pulled into the hotel parking lot on Long Island and looked back to see that Seneca had fallen asleep. Her cheek was bruised, and her throat red and raw. It could have been worse, and the thought of what could have been scared the hell out of him.

He helped Seneca out of the car. She was able to walk, but she was still a little shaky. He let her into his hotel room, and she went straight to the bathroom.

Max stood in the middle of the room and rubbed his face. Hell. He'd known it would piss off the Shifters if he went after Skinman, but he'd done it anyway. Not for XCEL, not for humanity, not for Seneca, but for himself. Now everyone he'd dragged into this had a death sentence.

It was his fault she was a target and his responsibility to protect her. He recalled the look on her face when she saw him. It was so honest and so beautiful and told him everything she felt about him. If she'd lied to him about Bart, there was a reason. And who was he to talk? He'd lied to her from the very beginning.

It was time he came clean, before he got her killed. He started pacing the room. This was far more complicated and dangerous than he had ever imagined. From what Bart had shared with him, the Shifters had Hager for a leader, and he would stop at nothing to bring death and devastation to Shifters, humans, this planet. The only thing standing between Hager and the world was Max. Maybe Noko was right. Maybe he was supposed to do something important with his life.

Max heard the bathroom door open. Seneca leaned against the doorjamb and looked at him. Her coloring was better and her eyes more focused. She'd shed her shoes and socks, revealing surprisingly delicate bare feet. As usual, she was gorgeous even with the bruises and torn clothes.

He had to tell her the truth.

"Are you okay?" he asked. "You need a doctor?"

She shook her head. "I'll be fine."

There was something about her quiet tone that seemed odd. "We have to talk. About Hager."

She tilted her head. "You didn't return my calls. Why?"

The truth. "Because I saw you meet with Bart."

Her eyebrows rose. "You followed me?"

He added, "And because you lied to me about it."

Seneca rubbed her bruised neck gingerly. "I know. I'm sorry. It's the only way Bart would meet me. He was afraid you . . ."

"I couldn't be trusted," Max finished.

Seneca dropped her hand. "Yes."

"He's right."

His words hung in the air between them, and the look on her face changed, softened. His body went on full alert even as she walked up to him and stopped a foot away. Her eyes were hooded, her lips full. "He's wrong. I trust you."

Max closed his eyes. "Don't."

He felt her hand on his face, her warm palm press against his cheek. She was close when he opened his eyes, and he grasped her fingers in his. This was going to be harder than he expected. "We need to talk—"

"I'm done talking," she said, and kissed him. For a moment, he didn't move. And then, every fiber of his being focused on her as he kissed her back. His mind began playing out what he wanted to do with her. His senses came alive, overpowered by one, single, promising desire—Seneca.

Tell her.

She wrapped her arms around his neck, giving him full access to all of her. His hands reached out of their own accord, finding warm fabric over soft skin. Everything he wanted was in his hands. His fingers slipped under her shirt, and he heard her moan against his mouth. He felt her unbuttoning his shirt, one button at a time, moving down. When she tugged the shirt out of his jeans, he sucked air at the sensation of fabric against his erection.

He kissed her hard, the surge of desire firing his soul. His body was no longer his, his mind lost. He belonged to her as much as she belonged to him. A faint *tell her* flashed in his thoughts and promptly evaporated in the heat. Everything could wait. The world could end. He was not stopping now.

Seneca dragged his shirt off his shoulders. He relinquished her just long enough to shed the garment and then lifted her shirt over her head. A black bra and hard nipples greeted him.

He pulled her to him, pressing bare skin to bare skin, and let out a long growl. This body, his body, felt every movement, every touch, every rub. The scent of her pheromones was so powerful, it threatened to drive him mad. She wanted him, but nowhere near as badly as he wanted her.

Seneca was kissing him, nipping at his lips while she un-snapped his jeans and carefully unzipped them. His erection pressed into her palms, freed from the confining fabric. He felt a groan vibrate through his chest when she cupped him gently, running her fingers along his length. He closed his eyes, savoring every touch as she wrapped her fingers tightly around him. For long moments, he couldn't breathe, lost in the chaos of sensation and the powerful urge to thrust into her.

Instead, he reached around and unhooked her bra. The straps slid down her arms and she let the bra fall to the floor. Her breasts were round and firm, with dark nipples that tightened even as he watched. He breathed in, breathed out, and then growled as he picked her up and laid her on the bed. She watched him with heavy eyes while he stripped off her jeans, sliding them down to reveal long, lean thighs, and firm calves. Black panties edged with lace smoothed over her hips and flat stomach.

He kneeled on the bed over her, their eyes locked as he slipped his fingers under the lace and rolled the thin fabric down over her legs until he stood at the end of the bed, holding silk in his hands and beauty in his eyes.

Every part of skin he'd revealed was exquisite, soft, and warm. She waited for him, naked and bold in her desire. He loved her this way—no holds barred. Then her lips parted and whispered, "I want you, Max."

He felt the words to his core, felt the hunger rise in his belly that only she could fulfill. He tried to harness his desire before it consumed them both. He was too close to the edge as it was, wanted her too much. When he thought he had himself un-der control, he removed the rest of his clothes, everything that separated them. He crawled across the bed, their eyes locked the entire time. His breathing was rough and fast, his muscles screaming with restless energy. Her pupils widened as he positioned himself over her.

"Now," she whispered.

He shook his head. He wanted to make it right for her, but he was close to losing any semblance of restraint. He dipped his head to wrap his lips around one taut nipple.

Seneca arched into him and dragged her fingernails down his chest. He felt her dig into his skin, exposing raw desire that sent shock waves through his body. He settled his thigh between her legs as he tasted the other nipple.

She wrapped her hand around his neck to pull him closer. Her hips rubbed his erection. He tried to hang on, was crazy enough to think he could, and then something snapped in his head. Whatever plan he once had was gone, leaving behind a primal force so fierce and basal that he could do nothing but surrender to it.

Max dropped to his elbows, moved her legs apart, and buried himself deep inside her. He savored the way her muscles gripped him and the heaven he'd found. She gave a cry and dug her nails into his back as he pulled out and thrust into her again and again, greedy in his need. Time spun out, their bodies parting and meeting in a reckless, frantic pace.

The sweet torture of pain and pleasure flooded his senses. Heat and passion, taut and tight—all melded in a potent mix that overwhelmed to the point of agony.

Moments later, Seneca sunk her nails into his shoulders and gave a shudder as she climaxed. The look on her face put him over the edge. He wrapped his arms around her neck, shielding her as he gave his body freedom—driving again and again, until release saved him.

◆ ◆ ◆

The sun was rising when Seneca finally roused. She sighed and reached for Dempsey, but the bed lay empty. The sound of the shower made her smile. She rolled over onto her back and stretched her body across the disaster of a bed. It had been a long time since she'd slept all night with a man. And Dempsey was a man on a mission. After the first furious time, he'd slowed down and taken his sweet time. Several times. She was probably ruined for life.

And he'd saved her life.

She'd thought she was dead in the parking garage. And he'd shown up just in time. She didn't think . . . She didn't believe in heroes. Demons, yes. She would have died there, and she was ready to. Because no one would have come to her rescue; no one ever had before. Until now. Maybe there was hope after all. Maybe she wasn't alone. Maybe there was a god or a Great Spirit or something else that intervened. Or not. But there was one man.

A cell phone ringtone broke her thoughts, and she sat up, wincing at the tenderness she'd earned last night. Dempsey's phone was next to the bed. She glanced at the bathroom where the shower was still running and decided to take the phone into him.

She slid off the bed and picked it up. "Hello."

"Uh, Seneca?"

"Apollo?"

"Yeah, it's me. Sorry to wake you."

"I was up. Dempsey's in the shower. I can bring the phone to him."

Apollo laughed. "I have a feeling that would make his day, but I'm in a hurry. Just tell him to call me back. I have news."

"On Hager?" she asked.

"You know about Hager?" Apollo replied, sounding surprised. Really surprised. Like, totally shocked. Suspicion flickered in the back of her mind.

"I know everything Dempsey knows," she said vaguely.

"I didn't think he'd—" Apollo said. "Anyway, I'm almost certain that Hager is the guy we've been tracking. He's operating the same way as the traitor on Govan—underground, building his empire. Which includes killing anyone who gets in his way. Ell must have overheard him on the ship, and he killed her when she figured out what he'd done."

Seneca felt the bottom go out from under her. *Hager? Traitor? Ell?*

Apollo continued. "Tell Max I set up a meeting with him and Carl at the diner at ten. Max will know where it is. Carl said he has something for him."

Seneca managed, "Okay. Thanks."

"Later." He hung up.

She disconnected and set the phone back down on the nightstand. The thoughts tumbled over one another in a blur of disbelief.

Hager was a traitor on the last Shifter planet.

Hager killed Ell because she found out he was the traitor.

Dempsey found Ell dead.

Dempsey and Apollo have been searching for Hager.

Because Hager killed Ell.

And that's why Dempsey is here.

For revenge.

Oh, God. How could she be so blind? It explained everything. Why he joined XCEL and put up with all the shit. Why he picked her. Lied to her. Used her. Her eyes burned.

"Who was on the phone?"

Seneca turned to find Dempsey standing outside the bathroom with a towel wrapped around his hips. She blinked the tears away, snagged her panties from the floor, and put them on. "Were you ever going to tell me? Or were you just going to kill Hager and walk away?"

He took a step toward her. "Who was on the phone?"

She pulled her shirt over her head. She'd slept with him because she thought he was a hero. Christ, she was a moron when it came to men. "Apollo. He told me about Hager and Ell and your traitor."

Dempsey swore. "Sonofabitch."

She grabbed her jeans and held them against her, feeling too naked in just the shirt and panties. "Don't blame Apollo. All he did was tell me what you wouldn't."

He ran his hand through his wet hair. "I was going to—"

"When?" she snapped. "After you got me into bed?"

Dempsey looked over at her. "You got *me* into bed."

Shit. He was right. "My mistake. Won't happen again. You didn't answer my question about Hager."

"I was going to kill him and leave," he said.

It was the truth at last. She knew because it wasn't what she wanted to hear. "Good. Because that's exactly what we're going to do. They replaced MacGregor yesterday. I guarantee Hager was responsible for that. I want him, and you're going to help me get him."

Then she walked past Dempsey, and he said, "I tried to tell you last night. And then—"

"My seduction was overwhelming, too much for you to resist. I know," she finished. She skirted him, slammed the bathroom door behind her, and locked it before shedding her clothes. Then she turned on the shower, stepped under the hot water, and cried.

CHAPTER
EIGHTEEN

Over breakfast in the diner, Max told her everything about how Hager had betrayed and destroyed the Shifters on Govan. He'd give the government locations of Shifter populations—targeting women and children first—so the government could wipe them out. He managed an underground network of spies who did nothing but feed info to the government. Every Shifter knew someone was behind the genocide, but no one could ever identify him.

"A few thousand of us secretly boarded a ship to escape the planet. We thought we left him behind when we departed," Max said. "But then Ell came up missing at the end of our journey. She left the sign of traitor in her own blood, warning us that he was on the ship. I just couldn't locate him before we crashed on Earth."

"You followed him here, to the city," Seneca said, remaining emotionless as she drank her coffee.

"By scent. And lost him. After that, XCEL was the only way I could find him."

"For revenge," Seneca added, her tone cool and professional. Max hated it.

"Yes," he said. "But Hager is working again, here. He'll rip this world apart like he did on Govan."

"How does he operate?" she asked. "What's his plan?"

"He wants power. He wants to be in control. On Govan, that meant working with the highest government officials to carry out the Shifter genocide. Here, I don't know."

Seneca looked him in the eye. "But if he wasn't your wife's killer, you wouldn't care what he did."

"Probably not," he admitted.

She leaned back in the booth, her eyes were wary and her expression tight. He should have told her last night, because he sure wasn't winning her over this morning. Although, it was probably for the best. He had no intention of leaving Hager alive and no delusions of his own mortality. There was only one way to take Hager and his entire operation out, and that was with the powerful explosive device lying in the bottom of his duffle bag. All he needed was to get inside Hager's headquarters with it.

"If he had that kind of power on Govan, then why did he come here with you?" she asked. "Why wouldn't he just stay there?"

Max shook his head. "I haven't figured that out yet. Something must have happened. The fact remains, he's here and he's rebuilding his network. This country is at serious risk."

"Bart said he was building an army of Shifters. What would he need them for?"

"Maybe for protection. Maybe for an attack. I don't know."

She stared at him for a few long beats. Finally, she said, "So basically you're telling me all this to keep me working with you."

He could say the other reasons—because he cared about her. Because he finally realized that he could trust her. Because he wanted her to have the knowledge so she could keep herself safe. But none of it would change the present or the future for them. So instead, he said, "Yes."

She blinked a few times and looked down at the table. "I appreciate your honesty."

He felt the heaviness in his chest at the subtle good-bye. It was the only way this could end. He could say he was sorry a thousand times and it wouldn't erase the betrayal.

"Neither one of us can go home," he warned. "It's safer if we stick together."

She lifted her gaze to his. "I realize that. We're partners, and we have a duty." Then her eyes focused on something behind him. "I think your friend is here."

Max turned just as Carl stepped into the diner. He stopped abruptly when he saw Seneca, but Max waved him in. Carl sat next to Max, across from Seneca, and ordered a coffee from the waitress.

"Carl, this is Seneca Thomas. My partner," Max said by way of introduction.

They shook hands but Max could sense the suspicion between them. He added, "She knows everything."

Carl raised his eyebrows. "Is that right?"

Her brown eyes studied him. "Including that you're a Shifter."

Carl gave Max a quick look. "Was that necessary? You know the position I'm in."

"He didn't tell me," she said. "I can see you."

Max grinned as Carl's mouth dropped open. "How is that possible?"

She spun her coffee cup and replied dryly, "Everyone acts so surprised when I tell them that. You must have had people like me on your last planet."

"No," Carl and Max said in unison.

"Great. How'd I get so lucky?" she murmured.

Carl asked, "Are there others like you?"

She shook her head. "I don't think so."

The waitress brought Carl his coffee, and he waited until she was gone before turning to Max. "Apollo said you found the traitor."

"His name's Hager. Running an underground operation and organizing the Shifters. We shut down his Skinman a few days ago, but it won't be long before another one replaces him. Have you heard of any other Shifters working for the government?"

"No," Carl answered. "I haven't seen any either."

Max exchanged a look with Seneca. Hager wasn't following the same pattern of working with the government. What was he up to, then?

"Hager has to be stopped. I don't need to tell you that," Carl said. "He's a threat, but we have other problems too. You asked me what happens to the Shifters you capture. They are picked up by a cryonics company called Smith Industries."

"Nicely generic," Max noted.

Carl nodded. "Officially classified as a private contractor hired to freeze and store Shifters. They set up facilities in all the cities XCEL operates in."

"And unofficially?" Seneca asked.

He looked at her. "There are minimal cryogenics capabilities at the facility here, not nearly enough to handle the number of Shifters coming in. Which means not all your captures are being frozen."

"Then what is happening to them?" she said with a frown.

Carl shrugged. "They're gone. The last audit they had? The incoming Shifters didn't equal the Shifters on hand. The contractor claimed some bodies were too damaged to bother freezing and were cremated. Of course, there are no remains to verify this, which means we're missing thirty or so bodies locally."

"So they could be using them for weapons development," Max said.

Carl nodded. "It's possible."

"I didn't know," Seneca said quickly. "I would never have agreed to that."

"I believe you," Carl replied with a little smile. "Maybe they *were* cremated and the facility just kept lousy records."

Max added another possibility. "Or their disappearance has something to do with Hager's army."

"Or all the above," Carl said. "The fact is, we simply don't know." He looked at Max. "Someone is going to have to find out for sure what is happening to the captured Shifters."

And that someone was Max. "Don't suppose you have the location of the local cryogenics operation?"

Carl reached into his pocket and slipped a piece of paper to Max under the table. "This is strictly confidential. You understand that if you decide to pursue this, and something goes wrong, I can't protect you."

"I know." Max checked with Seneca and found her staring at Carl.

She tapped her fingers on the table. "Carl Hannaford. I thought you looked familiar. Associate director for operations."

He nodded. "Yes."

"You've been in that office for over ten years," she said.

They all knew what she was getting at. The Shifters had only been here two years.

Carl said, "Mr. Hannaford had a bad heart."

Her expression was pensive, but Max had a good idea what she was thinking—Shifters were taking over. At this rate, he was definitely going to be working alone.

"You're on the Committee that oversees the XCEL operations," she said.

"That's correct."

"Our field office director was replaced by a Shifter," she said slowly. "We killed the replacement and our deputy has assumed control of the agency. But we could use your help."

Max nearly choked.

Carl smacked him on the back and asked Seneca, "What are you looking for?"

She leaned closer. "The Committee hasn't been informed of the current situation—our missing director, Hager, Skinman—and we'd like to keep it that way for a while longer so we can find and neutralize Hager."

Carl nodded. "I'll do what I can."

"Thank you," she said and looked at Max. "I have a plan."

"Am I included in this plan?" Max asked.

She lifted an eyebrow. "Oh, yes. You are definitely included."

◆ ◆ ◆

"I'm not sure I'm liking this plan," Apollo said as he sat in the driver's seat of the delivery van.

"You liked it enough to volunteer," Seneca replied.

"Seemed like a good idea until it occurred to me that I might not be too happy with what we find," he grumbled.

It was hard not to like Apollo. Six hours ago, they had intercepted a delivery out of the alleged cryogenics lab. The original drivers had been kind enough to share their destination after Dempsey "talked" to them. Four hours ago, they'd geared up and recruited Apollo to help complete the delivery. He'd used the driver's saliva to get his DNA and finished replicating his face and hair fifteen minutes ago. Now they were heading into what could prove to be a very bad situation. And he didn't *have* to do it.

She only wished things could have been different with Dempsey. Her mistake. Live and learn, and never make the same stupid mistake again. Although it was a shame because the sex was off the scale. She *was* ruined for life.

The road ahead ended at a barbed-wire fenced-in compound with a gate and a guy with rifle. She said, "There's the gatehouse. Drive up to it like you belong here."

"Into the fray," Apollo said. He pulled up to the warehouse complex gate and handed the armed guard a pass. The guard studied the pass and Apollo in turn. Finally, he nodded and waved them on. The steel gates swung open and then closed behind them.

"See? Easy. He never suspected you weren't the real driver," Seneca said.

Apollo looked at her. "Hopefully no one will look too closely at me."

She shrugged. "So he lost weight."

"Since last week?"

They drove through the industrial complex, their headlights reflecting off the perimeter of steel fencing and razor wire. No moon tonight thanks to thick cloud cover, which would work to their advantage since they were dealing with only humans. Hopefully. If not, then Apollo would be identified as a Shifter on sight and things would get really interesting, really fast.

At Building 12, Apollo turned into a parking lot and drove to the back warehouse doors. It was quiet. No movement, no other deliveries.

"Now what?" Apollo asked as he parked in front of a row of warehouse doors.

"We wait until someone comes out," Seneca said as she double-checked her gun before holstering it and zipping up her jacket to conceal it.

One of the warehouse doors began to lift, and light spilled out from underneath it. A man jumped off the dock and approached the van. He was stocky and ugly and human. There was a patch on his uniform that read "Butch." Not the smartest criminal on the block.

Apollo and Seneca stepped out of the van to greet him.

"You're late," he barked to Apollo.

"New chick," Apollo said, hitching a thumb at her. "Got us lost along the way."

"Well, you kept the man waiting," he said. "You know he doesn't like to wait. It's gonna cost you extra. Bring it in." Then he turned and climbed back up on the dock.

Seneca went to the back of the refrigerated truck with Apollo.

"Did you see anyone else inside?" he asked her.

"Couldn't get close enough. Worried?"

He whispered, "You bet your ass. Every time I do a job with Max, I get beat up."

She grinned. "What can possibly go wrong?"

"Christ," he said. "You sound just like him."

She didn't want to think about that comment too much. They pulled the gurney out, and the support legs dropped underneath the body. The black body bag stretched between them as they maneuvered the gurney onto the dock. Once inside, the warehouse doors closed behind them. Seneca counted two more human workers as they followed Butch down a wide corridor. She could hear him talking on the phone.

"They're here. I'll be ready in ten minutes."

Seneca looked back at Apollo, and he nodded that he'd heard it too. She checked her watch for the ten-minute mark. That didn't give them much time.

They all stopped in front of an elevator and waited as the oversized doors opened. Butch waved them in, and they pulled the gurney into the elevator with them. Butch pushed the red button at the bottom of the elevator panel.

If they were blown, there would be gunmen ready when those doors opened again. She slipped her hand inside her jacket and on her gun as the elevator began to drop. Apollo was armed as well, but there was a minor problem. The elevator walls were heavy steel. Ricochet City. They wouldn't have a chance.

"I hope this is a good one," Butch said to no one in particular. "You know we only accept the best here."

Seneca said, "He's prime."

Apollo cast her a quick glance that she ignored. So they only wanted the best. That could mean anything. One thing was for certain, though: XCEL agents had been lied to, and she was not happy about that.

The ride seemed to take forever before the elevator clunked to a stop, and the doors opened. Seneca had gun in hand, but it looked clear. They pushed the gurney out and into a well-lit room that resembled a medical facility. Her heart sank as she scanned the expensive, stainless steel equipment lining the walls and rows of deadly looking instruments lying in steel pans. There was a door on the left and a long white hallway extended out straight ahead with a series of doors on either side.

Butch unzipped the body bag. "Let's see what you got."

Apollo moved behind him while Seneca stayed next to the gurney. Butch hummed a few times as he poked and prodded the Shifter body.

Seneca tapped her foot. "Well?"

"Give me a minute," Butch said, annoyed at her impatience. "I need a slice to make sure he's healthy."

A slice? She hadn't expected that. Then Butch picked up a razor-sharp surgical knife, and her heart stopped.

"Then you can't use him," she said quickly.

Butch gave a chuckle. "You ever see how fast these bastards heal? He won't even miss it."

Just as he bent to cut the skin, the body moved, and the Shifter in the body bag grabbed him around the neck. Butch's eyes widened, and his expression quickly turned to shock and terror.

It was priceless.

◆ ◆ ◆

Max held Butch by the throat and drew him to his face. "It's assholes like you who give humans a bad name."

"Don't kill him," Seneca said. "We might need him."

Max growled and threw Butch across the room. He bounced off the wall hard and landed on all fours, looking like he was going to have a heart attack right then and there. Max rolled off the gurney and stepped toward him. "You make a sound and I'll rip your throat out. You won't even miss it."

Butch scrambled back against the wall with a little yelp. Max scanned the room for the first time, and a bad feeling settled in his gut. This was an operating room.

Seneca checked her watch and walked to the side door to put her ear against it. "We have about two minutes before they show up. Apollo, watch the door."

He pulled out his gun and got into position.

"Just enough time to extract some information," Max said, drawing his Shifter frame up to dominate the room. Butch turned white.

Seneca eyed Max as she headed for a corridor at the back of the room. "Don't kill him. I mean it." Then she disappeared down the hallway.

Fine. But she didn't say anything about scaring the living shit out of him. Max stood in front of Butch. "Who's coming?"

"A scientist," he said, his eyes huge as he stared at Max. "Name's Franklin. Dr. Franklin."

"What does he do with the bodies?"

"No, no. You . . . you'll kill us," Butch stuttered. Sweat was soaking his uniform around his neck and armpits.

"Answer my question or I will," Max said, moving closer.

Butch grimaced. "He works on them."

"How?" Max asked.

Butch just shook his head over and over, and the smell of his fear filled the room.

"You're really pissing me off, Butch," Max warned.

"He . . . He . . ."

"He forces them to shift under UVC light," Seneca finished from behind him. Max turned to find her walking toward him from the hallway. Her eyes glistened when she looked at him. "I found them. In various stages of transformation. None of them were alive."

Max rounded on Butch, who covered himself with his hands. "I didn't do it—it's not me! It's not me!"

If Seneca weren't standing right there, he'd rip Butch to pieces.

Apollo said, "That doesn't make sense. We can't shift under UVC light. Everyone knows that."

"We can," Max said. "It just doesn't work."

Seneca replied, "But if you could, you'd be able to go up top and shift at will."

Max growled. "The perfect army."

"Right." She held up a large syringe containing liquid to Butch. "What's in here?"

"A formula that Dr. Franklin is working on, that's all I know." Then his eyes widened at Max. "No, wait, I know more. A lot more."

Seneca slid a glance at Max and smiled a little.

Then the side door opened and a man in a white coat walked in. Glasses, a beaklike nose, and a thin body. Max could snap him in two like a twig. He froze when he saw Max in Primary Shifter form.

Apollo leveled his gun at the scientist's head. "Dr. Franklin, I presume."

"Yes, I am," he said, lifting his chin in arrogant defiance. "Go ahead, shoot me."

Seneca walked up to him. "You'll wish we did by the time we're done with you. XCEL agent, Seneca Thomas. You're under arrest."

CHAPTER
NINETEEN

Hager pulled a dusty bottle from its cubby hole and blew on it to reveal the label. 1969 Inglenook Pinot Noir. An excellent wine for a bad day.

He handed the bottle to Puck to uncork and decant. The little man scurried to his duties as Hager took his seat in the cool chamber, silent in his thoughts. He scanned the news on his BlackBerry. It wasn't good. A man with less self-control would be furious, lashing out at those closest to him. But Hager needed the loyalty of those close, to protect him. No, all his energy was focused on taking this situation and making it work for him.

Max Dempsey and his partner had single-handedly put his program months behind. Skinman's inventory was useless. Word had gotten out that his organization was targeting XCEL agents, and they'd been warned. Suddenly, XCEL agents were scarce, making Hager look like a fool. His replacement for MacGregor had been discovered and terminated. Dempsey had even thwarted a kidnap attempt on Seneca Thomas.

And now the laboratory had been discovered and shut down. There were many layers between him and Dr. Franklin. He was safe enough, but he'd lost precious time and invaluable research. Now he'd have to start over and find another way to create a militia. *His* militia. He would not be betrayed by another government. This time, the government would bow to him.

Puck finished decanting the wine hastily, wasting some of it down the outside of the glass decanter. Hager breathed in and out with controlled effort as Puck asked, "Want me to pour you a glass?"

Hager shook his head. "Too soon. You can go."

Puck frowned, looking from the glass to the decanter. "You sure?"

"Some things can't be rushed, Puck."

"True." Then he exited the room, leaving Hager to think. Dempsey and Thomas had outsmarted him too many times, undermining his reputation. He needed to show his inner circle of borough lords and his budding militia that he indeed had the power, the reach, and the cunning to run this organization.

After careful thought, Hager dialed a number on his Black-Berry and waited. His best tracker picked up on the first ring. "Yeah, boss."

"Bring Seneca Thomas's informant."

"You want him dead or alive?"

Hager poured the wine from the decanter into his glass. "Alive."

"I'll do my best."

Hager hung up and picked up his wineglass. He swirled the red pinot in the light. "*Now* is the time."

◆ ◆ ◆

Seneca rubbed her eyes, trying to coax her body and mind into a sleep schedule that was totally out of whack. Staying in the hotel room with the blinds closed all the time wasn't helping. She had nothing to ground herself to, no sense of day and night, no touchstone in the chaos that had become her life.

Dr. Franklin and Butch were in custody. XCEL was sweeping the facility for intel. She and Dempsey had slept for a few hours. And now it was late afternoon again. Of what day, she had no idea.

Seneca dialed Noko on her cell phone while Dempsey was in the bathroom. She sat on the hotel bed where they had made love and tried to pretend it didn't matter. The sucky part was that it did. All her feelings and emotions were in a jumbled mess. Nothing was as it seemed. Nothing was as simple as she'd once thought.

Noko picked up the phone on the third ring. "Hello."

"Are you safe?" Seneca asked.

"Of course."

Seneca rubbed her forehead. "Nothing out of the ordinary?"

"Aunt Lavina is adding too much salt to her sauces. Uncle Joe still smokes his pipe and gives Chicklets to all the grandchildren."

In other words, things were normal. "No one stalking you?"

"Only you."

"Good." At least one thing was under control. Noko was safe.

Noko asked, "How is Max?"

Seneca glanced at the bathroom door where the faucet was running. Then her gaze fell to his duffle bag on the floor. Normally he took it in the bathroom with him. In fact, he took it everywhere with him, which was a little odd.

"He's fine," she said absently as she got up and walked over to the bag. She leaned over and peeked inside. She shouldn't pry. On the other hand, even though he'd spilled a lot at the diner, it didn't mean he was spilling any more. She needed to take more initiative in getting her answers.

"He lied to me about everything," she said. "About why he joined XCEL, about why he's working with me."

Seneca reached down and widened the opening with one hand but still couldn't see much. Screw it, she was checking the bag. She knelt down, cradled the cell phone on her shoulder, and opened the bag.

"So you feel betrayed," Noko said.

"Hell, yes," Seneca replied. She worked through his shirts and jeans and guns. Nothing unusual.

"Perhaps his reasons were personal."

Her hand hit the bottom of the duffle with a weird sound, like it was hollow. She tapped lightly. Definitely hollow.

"Well, he's my damned partner so his personal crap affects me too."

Another hum. "You wouldn't feel betrayed if you didn't care for him."

Seneca slipped her fingers around the bottom and lifted it up. "I care about all my partners. They keep me alive."

"Not like this. You love him."

Her fingers wrapped around a small rectangular package and pulled it out. It was a white block of soft claylike plastic wrapped in cellophane and it looked an awful lot like C4 explosive. Enough to take out a few rooms. And whoever was in them.

She couldn't answer, paralyzed by sudden clarity of what this meant. His entire mission in life was to kill the man who murdered his wife. There was no other future for him, at least not that she'd seen. He didn't care that his apartment had been trashed; he didn't have any plans; he didn't care what XCEL or anyone else thought of him. No dreams. No goals.

Dempsey was going to kill Hager and himself too.

"Seneca?" Noko asked.

"I don't love him," she said.

"Are you certain?" Noko asked.

"No," Seneca whispered. She'd been so concerned about herself, about her country and her people. About everything and everyone *she* loved and wanted to protect. But his loves meant as much to him as hers did to her. He felt as much pain as any human. He hurt and he suffered, probably more than she would ever know.

Seneca sat back on her heels. But she did know. She'd been there in his mind, felt his agony and his grief. Had seen the only thing that mattered to him dead on the floor. Was she any different than him? Did she not wish every day to find the people who killed her parents? Wouldn't she give her life for that one moment when she could exact revenge?

"I have to go," she said to Noko. "I love you."

"I love you too," her grandmother replied. "I know you will find your way."

The phone went dead in her ear. She put it in her pocket and got to her feet.

"Looking for something?" Dempsey asked from behind her.

Yes, but I'm not going to get it, she thought. *And neither are you.*

Seneca turned around slowly to face him. He was naked without a hint of modesty, and for a moment, she totally forgot what she was thinking. Until his gaze dropped to the C4 in her hand.

"I'm assuming there's a detonator that goes with this?" she said.

His eyes lifted to hers, and he was not happy.

"How were you going to do it?" she pressed. "Absorb the plastic into your body? Blow up Hager, his thugs, his place?"

"Something like that," Dempsey said and walked over to take the C4 from her. He set it in the bag and zipped it closed. Then he turned and gave her a smile that didn't reach his eyes. "Not that it's any of your business."

He crossed the room to where his clothes were laid on the bed.

"Was I part of that plan?" Seneca asked.

"No, and if you have to ask, you don't know me at all."

Of course she wasn't part of it. He was going to use her until he didn't need her anymore, and then take Hager out by himself.

"Why a bomb? Why not just kill him?"

He pulled on a pair of boxers. "Hager needs to be taken out along with his plan and his minions, or someone else will step in. Shifters are nothing if not opportunistic."

He'd lost everything he cared about years ago. He would die with Hager, just like he died with Ell and everything else that mattered to him.

"You could do it without killing yourself in the process," she said. "I can help you."

"This is personal," he said, sounding very irritated but honest.

"What about world peace?"

He gave a short laugh. "You, of all people, know that will *never* happen. Once we're extinct, you'll find something else to kill each other for. Shifters won't change that. They just might speed it up a little."

His bitterness and his finality left dread in her heart.

"I saw what Hager did to her," Seneca said. "She was choked to death with the necklace that was in your apartment."

Dempsey frowned at her. "How do you know that?"

She brushed past his question. "I don't blame you for hating him. For wanting him dead. But that can't be your sole purpose in life."

"It is." Then he walked into the bathroom and started brushing his teeth. She followed him and leaned against the doorway, trying not to act as scared and helpless as she felt. "There has to be *something* about this planet that you like."

He looked at her in the mirror, and she gasped at the intensity. His eyes were heavy and dark, and in them she saw enough sexual energy to set her on fire.

Her? Them? Sex? That was the best he could come up with? Granted, it would be the top of her list too, but was that it? That was the something?

Dempsey finished brushing his teeth and was wiping his face with a towel when she unsnapped her jeans. He heard it and looked at her. His brow furrowed as she slowly unzipped the jeans and tugged them down over her hips. She wasn't sure when she'd made the decision, and it was too late to analyze why.

Max didn't move, the towel motionless in his hand, his eyes

on her. Heat rose in her belly, and she slid her hand up her stomach, taking her shirt with it. He watched her as if she were the only thing in the world. And to him, she was. Her and revenge.

Dempsey tossed the towel aside. His breathing had quickened, his body taut, his erection full-on under the shorts.

"Do you know what you're doing, Seneca?" he rasped.

No, I don't. But maybe, just maybe I can beat out revenge. She peeled the shirt up over her head. The steam from his recent shower settled over her skin, making it slick under her fingertips as she traced a long line between her breasts. Dempsey stared at her fingers, his lust barely leashed. The man and the beast, that was what she wanted and needed.

She ached all over for him, for what he was and what he'd been through and for the sacrifice he was willing to make. She tossed her shirt to him. He caught it with one hand and brought it to his nose. A growl reverberated through the tiny bathroom as he inhaled her scent.

"No regrets," he said, his voice rough. "I'm not moving until you say it."

She half smiled, half laughed with the heady mix of need and power flooding over her. *Say it.* She couldn't even think it. Instead, she closed her eyes, slipped her fingers under her panties, and stroked herself, feeling the fullness and throbbing. That was how much she wanted him.

Suddenly, she was grabbed by the arm and spun toward the sink. She opened her eyes as Dempsey yanked her jeans and underwear down to her knees and pushed her against the granite counter. His erection burned her bottom, and in the mirror, his eyes burned her soul.

Her nipples reflected back hard and dark, her skin dewy and blushed. She braced herself against the sink as he reached around and found her clit. She cried out as he rubbed her firmly, expertly.

She was soon lost in the growing wave of ecstasy. She reached up behind her and gripped him by the neck for support as the climax rose, crested, and took complete control of her, making her feel split in two as it imploded. Her body shuddered in the aftermath, leaving her breathless.

Dempsey pressed his mouth to her ear. "Say it."

He wouldn't continue if she didn't. Wouldn't be tied to her. She had no choice.

"No regrets," she whispered.

A second later, he was inside her. He wrapped his arm around her waist to hold her to him as he gritted his teeth and drove into her again and again. She felt all his hunger and all his desire. The hurt and the passion. And then she was as lost as he was, gripped by another climax.

The bathroom filled with Dempsey's final guttural shout and her moan of release. When she recovered, she was lying upon the cool granite. Dempsey leaned over her, using his hands for support, his head down, sucking air.

Seneca looked up at herself in the mirror, her face glowing, but her eyes full of regret. She hoped he didn't look at her because he'd see the lies and confusion. She'd done it to give him a reason to live; at least that was what she told herself. But what if it didn't work? What if his loss was too great for her to overcome? If she wasn't enough?

TWENTY

Max stood on the other side of the glass and watched Seneca interrogate Dr. Franklin. She was playing into Franklin's demigod mentality and it was working. Her style was persuasive and nonthreatening, and Franklin was chatting away like they were old friends.

Carl came in and sidled up to him. "That was a pretty risky operation you pulled off. I'm glad to see it turned out okay."

Max eyed his old friend. "It was less risky than you taking over command of this agency. Nice to see you're still alive."

Carl chuckled. "That's because they don't know what I am. Only you and Seneca do."

"You can trust her," Max said.

"I know."

There was a silent understanding in that statement. Seneca had always been loyal, but she was different now. He'd seen her anger and disgust at the good doctor's work. It didn't matter to her that those victims were Shifters. It was still wrong.

"How long do we have before the Committee shuts us down?"

"A few days," Carl said. "We're running on a shoestring as it is, moving base operations from location to location to stay one step ahead of Hager's people. I'm playing it as an operational exercise, but it won't be long before the Committee figures out that it's not."

A few days. It would have to be enough. "What about the other XCEL agencies around the country?"

"They are investigating their cryogenics facilities and making sure no more bodies leak out. I gave that project to the Committee to keep them occupied."

Carl knew more about the politics of this government than Max ever wanted to understand. "Find anything useful in Dr. Evil's lab?"

"Just that he was trying to create a formula that negated the effects of UVC light so Shifters could transform in daylight. From what my tech guys say, he was very close," Carl said. "Lucky you found it when you did."

Max nodded. "Plus it'll really tick off Hager."

Carl gave a sigh. "Imagine if Hager had a hundred Shifters who could shift at will—day or night?"

"XCEL would never be able to handle them all," Max answered. "The only thing that keeps Shifters from walking around in Primary form during the day is the fear they'll be destroyed on sight, of not being able to shift back to human to blend in with the locals when threatened. But if that barrier was eliminated—"

Carl finished. "It'd be all-out war."

"And that's exactly what Hager wants," Max said. "This country would be thrown into utter anarchy. He'd terrorize the citizens and destroy this country from the inside out. Then he'd have a chance to grab a piece of it, and eventually, all of it."

"Sonofabitch," Carl said.

"Agreed." Then Max noticed that Seneca was getting upset, and Dr. Franklin's voice rose.

"You don't understand," he was saying. "I am doing important work. No one has ever operated on aliens. Can you not grasp the opportunity we have been given?"

Max watched Seneca lean over the table. "You are experimenting on people, murdering them."

"They aren't people," Dr. Franklin said indignantly. "They are simply another life-form. A new species."

"Like a new kind of bug?" she said softly.

"Uh-oh," Max said. He knew that tone.

"Yes," Dr. Franklin replied, looking pleased that she understood. "Like a new beetle. We must study them to understand how they function, their remarkable ability to control their DNA, their physiology, social structure, sensory and neurological capabilities."

"Is she going to kill him?" Carl asked.

"Quite possibly," Max answered. In fact, he was a little surprised that she hadn't already.

Seneca's hands curled into fists on the table. "So this is for science?"

"Absolutely," Dr. Franklin said.

"It didn't bother you that your sponsor was a Shifter?" she said.

He blinked several times. "Their presence here is being covered up at the highest levels of our government. How else could I get my hands on test subjects?"

With humans like that, who needs Shifter enemies, Max thought.

Seneca tapped her fingers on the table. "But you don't know your sponsor's name?"

Dr. Franklin shrugged. "I don't care."

Max heard a ring, and Seneca pulled out her cell phone, read it, and frowned. Then she looked at him through the glass, and he knew something bad had happened.

She stood and Dr. Franklin jumped to his feet as she walked toward the door. He said to her, "Is that it? What about my lab? My research notes? Those belong to me."

Seneca stopped and turned to face him. "Oh, yes. There is one more thing." Then she punched Dr. Franklin in the mouth. He grabbed his face with a scream and dropped like a brick. She leaned over him, and said, "That was for the *people* you killed, you monster."

Then she walked out.

Carl looked at Max in utter shock and respect. "Remind me not to piss her off."

Max smiled for the first time all day. Now *that* was the woman he knew and loved.

"You really care about her," Carl added.

Too much. "She's my partner."

Carl's eyebrows rose. "I think she's a little more than that."

Much more. Max turned for the door to meet up with her. "She can't be."

◆ ◆ ◆

"Are you sure this is the place Bart wanted to meet?" Dempsey asked her. He was standing next to her in the shadows of abandoned factory buildings in Red Hook.

It was late again—dark, stinky, and bitter cold with the breeze off the bay. Why was it always that way? One of these days, she'd like to try a nine-to-five job with HVAC and donuts. Like normal people.

"This is the address he texted me from his phone," she told him.

Dempsey studied the cluster of dark buildings surrounding them. He was in human form, but his eyes flashed iridescent as he used his Shifter vision. "Does he always text you?"

"Sometimes. Depends how much he's had to drink and how coordinated his fingers are. But—"

Dempsey turned and looked at her, and Seneca's heart beat just a little faster. She liked the way he did that—all intense and serious, and with just enough smolder to let her know he was thinking about her—probably naked.

"But what?" Dempsey asked, his voice soft.

She said, "I've been trying to call him back for two hours. No answer, no reply."

Dempsey shrugged. "Maybe he passed out somewhere."

"Maybe," Seneca said, but it didn't ease the free-floating anxiety she was battling. Something didn't feel right. Bart was ten minutes late. He was *never* late.

Dempsey turned his gaze to the night sky. "Nice way to deck Dr. Franklin."

She bit her lip. It was very unprofessional, and MacGregor would have kicked her butt for doing it. But she'd been so furious and sickened with his psychotic babble. And then when he had the nerve to ask about his research papers . . . "I didn't have a gun with me."

Dempsey smiled at that. "You realize that the Shifters he was working on were criminals that XCEL had caught."

She hadn't forgotten that part, or the fact that she'd joined XCEL to rid her planet of Shifters. Or that if they got rid of the Shifters, that would include Dempsey. She was purposely trying not to go down that road.

"They still deserved better." She checked her phone again. "Bart is fifteen minutes late. I don't like this."

"Neither do I." His voice was raw and thick. He'd shifted. "We have company."

Seneca reached for her guns as shadows burst from the buildings all around them.

"What the hell!" she said as she fired into them.

"Follow me!" Dempsey roared. Five Shifters moved in as she ran with Dempsey, getting off shots when she could. She had both her Glocks, the tranq gun, and a protective vest, but no night vision.

Dempsey lunged at the Shifter standing between them and the closest building and knocked him out of the way. Seneca sprinted past him toward the nearest door. She kicked the warehouse door and its hinges broke. She pushed her way inside and hid behind the doorjamb. That was when she noticed that Dempsey wasn't with her. She peered out to find him fighting off the five attackers single-handedly. Loud grunts and screams echoed between the buildings.

He tells me to take cover, and then he plays hero. She was going to kill him. She stepped outside. "Hey, dickheads. Aren't you forgetting someone?"

For a moment, none of them paid any attention to her.

"Hello!" she hollered and waved her guns over her head. "Wanted woman here."

Then two of them peeled off and came after her. That left Dempsey with three and a fighting chance. She turned and ran back into the building and through the littered rooms. Without night vision, she had to rely on the ambient city light filtering through grimy windows. She tripped over uneven floorboards and skirted rusted machinery. A set of stairs appeared up ahead. The stairwell was partially blocked by fallen beams, but she managed to squeeze between them.

The Shifters were right behind her, and she heard their voices when they reached the bottom and realized they couldn't fit. They'd have to shift back to human, which would give her time. She raced up the stairs, feeling pretty good until she heard wood creak and splinter.

Or they could just use their superhuman strength to clear the beams. Damn Shifters. She moved her ass, heavy footsteps behind her. The trick was keeping them interested but not too close. When Dempsey was done outside, he'd come after these guys.

She hoped.

Moonlight illuminated the soaring second-floor space. Long conveyor belts stretched the length of the open area and catwalks crisscrossed the ceiling three stories up, linking steel storage tanks. Thick chains hung down like nooses. The Shifters were closing in behind her. She holstered one of her guns, jumped up on a conveyor belt, and ran as fast as she could over the busted track, tossing everything she got her hand on behind her to slow them down.

A catwalk ladder was dead ahead and Seneca sped up, hit the end of the track, and leaped onto the ladder. It gave a groan as she slammed into it and prayed it held together, at least until she got to the top. The catwalk was just within reach when they wrenched the ladder hard to the right and she nearly lost her grip. The Shifters shook it again, and her feet slipped off, leaving her hanging by one hand. She fired at them and scrambled to regain her footing.

With one mighty lunge, she reached for the catwalk and pulled herself up through the small opening in the grating. One of the Shifters was climbing the ladder right behind her. She crawled on her hands and knees out of reach as he poked through and made a grab for her. He grunted as he tried to push himself up farther, but his shoulders were stuck.

"Today is not your day, buddy." She gripped his head with one hand, concentrated, and said, "Shift."

His eyes widened, and his body fought the terrible transformation without success. He stared at her as the contortions consumed him. Seconds later, he dropped and landed headfirst on the floor. The other Shifter stood over him as he flailed in agony. Then he looked up at her.

"Surprise," she said, pulling herself to her feet.

The Shifter growled and ascended the ladder. She waited, knowing she was out of reach. *This is going to be a lot easier than I planned,* she thought. Right up until he got to the top, climbed over the railing, and dropped onto the catwalk in front of her.

Shit. She pulled out the tranq gun and shot at his chest. The cartridge passed through him and hit the wall. His face split into a big grin.

"Right," she said, tossed the gun over the railing, and ran.

The metal structure shook as the Shifter chased her. She heard bolts snap and metal whine. The maze of catwalks bounced and flexed with every step. A few of the grates were missing and she leapt over those with the Shifter close behind her.

Seneca turned a corner and realized that it dead-ended at a massive steel tank. She stopped and glanced through the grates—at least three stories down. The Shifter had her trapped.

He chuckled as she turned to face him and backed up. They moved in unison—him advancing, her retreating. She looked down again, searching for Dempsey. All quiet below. She pulled out her Glocks, knowing they were useless at this point.

Then a grate popped several screws when she stepped on it and gave under her weight. A plan formed as she lifted her foot off the bad grate and took a giant step back.

"You think you can beat us," he hissed, enjoying his advantage. "You pathetic piece of flesh. I could slice you in half."

She countered, "Maybe. But I have something you don't."

"Your little guns?" he said.

She just smiled. "Come any closer, and I'll show you."

He stepped on the loose grate and reached for her. She aimed and shot at the few remaining screws holding the grate up. He threw his head back and laughed. Then he was gone, crashing through the metal and hitting the concrete with a bone-crunching thud.

"I have brains." She leaned back against the tank to calm her pounding pulse and closed her eyes for a moment. That was too close. How many lives did she have left?

Then she pushed off the tank and made her way back down. She'd just reached the bottom when Dempsey came running in, still in Shifter form. She scanned his formidable Shifter body. No injuries that she could see, and for that she was grateful. He looked powerful, and for the first time, she realized there was beauty in his Primary form. She'd been too busy hunting them to notice.

"Are you okay?" he asked.

She reloaded her guns. "You know, I'm getting damned sick of being ambushed. I assume the others are dead or gone."

"Both." Dempsey checked the fallen Shifter. "He's dead. Where's the other one?"

"I shifted him and he fell three stories on his head. He's a goner."

Dempsey stood up and shifted back to human. "And I have a feeling Bart isn't doing too well either. They used his cell phone to set us up."

She'd tried to come up with another explanation, but now foreboding loomed. Bart was in serious jeopardy, she was sure of it. "Let's check his place. Maybe his phone was lost or stolen."

Dempsey gave her a dubious look. "Your optimism is sweet."

She walked by him, guns at the ready. "There's nothing sweet about me."

◆ ◆ ◆

Bart's place could be described in three words: tiny, dirty, and orange. Max scanned the disaster that stretched from the corner kitchen to the living room to the bathroom. "I can't even tell if it's been ransacked."

Seneca was wading through piles of clothes, empty bottles, and pizza boxes toward the kitchen area. "I can't believe anyone *lives* like this."

Max headed to the bathroom, which was the only other room in the apartment. If Bart had left anything behind, it'd be here, somewhere in this sea of garbage. He stopped, catching a faint scent. "Shifters."

Seneca had her guns out in a flash. "Here? Now?"

"It's been a few days. One, maybe two Shifters," Max said. "It's a little hard to separate the scents in here."

She holstered the weapons. "I can imagine. This is one place I wouldn't want super olfactory powers. Picking up anything else?"

Max followed the scent to the couch. "Yes. At least one of them was female."

Seneca stared at him. "A female Shifter? I thought you said they were wiped out."

"All the children were lost, but a few women survived."

"Enough of them to save your people?" she asked.

It was his turn to stare. *To save his people?* He wasn't used to hearing that or even having anyone care enough to think about it. "Probably not. Our race is destined to die out here."

Seneca pursed her lips, her expression pensive. What was she thinking? He didn't know anymore. The way she looked at him now was so different. She'd given herself to him. She'd defended the Shifters as her own to Dr. Franklin. She'd changed.

He turned his attention back to the room. "I don't see any signs of a struggle, although that's debatable."

Seneca nodded. "I'll start at this end; you take that end. Maybe we'll get lucky and find him passed out somewhere under this mess."

An hour later, they'd finished working through the two-room apartment. No Bart, and no clues to where he might be. Max also realized they were back to square one again. How were they going to find Hager now?

"I'll send the cleanup crew in to see if they can find anything we may have missed," she said and stopped in front of him. She was noticeably exhausted.

"And we need to locate another XCEL informant." Max wiped a smudge of dirt from her face. "Bart's not alive, you know."

"I know."

She looked so vulnerable at that moment. He reached out and wrapped his arms around her to hold her tight. Her world, what she loved, was unraveling around her. He knew from personal experience that it was hell.

Then a thought struck him. "Can our techs follow the cell phone signal?"

Seneca leaned back and looked at him, renewed by a glimmer of hope. "They should at least be able pinpoint the location the last text message was sent from."

"Then we have a shot," he said, releasing her. "Let's get out of here before we contract something deadly."

Just as they stepped out of the apartment, Max noticed one of the neighbors peeking out her door. The old woman slammed the door shut when she saw him.

Seneca exchanged a look with him. "Nosy neighbors. My favorite kind."

She walked up and knocked on the door while Max scouted the hallway. The apartment building was run-down and loud. Voices carried from floor to floor. A perfect setup for eavesdropping.

The woman opened the door, a chain stretched across the few inches. Max moved behind Seneca for a better look. She was in her sixties with white hair that stuck out in every direction. "What do you want?"

Seneca said, "I'm sorry to bother you, but we are looking for Bart. He lives next door."

The woman glanced up at Max, and then back at Seneca. "Ain't seen him lately."

"When did you see him last?" Seneca asked.

The woman frowned. "Are you a cop?"

"Friends of Bart," Max said.

She glared at him. "Not you, *her*."

Seneca replied, "No, we're friends. I haven't heard from him in a while and I'm worried."

She muttered, "I told him not to trust them."

Seneca asked, "Trust who?"

The woman stared directly at Max. "The ones like him."

Max froze. Could she see him?

Seneca gave a little laugh. "Like what?"

"Monsters," the woman said, her eyes fixed on him. "They come and go all the time. I told Bart, one of these days, they gonna kill you. You ain't like them."

"Well, I'm not one of them," Seneca said, evenly. "You can trust me."

The woman looked at her and chewed on her lip. "He ain't been home in two days. Don't know where he is."

Seneca nodded. "Thank you for your help."

The woman flicked her gaze to Max and motioned for Seneca to move closer. Max heard her whisper, "Bart keeps all his good stuff in his mailbox."

Seneca thanked her again. The woman gave Max a final dirty look and slammed the door shut. They walked down the stairs toward the front of the building where all the mailboxes were located.

"She could see me," he said.

"Yes," Seneca replied quietly. "I wonder how many more of us there are?"

CHAPTER
TWENTY-ONE

diots. It took every bit of Hager's self-restraint not to throw his BlackBerry at Louie.

"Is there no one who can catch these two?" he asked the lone Shifter from the five he'd sent out to capture Dempsey and Thomas. Louie was in human form and battered. There were odd bumps under his clothing, and he could barely walk. Too bad. He got paid plenty for his injuries.

Louie rubbed his head. "You don't understand. Max is good . . ."

"He's no different than you," Hager insisted. He stood and paced the perimeter of his cell, the only safe place he could live. And every day, it felt smaller and smaller. He was beginning to hate this planet and its humans. One day, he'd rectify both.

"But *she* isn't," Louie said. "She forced me to shift."

Hager stopped dead in his tracks. "She *what*?"

"She put her hand on my head and said, 'Shift,' and *I did*. And let me tell you, it hurt like hell and I'm still not healed right."

Hager frowned at the man. He was dead serious. "Did she use something? Technology? Drugs?"

Louie shook his head. "Nothing. Just her hand. I couldn't stop it from happening. I couldn't control the transformation. You can offer me all the money you want, but I'm not going after that woman again."

Seneca Thomas could force Shifters to shift with her bare hands. Hager had never seen or heard of such a thing. It was unique and, therefore, valuable. In fact, he could use a woman and a weapon like that. All he had to do was convince her to work for him.

Or maybe it wasn't *her* he had to convince.

"Go heal yourself," Hager said. "And send Puck in on your way out."

Louie nodded and left. Seconds later, Puck shuffled in.

"I want to talk to Max," he said. "Make sure he gets a throw-away phone."

Puck gave him a wary look. "You really think you can stop 'im with talking?"

Hager pulled on his jacket and stuffed the BlackBerry in the pocket. Every man had his price. Every situation could be turned to an advantage. "Yes, I do. It's time."

Puck screwed up his face. "Time for what?"

"Call in all the borough lords for a meeting. Set it up for tomorrow night." He headed out of the wine cellar. "Tell them we're arming."

Puck asked, "Where are you goin'?"

Hager answered over his shoulder. "To see an old friend."

✦ ✦ ✦

In the apartment building entryway, Seneca sifted through the papers they'd retrieved from Bart's mailbox. The building super was more than happy to hand over the keys after she offered him a month of Bart's rent. She only hoped it was worth it. There were overdue bills, unpaid parking tickets, a bag of a white illegal drug, and an envelope with a hundred dollars in it. One man's life, in a box.

Dempsey said, "This is his good stuff?"

"It would appear so. I don't see anything useful in here. No notes or contact information." She sighed and slid the papers back into the mailbox.

"Wait a minute," Dempsey said. "Give me the parking tickets."

She eyed him as he studied them. "Feeling generous?"

"No," he said, and waved the clutch of tickets. "But Bart has a car."

It took her two phone calls and a few hours to track down Bart's car. They located it in a NYPD impound lot. It was a quiet drive to the lot. Seneca concentrated on the fact that they had another chance to find something Bart may have left behind. Because one thing was clear: Bart hadn't skipped town in his car.

Cars of all makes and models were lined up in the pound.

"Should we tell someone that Bart isn't coming for his car?" Dempsey said.

Seneca shook her head. "We don't know he's not coming back. Maybe he got spooked and is on the run."

They found Bart's 1998 Buick LeSabre unlocked and full of

trash. No surprise there. Seneca endured the stench from liquor flasks, food containers, urine, and vomit as she searched the interior and glove box. She stuffed a few scraps of paper she found in her pocket. Then she looked through the rearview mirror to find Dempsey staring at the trunk. "What's wrong?"

"Pop the trunk," he told her, and she obliged.

Over the top of the trunk, she saw him frowning. With great dread, she got out and walked around the back of the car.

Bart was wrapped in layers of plastic and stuffed in his own trunk.

Dempsey said, "I think it's safe to tell them he won't be picking up his car now."

◆ ◆ ◆

"Our crime scene unit said he'd been dead at least twenty-four hours," Carl said. "Strangulation."

Seneca was pacing Carl's office at the newly relocated makeshift XCEL headquarters, her head down and face pale.

Max asked, "He had his wallet?"

"Yeah, looks like they just wanted the cell phone."

"My informant," she repeated for the third time as if she wasn't even listening to them. "This is my fault."

"Every informant takes that chance," Carl told her, but she didn't stop pacing. Max watched her. She was running on empty—no sleep, no food, no answers. He could do that, but then again, he wasn't entirely human either.

"Did the trace come through for Bart's text message?" Max asked.

"Just got it," Carl said and slid a printout across the desk. "Times Square. Sorry."

"Damn, damn," Seneca said, stopping. "*Damn!*"

Max agreed. Chances were pretty slim that Hager was working out of Times Square. "Anything else?"

Carl sighed. "We found MacGregor's body in a sewer drain near his house. I'm betting that Hager was involved."

Seneca stopped and gaped at Carl, pain etched on her face. Then she covered her eyes with her hands. "This can't be happening."

"I've told our units to follow up every lead we get," Carl said, giving Max an apologetic look. "I'll call you if we find something promising."

"Thanks." Max stood up.

Seneca was beside herself. "We should talk to MacGregor's neighbors."

"No," Max said, softly.

She blinked a bunch of times, her eyes red and tired. She needed sleep. "I'm not going to just sit here and wait for the fucking lead fairy to present us with clues."

She *really* needed sleep. He nodded good-bye to Carl and took her by the arm. "I have a plan."

That got her as far as one of XCEL's surveillance vans. She slid into the passenger side, ready to rumble. "Where to?"

Max hitched his head to the rear of the van. "The cot in the back."

As he expected, she didn't like that. "That's your plan? Are you kidding me?"

This wasn't going to be easy. "You cannot function without sleep."

"Watch me," she said, crossing her arms.

Stubborn woman. "Let me rephrase. You can't operate safely without sleep."

She frowned. "Are you afraid I'm going to put you at risk? I think we're well past that."

He decided to change tactics. What she needed was a challenge. Something a little dangerous to keep her interested. Max leaned closer and traced the V-neck of her shirt with his finger. "Tell you what. You give me ten minutes. You, me, and the cot."

She narrowed her eyes, but there was a hint of the challenge he was hoping for. "And if I'm not asleep by then?"

He sighed. "Then we'll go after bad guys everywhere."

"I love it when you talk dirty," she said, a slight smile curling her lips.

"All I have to do is mention guns. Now get in the back."

He followed her through the equipment and weapons to a small cot normally used for sleeping and injured agents. Max lowered it while Seneca looked at it and then at him, not knowing what to do next.

"Relax," he said.

Seneca raised an eyebrow. "If that's your entire plan, then we may as well stop now."

Max smiled. He'd spent most of the last few minutes working diligently on this plan. He wrapped his hands around her waist and kissed her. With his fingertips, he stroked her lightly from her breasts to her thighs. With every caress, her muscles relented and the tension subsided. It took a few minutes, but she finally wrapped her arms around his neck. He unsnapped and unzipped her jeans, and then whispered, "Sit."

She moved to the middle of the cot, and he dropped to the floor in front of her. Her eyes followed him as he tugged her jeans off, and then loosened and unbuttoned her shirt.

She licked her lips. "You know, Hager could be anywhere in this city."

He exposed her black bra and black panties and felt the blood rush to his groin. This was going to be a lot harder on him than it was on her.

"We could be out there now, checking the hot spots . . ." She gave a little shudder as he slipped her shirt off.

Max slid the bra straps over her shoulders and pulled it down to reveal her breasts. She inhaled sharply as he leaned forward and wrapped his lips around one nipple. He felt her breathing quicken and deepen. Then he moved to the other one and gave it similar treatment. Seneca moaned a little and arched into him.

Just when he thought he had her, she murmured, "Maybe Hager *is* at Times Square. You never know. We should follow up."

A lesser man might have quit, but there was no way he was leaving her like this. Max put his hands around her waist and then under her bottom, slowly removing her panties. Seneca lifted her hips enough for him to slide them off.

"Aren't you worried we won't find him?" she asked.

"No." He was, but at the moment, he didn't care. He was on a different kind of mission. He kissed her to shut her up and ran his palms along her thighs, spreading her legs so he could position himself closer. His thumb rubbed the sweet spot gently, then faster, and her breathing became deeper as he matched his kisses to the caresses.

"Max," she said against his lips, her voice hushed. His body responded hard and fast, but he held himself in check. This wasn't about him.

Her arms locked around his neck and she moaned, pushing her hips toward the pressure of his thumb. He concentrated on her body and the small nuances that told him what she needed. Her skin began to flush, heat rising in her face and chest as she kissed him hard.

Finally, she broke off the kiss and dropped her head back. Her expression was pained, but he knew where she was. He flattened his thumb and slowed his motions until she gritted her teeth and he watched her face as she climaxed. It suddenly dawned on him—he'd live for this. To see her do this in his arms.

But then what? Life like this? Making love in a van because they couldn't go home? Killing Shifters all night? Worrying about every person they ever knew being used for ransom? He'd seen this before, and it never ended well. Too much blood would be spilled to make it work. There was only the present, and for now, she was his.

Her face softened, and she collapsed into his arms, her body trembling. He held her close and caressed her neck as she recovered. He inhaled her scent—moist and sexy.

"I'm not tired," she said, but she sounded otherwise. Besides, she wasn't getting off so easy. If he let her go now, she'd drag her exhausted ass back to work.

"I'm not done yet."

She leaned back, her eyes hooded. "What else did you have in mind?"

He grinned. Her eyes widened as he spread her legs and dipped his head between them.

◆ ◆ ◆

Seneca surfaced to a gentle shake. She swatted at the hand. It was safe and warm where she was, and she didn't want to come out.

"We have to move, Seneca," a deep voice said.

Mmm. She snuggled in the blankets, aware that she was completely naked. Then she remembered several amazing orgasms and Max.

Max. Sexy, amazing Max.

She opened her eyes and looked up at him. He was smiling at her but something was wrong.

"What time is it?" she asked, waking in a hurry.

"Noon."

She sat up, taking the blanket with her. "Did we get a lead?"

He shook his head. "Not quite. Apollo called me. He's in trouble."

TWENTY-TWO

They found Apollo in the alley behind their boxing gym under a pile of cardboard boxes. Sunlight streamed between the buildings. Max smelled the scent of Shifters and blood even before he saw it.

"Oh God," Seneca said as she knelt beside Apollo.

His face had been battered, both his eyes purple and swollen shut. His workout clothes were caked in mud, his mouth was cut, and blood streaked his shirt. There were numerous bruises and slashes on his arms.

"What happened?" Max asked as he pulled the trash away from his friend.

"Remember I told you that every time you have a plan, I end up in the middle of it?" Apollo said, his speech slurred.

Seneca checked his eyes. "Who did this to you?"

"Shifters," Max answered for him.

Apollo grabbed his arm and whispered, "We gotta talk. Privately."

That didn't sound good. Seneca looked from Apollo to Max with a strange expression on her face, like she wanted to say something but changed her mind. "Noko isn't here to heal him."

Max asked him, "How many were there? Did you recognize any of them?"

Apollo shook his head. "Is anyone listening to me?"

Max told Seneca, "Let's get him into the van. If he shifts, he'll heal faster."

Seneca nodded and together they lifted Apollo, each of them taking an arm. They walked him to the van and laid him down in the back.

Seneca handed Max the first aid kit. "I'll drive us to a safer location." Then she moved to the front of the van. The second she was out of sight, Apollo slapped a cell phone in Max's hand. "Hager wants to talk to you. *Just* you. They were pretty adamant about that."

So Hager was behind this. He should have known they'd start going after people he cared about. Luckily, that was a very short list. Max waited until the van was under way before he flipped open the cell phone and checked the phone list. There was only one number on it. He dialed, and it picked up on the second ring.

"Ah, I see you received my message," a man answered.

"Hager," Max said. He finally had the murderer, and all he could think to say was, "It's about time you stepped out from behind your goons."

"Well, my goons got the message across, didn't they?"

Max glanced at Apollo, who had morphed to Shifter form. His eyes were closed, and his breathing was even. He'd survive, for today, but what about next time?

The rage threatened to swamp him and undermine a mission he'd worked on so hard and for so long. Max wanted nothing more than to tell Hager that he knew he killed Ell and all the other Shifters back on Govan. He wanted to, but he realized if he did, he'd lose a key advantage.

"What do you want, Hager?"

"You. I'd like you to join my organization. And bring in Seneca, of course."

Max tamped down his anger and settled for a heartfelt, "Fuck you."

Hager chuckled. "Now, now, you must give me a chance to explain. You see, if you don't join me, I'll need to resort to drastic measures."

"You want me? Come and get me," Max said.

"We could do it that way, but there would be a lot of blood and death. Besides, family is so much more important. I think Seneca would agree."

Max stilled. *Noko.* "If you can find them."

"Oh, I already have."

Max cast a quick glance toward the front of the van where Seneca was driving. Noko would be the one thing she would surrender for. In a heartbeat.

Hager continued. "Besides, now that XCEL is no longer in business—"

"What?" Max said.

"Oh, you haven't heard. The operation has been shut down by the brilliant committee that oversees it. You have nowhere to go, Max. And no one to protect you."

Max kept his tone even. "I don't believe you."

"Yes, you do. You knew it was coming. And so did Seneca. Think about my offer. You have six hours." The phone disconnected, and Max closed the cell phone.

"What'd he want?" Apollo asked.

"He wants me to join him. And bring in Seneca."

Apollo rolled his head back and forth. "You really gotta stop pissing people off."

"Doesn't matter. I won't do it," Max said.

Apollo grunted. "Figured as much. Although—"

"What?"

"It would be the perfect opportunity to see Hager's operation," Apollo finished.

Hell. Apollo was right. How else was Max going to get inside and get to Hager? He could blow them all up, which would be ideal except that Seneca would have to be there too. Unless he figured out a way for her *not* to be there.

"You know I can't help you with Hager. Not in this condition," Apollo said. "I need at least twenty-four hours."

Max squeezed his shoulder. "It's okay."

Then Apollo opened one eye with considerable effort and looked at him. "Get the bastard."

"Plan on it," Max said.

❖ ❖ ❖

Once Apollo was settled in a hotel room, Max called Carl from an adjoining room. As soon as he answered, Max asked, "Did the Committee shutdown XCEL?"

Carl replied, "Yes. And all the other agencies around the country. For assessment, they said, which is bullshit because we all know if XCEL comes back, it'll be a very different agency."

Max had never heard Carl sound so bitter. "You'll still be part of the process, though, right?"

"I don't know, I haven't been tapped yet." Carl sighed. "How did you find out?"

"I talked to Hager. He offered me a job."

Carl gave a short laugh. "Unbelievable. Look, I know it seems bad, but come into the office, and we'll figure something out. They haven't locked the doors yet."

"We'll be there shortly," he said as Seneca walked in from the bathroom and lifted an eyebrow in question.

"See you then."

Seneca crossed her arms and stood in front of him. She looked beautiful, and he wished they had more time. For everything—for sex and laughter and life.

She said, "Are you going to tell me or do I have to beat it out of you?"

He eyed her. "I kind of like the sound of the second option."

She gave him a no-nonsense smirk, and he went with option one. "Hager's men attacked Apollo to send me a message. And provided a cell phone so I could talk to Hager directly."

"How nice of them. And?"

"Hager wants me to join him." Max left out the part where Hager wanted her too. Knowing her, she'd jump at the chance.

Seneca blinked. "Join his organization? Are you kidding? Does he know that the woman he murdered on the ship was your wife?"

"Doubtful."

Seneca shook her head. "So what did you say to him?"

Max smiled.

Seneca smiled back. "How did he take that?"

"Not well," he admitted, and then added, "He knows where Noko is."

Her smile faded. "I'll warn her."

"She's already being watched," Max said.

"My relatives can handle it," Seneca said, but she didn't sound convinced.

"And the Committee shut down XCEL."

Seneca took a step back in obvious shock. "What? No. They can't."

"They can, and they did. Hager told me; Carl confirmed."

She ran her fingers through her hair and turned away from him. "I can't believe this. How can they do this now, of all times? We're on the verge of war here, don't they understand that?"

"Apparently not."

"Idiots," she continued. "Friggin' short-sighted, bureaucratic dickheads. How do we fix this?"

It would be the perfect opportunity to see Hager's operation. The thought kept coming back to him. "I don't know."

Seneca narrowed her eyes at him. "Out with it, Dempsey. How do we stop Hager?"

The perfect opportunity. And maybe the only opportunity. He didn't have a lot of choices left. Whether Seneca agreed or not, he was going to have to take Hager's offer.

"I might have an idea, but I'll need Carl's help."

◆ ◆ ◆

Seneca walked into their temporary headquarters like a woman on a mission. She was beyond furious, beyond reason, and she didn't give a damn. The Committee was going to get an earful from their most effective agent. But as she walked through the room, the hair on the back of her neck went up. Something felt off, and it wasn't just that Price was at his desk and rest of the place was empty except for stacked boxes.

"I guess they weren't kidding," she said to Dempsey. He was very still, his eyes scanning the room. It felt dead, like a morgue. Lifeless.

Price looked up when they walked by and said, "I'll need your weapons and passkey to this office."

Seneca kept walking. "Bite me."

She pushed open Carl's door and found him behind the desk. "What the hell happened?"

Carl smiled at her. "And a good day to you too."

"Not in the mood, Carl," she said, planting her hands on his desk. "How can they shut us down?" She waved a hand toward the window. "Do they think they have someone else who can do a better job?"

"You get no arguments from me," Carl said. "Calm down. We'll discuss—"

"Discussion is not going to solve this," she snapped. "Discussion is not going to find Hager."

"But a real, planned strategy might," Carl said. "Sit down. Please."

Seneca pursed her lips. She'd give him thirty seconds. After that, she was taking her guns and shooting something. She sat next to Dempsey, who was unusually quiet. Everything was wrong. The office, the people, the boxes, the boss. "Where are the other agents?"

"Handing in their gear and doing exit interviews. You're supposed to report too," Carl said, leaning his elbows on the desk.

"We can't do that," Dempsey said.

"I know, but we'll have to move fast." Then Carl rummaged through the files on his desk, for a few seconds. "Seneca, I need the file on Price's desk with the Committee's last report. And don't hurt him."

She wrinkled her nose. "You take all the fun out of working here." But she got up, opened the door, and closed it behind her. Price sat at his desk, watching her as she approached. Her skin began to crawl. Price was acting extra weird.

Then he lifted a gun from under his desk and shot her. She felt a sting in her stomach and looked down to find a tranquilizer dart embedded there. She yanked it out, but the damage had already been done.

The office spun violently. *No.*

She opened her mouth to yell, but nothing came out. Her body had became numb in seconds, her muscles uncooperative.

Price wavered in her vision as he stood up and walked toward her, his face twisted in a smile. Shifter shadows converged behind him, ebbing and flowing against chairs and desks.

She felt the carpet under her knees and realized she'd fallen.

Her fingers fumbled clumsily for her gun, but just when she thought she had it, someone yanked it away. Her hands dropped and she fell backward, staring at the long panels of fluorescent lights.

Max! she cried, but there was only silence.

Price's face entered her line of sight, and she heard him talk in a faraway voice. "Bite me, Seneca."

Then she passed out.

TWENTY-THREE

C arl leaned back in his chair after Seneca left to get the file. "Do you miss the good days, Max? Back when you and Ell actually had a life together?"

It was an odd question. "Sometimes."

Carl drummed his fingers on the desk. "It would be nice if you could have that again with Seneca. I know you care about her a great deal."

The strange feeling Max had when he first walked in turned to wariness. His old friend stood up from behind the desk and walked over to a window that overlooked rooftops. "What would you sacrifice to have that again?"

Max looked at the door behind him. What was taking Seneca so long? "Why are you asking me this now, Carl?"

Carl turned to him. "Is it too much to ask for a life? To ask for peace? For a home. For happiness. We deserve that much, don't we? Doesn't everyone?"

Max pushed up from his chair, his body going into full-ready mode. "Yes, we do. And we aren't going to have it with Hager around."

"I fear we won't have it with humans either."

"We haven't given them a chance yet." Max moved for the door. *Where was she?*

"I think we have," Carl said. "And they failed."

Max was about to turn the doorknob when Carl's voice stopped him.

"I have very few friends left, Max. You are one of them." Carl gave him a crooked smile. "I don't want to lose you."

The smell of Shifters seeped in around the door. Max stared at him. "What have you done?"

"What was necessary."

Sonofabitch. Max morphed into Shifter form and smashed through the door. He rushed into the office to find it full of Shifters—some in human form with weapons, some in Primary form. In the center was Seneca, gagged, unconscious, and tied to a chair. Price stood behind her, grinning like the bastard he was, with a gun to her head. "Shift back to human, or I'll blow her brains out."

Rage flooded his body and Max growled low in his chest. Price's eyes widened, but he lifted Seneca's head by her hair and put the gun to her temple.

"Don't do it, Max," Carl said from behind him. "You'll die, and so will she."

Max swung around to face him, and realized he'd joined Hager. "You set us up."

Carl didn't look at all sorry. "This *is* the only way, Max."

"Have you forgotten what he did?" he asked.

Carl shook his head. "No, but this is the best chance we have. Shift back now, Max. Please. Hager wants you both alive, but he didn't specify how much."

Max could move fast enough to take out Price, he knew that. But he couldn't risk Seneca getting killed in the melee that followed. On the other hand, she'd blame him for not trying. There was no winning this. He looked at her, the way her black hair flowed around her face, the beauty inside and out that he couldn't risk. With his last breath, he would save her.

"I shift, she lives," Max said to Price.

He lifted his chin. "Of course."

"And when the time comes," Max said low, "I'm going to rip you limb from limb."

Price blanched. Max shifted. Seconds later, he was pelted with tranquilizer darts.

◆ ◆ ◆

Seneca could hear men talking. She was cold and damp, and laid out on something hard. Her head weighed a ton and pounded steadily. Her neck and shoulders hurt. Her throat was like sandpaper. She opened her eyes to pitch blackness. When she tried to touch her face to see if her eyes were really open, she realized her hands and feet were bound together.

Where was she? Where was Max? Her eyes adjusted slowly, and she noticed a thin strip of light outlining a door to her right. A door meant a room. It smelled of mold and dirt, like somewhere underground. Had to be Hager's lair. She tried her restraints again, but the straps were tight around her wrists and she was lashed to the table with a big strap over her chest. She wriggled but there was no way to reach the strap.

For a long moment, she imagined what she was going to do to that weasel Price next time she saw him. Death was too good for him. He'd betrayed her and Max. And Carl too? She didn't know.

Another even more disturbing thought arose above the throbbing in her head: She was alive. Why? She'd heard enough about Hager to know that he'd do just about anything with little to no provocation. So why spare her?

Outside the door, voices rose and drew closer. Shadows moved across the sliver of light.

"You promised peace this time," someone said. "This is war." His accent was thick and Irish.

Another voice replied, "In order to have peace, you must be prepared for war, Puck. I'm simply ensuring our superior position."

The one with the accent said, "Like on Govan? When you traded Shifter lives for a superior position? A life of luxury while others died."

They were talking about how Hager had betrayed the Shifters. Seneca closed her eyes and hung on every word. One of them had to be Hager. Who was the man with the accent?

Hager said, "You didn't complain then. Your life was good. You had everything you ever needed."

"Until the government betrayed us, and we lost it all."

Seneca smirked. Hager betrayed his people to the Govan

government and then the government betrayed him? Now, *that* was justice.

Hager said, "It worked out to our advantage too. We moved to a better home with these humans. Nearly perfect DNA to replicate. The plan is going exactly as we agreed."

Moved to a better home? Wait. She'd been told that they crashed here by mistake. But what if they didn't? What if Hager *targeted* Earth on purpose? She suddenly felt sick to her stomach.

"I like these humans."

Hager replied, "Well, they don't like us, and that's all that matters. We destroyed the ship. We can't flee this planet like we did the last one. There are no other options. We live here in peace, or we die here fighting. One way or the other, we will be accepted."

Seneca felt her mouth open in disbelief. Hager destroyed the ship. It was no mistake. He had stranded the Shifters here. Why?

The other man said, "You destroyed it because you were afraid the Govan government would find out that you stole it from them."

Unbelievable, Seneca thought. He stole the ship and then used it to transport as many Shifters as he could here. Those Shifters thought they were leaving to find a new home. All they were doing was providing Hager with an army. What kind of monster did that? He had to die.

The Irishman stuttered. "We . . . we ruined our people . . . We have no children. No future."

There was a short pause. "You and I agreed when we left Govan that we would do whatever was necessary to survive. If that means we fight for our place, then that's what we do, little brother."

Hager had a brother? Oh great, there were two of them.

"And what of the humans?" the brother asked. "Do you plan to wipe them out too?"

Seneca froze, waiting. Hager replied, "Not at all. In fact, they will serve us. We can live forever through their bodies. We're immortal here, Puck. *Immortal.*"

Seneca felt horror ice up her veins. It was a scenario she had never imagined in her worst nightmares, and she'd had some bad nightmares. She couldn't let that happen. Not to her people. Not to Max or the Shifters. They didn't know any of this, she was sure of it. If they did, Hager wouldn't be alive right now.

The door opened, and she pretended to be unconscious. She heard them approach and fought the instinct to open her eyes. Although, if they wanted her dead, she'd already be dead.

"She's still out."

Hager said, "Good. Move her to the chamber before the others arrive. I want her to wake up surrounded by Shifters."

Bastard. Like she needed one more reason to hate him.

"She won't join us," the brother said. "She's stubborn."

Stubborn? They had no idea.

"I can be very persuasive," Hager said, with a chill in his voice.

"And then what?"

"Then we either have a celebration or an execution."

Hell.

Seneca waited for Hager to leave the room. She felt his brother gently remove the thick strap that held her to the table. Her mind raced through her options and settled on the only one that held a glimmer of hope.

"Your name is Puck?" she asked.

The man stepped back, surprised by the fact that she was awake. She turned her head and looked at him, silhouetted in the doorway. He was a small man, hunched and old. But the light behind him highlighted the biggest Shifter shadow she'd ever seen. Larger even than Max. Powerful, pure energy pulsed around him, his frail human figure nearly lost inside it.

He stepped closer to her. "I am. How do you feel?"

She studied his face and found genuine kindness. What was he doing with the likes of Hager? "I have a headache."

"Aye, I bet you do. I apologize for this . . . situation."

She sat up slowly and swung her bound feet over the edge of the table. "It's not your fault. Your brother means a great deal to you. I understand that."

Puck's shoulder rounded slightly and he bowed his head. "He is all I have left."

"I know what your people have suffered." Seneca eyed the distance between them. She couldn't jump far enough to force-shift him. She needed to get him closer. She needed common ground. "Do you think, when he's done, there will be peace?"

The little man looked up at her with great sadness. "I hope so."

"Did it work on Govan?" she pressed.

He shook his head. "No."

"How many lives were lost there? How many more will be lost here? Or does he only care about his own life?"

Puck winced. "He's smarter than I am. Always has been."

She smiled. "Smarter doesn't mean right. Right is what's in your heart. Think with your heart, Puck."

"My brother doesn't like it when I think." Puck moved to a small table against the wall and picked up a syringe full of something she was sure was meant for her. Seneca's pulse sped up. She didn't have much time left. He was going to drug her again. "You're right, you know. I won't join you."

Puck came to her, syringe in hand. "My brother always gets what he wants."

"I'd rather die than betray my people. I'd rather fight your brother than do what I know in my heart is wrong."

Puck held the needle inches away as he stared at her. *Please,* she thought. *Please listen.*

"We aren't different from you," she whispered, fear lacing her voice. She couldn't win this alone. She needed help. "We're all related, Puck. We all love."

Puck's face reddened as he jabbed the needle into her shoulder. "I am sorry."

◆ ◆ ◆

UVC light flooded Max's tiny cell. His head was cloudy thanks to the aftereffects of the tranquilizers. He'd been stripped down to his jeans. And Seneca was nowhere to be seen, which worried him, a lot. It occurred to him about five minutes after he woke up here that Hager didn't need him. If he had Carl, then he knew all about XCEL and the Committee, and probably a whole lot more than Max could ever give him. And Hager knew Max would never agree to work for him.

Which left only one conclusion: Hager had wanted Seneca all along. And the only reason he would want her was if he had discovered her ability to identify and force-shift Shifters.

"Shit," Max said under his breath. He should have realized

that the first time they tried to grab her in the parking garage, but he thought it was for the XCEL agent contract. He'd missed a vital clue.

Which led him to the next question: Why was *he* still alive? An excellent question, and one he'd been thinking about for the past hour. The only reason he could come up with was as incentive—to force Seneca to work for Hager. She would do it for him. He knew that without a doubt.

Max laid his head back against the cold concrete wall. He'd trusted Carl with his life and Seneca's. How could he have not seen that betrayal? And now Seneca would be at Hager's beck and call, and Max would be her motivation. He clenched his fists tightly at the thought of Seneca bound and broken. He'd rather die than reduce her to that.

He studied the cell again. Four solid concrete walls. One small door bolted shut. UVC light overhead, ten feet up and protected by thick glass. He'd already tried to smash the door in his human form with no success. The light was too high to reach and there was no way to destroy the UVC bulb. If only he could shift, he was certain he'd be able to get through the door.

But if he shifted under the UVC light, he could die right here and Hager would live on. He'd never attempted to shift in the UV rays of daylight. On the other hand, Shifters had an uncanny way of adapting to their changing environments. Maybe he'd be the lucky one. Besides, he only needed to be alive long enough to save Seneca.

Max looked up at the light. He had two choices: Take his chances to shift and save Seneca, or sit here and be used to control her.

Max got to his feet and felt something in his pocket. He reached in and found Ell's necklace. It spun on the chain, its inner light brilliant. Ell had always believed in hope, blindly and without reservation. A crazy faith that he never understood. And she always had faith in him, even when he didn't.

Noko's words echoed in his mind. *You have a purpose here. Listen carefully, and you will find it.*

He clenched the necklace in his fist. He'd found it.

Max closed his eyes and concentrated on every cell of his being. He thought how it would feel to fly, high above like an eagle, seeing a perfect Earth. He dredged up tiny scraps of hope from the people he cared about. He prayed to a god he didn't have.

And made his choice.

CHAPTER
TWENTY-FOUR

Seneca awoke in the center of a low, underground chamber. She lifted her heavy head. Through the drug-induced fog, she saw a half dozen Shifters lining the walls and chatting among themselves.

Straight ahead was a distinguished forty-something man in a gray suit sitting in a leather chair with his legs crossed, watching her. *Hager*. Behind him was Puck, quietly staring at the floor.

She looked around for Max but didn't see him. The fog dissipated a little more, and she took a split-second inventory of herself. Rope bound her hands on her lap, and each of her feet was tied to a chair leg. Aside from the drug hangover, she appeared injury-free. So far.

She was still underground, in a low-arched wine cellar about thirty feet wide and longer than she could see. Racks of wine hugged the walls and created partitions down the length of the wide tunnel. No windows and no doors in sight. She couldn't turn her head to see anything behind her because it felt like it would fall off.

"Welcome back to the living," the man in the gray suit said. The room became noticeably quieter as every head turned to him. He stood and approached her. "The name is Hager. Welcome to my humble abode."

"Fuck you," she whispered, her throat raw.

One eyebrow cocked. "How eloquent."

"Okay, try this. Fuck you, you miserable piece of shit. Better?"

He laughed. "You are exactly how I imagined. I have an offer for you."

Go to hell, dickhead, she thought as she tried the ropes, but they were nice and tight. Her limbs felt tired and sluggish. If she had better control, she'd rush Hager, taking the chair with her. Then she'd force-shift his ass, maybe a few times. She'd never attempted that, but who knew? It might even kill him. That'd be worth the price of admission alone. Right now, though, she needed more time to recover.

Hager continued. "As you may be aware, we are creating a consortium of Shifters to protect ourselves."

"That's bullshit. You're building an army."

He ignored her and waved to the others. "These are my borough lords."

She scanned the group of men, who stared stoically at her. All Shifters. All looking perfectly human and normal. "And here I thought you guys just wanted world peace."

"Peace takes too long on your planet. So we've decided to do it our own way," Hager answered. "And we could use someone with your talents to make this transition of power a more pain-less process."

"Transition of power. Wow, you make it sound so easy."

"I'm giving you a wonderful opportunity," he said. "And of course, you would have special privileges."

She shook her head slowly. "What could you possibly give me to make me even think about working for you?"

"Max Dempsey. He's here. And he's alive. For now."

The blood froze in her veins, clearing her head with remark-able speed.

"On the other hand, if you refuse," Hager continued, "then we would have no choice but to terminate him."

It shouldn't have surprised her that he'd use Max to force her to work for him. She cast a look at Puck, but he just pressed his lips together and looked down at the ground. "And what would we be doing in your organization?"

Hager smiled. "Max would be protecting you. I wouldn't want to take any chances with your precious gift."

Her gift. Ah, all her brain cells clicked in unison. And that explained why she was alive and why he wanted her to join him.

Hager crossed his arms over his chest. "You can force Shifters to shift against their will."

There was a collective gasp from the Shifters lining the walls. So Hager hadn't told them. *What else hasn't he told them?* she won-dered. It might be worth finding out.

She laughed lightly. "That's impossible. No one can do that."

"You can."

Seneca looked at the closest borough lord, a handsome, thirty-something guy with short brown hair and a deep chin dimple. He looked like a stockbroker. "Sounds crazy to me. Do you believe him?"

The dimple guy gave her a cocky smirk. "He's the boss."

"Yes, he is," she said. "After all, he got you this far, right? You *all* owe him. He saved your asses when he found a ship to leave Govan. He crashed the ship on this perfect planet with the perfect race to replicate. I mean, talk about lucky."

She watched Hager's eye twitch as she continued. "Because none of this would have happened if the Shifters weren't betrayed on Govan. You could have stayed there with your families, happy and lazy. Mowing your lawns on the weekends, working those day jobs to buy ponies and pizzas. But then there was the traitor, the one who turned in your wives and your kids to the government. Who fed the genocide."

Seneca sensed the change in the room as the Shifters began to frown. She leaned toward dimple guy. "Who'd you lose?"

"That's enough," Hager said tightly.

The Shifter squinted back at her. "What are you saying?"

She rolled her shoulders. The fog from the drug was wearing off nicely, which was good because things were about to get really interesting. "I'm just pointing out the odds, that's all. Now you have a chance to start over again, with Hager here as your king." Then she smiled at him. "Maybe Hager is the lucky one."

The Shifters were all staring at Hager, thinking. Thinking was good. It took time, and time was what she needed. Seneca placed her feet firmly on the hard floor. Hager stood six feet from her. If only she could get him to move one or two steps closer.

Hager glared at her. "Don't listen to her. She's just trying to save herself."

"You should know," she said with a smile. "That's what you do best. Right, Puck?"

Every Shifter turned to Puck, who was watching her and frowning deep in thought. Then Hager stepped in and blocked out his brother. His face flushed with fury. "He's an imbecile."

One more step and he'd be within reach. "Tell them the truth, Puck. They deserve to know what happened to their families. Who betrayed them to the Govan government. Who orchestrated their escape. Who stranded them here with no options but to work for him?"

Hager pulled out a gun. "Your services are no longer required."

Hager aimed the gun at her head. Time was up.

A small voice arose, laced with a thick Irish accent. "Hager did it."

Her relief was shattered by a flash of light, and Seneca closed her eyes, bracing for the bullet. Suddenly, she was yanked by her shoulder and hurtled against the wall, chair and all—amid a chaotic roar of yells and destruction. It took her a moment to realize that she wasn't dead, only that the lights had been knocked out.

The chair had broken in half, and she struggled to kick loose of it. She managed to free herself and rolled to her knees to find mass pandemonium, furniture splintering and bottles smashing. Shifter shadows collided—some slashing, some running. One shadow looked familiar, and her chest tightened when she realized it was Max.

He was alive.

Then gunshots filled the air. She hit the floor as bullets ricocheted around her and voices yelled, "XCEL!"

✦ ✦ ✦

XCEL agents flooded in behind Max, following his lead as they rushed the room. He hadn't expected to find Carl leading them here to wage war against Hager. They weren't even upset to see him in Shifter form. All he cared about was that they were here. Amid the bedlam, he tried to reach Hager, but there were too many Shifters in the way. Max slashed at a Shifter's face and he dropped in his tracks.

Max looked up and saw Hager escape down the tunnel. He cast a quick look at Seneca. She looked dazed but safe, and XCEL would protect her. He pushed past the remaining Shifters and followed Hager through the tunnel. Hager disappeared through a doorway up ahead and Max raced through it, taking the stairs three at a time to the top. It opened to a small, decrepit office with one door that led to a shipyard—and daylight. Hager was running across the deserted yard.

Max blinked a few times to let his Shifter eyes adjust. "XCEL isn't going to like this."

Then he ran outside, just in time to see Hager duck behind a building near the water. He was still in Shifter form, and Max looked around quickly before following him. The shipyard hugged the Hudson River, and a band of buildings across the river reflected off the water. In daylight, Shifters were bound to Primary form. Max wasn't any longer, thanks to the successful shift under the UVC light, but he wasn't going to push his luck.

Max chased Hager around the corner of the building, past a stack of crates, through abandoned vehicles, and into a narrow alley. He felt the attack a split second before the crushing blow to his chest knocked him back. The cold axe head sunk deeply into him, leaving him in excruciating pain and unable to breathe.

"You ruined everything!" Hager yelled as he ripped the axe out and pulled back to swing again. He struck Max in the shoulder, and bone shattered. Max dodged the third strike, but it grazed the side of his head, sending blood everywhere and blinding him in one eye.

Pain crippled his senses as he blocked the next swing with his arm, breaking the axe handle in half. Max slashed at Hager with his other hand, shredding Hager's arm. The Shifter howled and stumbled backward, holding his arm as he turned and ran.

Max staggered to his feet and limped after him, struggling to draw air into his lungs. The wounds were deep and critical, and he realized he wouldn't be able to keep up with Hager. He could feel blood pour out, his body turn cold and slow.

Sirens invaded the shipyard, echoing between buildings. *Humans were here. Humans could see him*, Max thought. But he couldn't do anything about it as he stumbled forward. His thoughts spiraled inward, darkening along with his vision. He made it to the next corner of the building, following Hager's trail of blood. Hager wouldn't get far, not after being outed as the traitor. If XCEL didn't catch him, the Shifters would.

Max kept moving, doggedly tracking Hager. His only regret would be that he wouldn't see Seneca again. He envisioned her face in his mind, felt her warmth in his dying heart and fresh regret in his soul.

Shouts rang out behind him and feet pounded toward him. He should shift. He should do it now before it was too late. Then he heard voices up ahead, arguing, and he leaned against the building for support. He moved forward to get closer, barely feeling his feet on the ground. The figures of two Shifters appeared.

"Get out of my way, Puck!" Hager yelled at a much-larger Shifter blocking the alleyway between the buildings.

The other Shifter shook his head. "She was right. You don't want peace. You never did."

"Fuck her, she's nothing," Hager growled.

"Like me?" Puck replied. "You used me. You lied to me like you did everyone."

"So what?" Hager said.

"I'm your *brother*."

"Right now, you're in my way." Hager lunged at him. "Now, move—"

The larger Shifter grabbed him, spun him around, and broke his neck so fast that Max almost missed it. Then he let Hager drop. For a minute, Max just stared at his sworn enemy's dead body. Hager, the killer of his wife, the betrayer of everything he held sacred, was finally dead. And Max felt nothing. No relief, no joy, no resolution.

The only thing in his mind was Seneca's face fading away.

◆ ◆ ◆

"We found him, but he's in bad shape," Carl said to Seneca as they ran side-by-side through the shipyard that had become a circus of law enforcement, bystanders, and media. Shifters in Primary form were dead or dying following the assault. TV and police helicopters hovered over the scene, bringing the horror to the unsuspecting public.

Her legs were like rubber, sabotaged by the fear that she was too late. Carl yelled over the racket. "I should have clued you both in about the double cross, but I couldn't risk Hager finding out. I couldn't trust anyone."

"Forget it," she said. "You did the right thing bringing XCEL in. Just how bad is he?"

"Very, I'm afraid," Carl said as they turned a corner and slowed at a cordoned area. Seneca ducked under the tape and pushed past Witley and the other XCEL agents standing guard over Max in Shifter form. He was stretched out on the dock in a pool of blood with Apollo beside him.

She fell to her knees, horrified at his condition. There was so much blood, everywhere—his chest, his shoulder, his face. She put her hands on him, not knowing how to make it stop.

She looked up at Apollo. "Can you do anything?"

"I tried, but . . ." Then his voice trailed off, and he just looked at her, his expression grim. Her heart sank.

"Seneca," Max whispered.

"I'm here. Just hold on." She pulled her shirt off and shoved it into his gaping chest cavity. It was soaked in seconds and helplessness gripped her. "Help me, Max. Tell me what you need."

His eyes opened and focused on her with obvious effort. "I'm sorry."

She felt her eyes burn as she pressed against the wound, but it didn't seem to be making any difference. "Next time, duck."

"Won't be a next time, Seneca."

Tears filled her eyes. "Just shut up and help me here."

His eyes closed. "I love you."

"Fine, good. Now heal yourself so we can live happily ever after."

He didn't reply, and she knew he couldn't heal this. It was too much. She was going to lose him. Panic laced her words. "Max, can you hear me? You have to concentrate."

"Change me back to human."

She blinked at him in disbelief. "What?"

He labored for every word. "I don't want to die like this. Force-shift me."

Her hands were in blood up to her wrists. "No, you need to stay in Shifter form so you can heal. Apollo, give me your shirt."

Max gasped for air. "Please, Seneca. Let me die as a human. Do this for me."

Apollo handed her his shirt, and she pressed it to Max's chest. It was instantly soaked, worthless. She sobbed, her heart breaking into a million pieces.

"Now," he said weakly. "Now, Seneca."

He was slipping away from her. She couldn't deny him. Tears streamed down her face as she called upon her ancestors and her god for strength and courage, hope and faith.

Just this once, she prayed, *just this once give me what I need. I understand now. I believe.*

"Stay for me," she whispered to Max.

Then she placed her bloodstained hands over the wounds where his life force was seeping out. She heard air rattle in his lungs, felt him seek peace.

She closed her eyes, let the power flow through her hands, and said, "Heal."

TWENTY-FIVE

Max floated in and out of consciousness for what seemed like an eternity. Every time he surfaced, Seneca was there. Her voice eased the pain, her scent healed him, her warmth gave him tranquility. She talked to him, telling him the latest news, reading from the newspapers, and encouraging him to get better.

In his mind's eye, he could see the turmoil the revelation of the Shifters' presence was causing. The story had broken, and the shock to humanity was cataclysmic. There were government hearings and finger-pointing. The international community was terrified. XCEL was under scrutiny, and the nebulous Committee had been disbanded. There were alien haters and doomsday believers who proclaimed the end.

Then Seneca would tell him that there was also hope. About the people who just wanted answers and knowledge, who were willing to listen. Government officials who supported a dialogue and cooperation with the Shifters.

She talked about her past and her fears. Her grief over losing her parents, and the anger she'd never quite relinquished until now. About the healing power she'd been given and how she wanted to use it for something good, to treat and cure his people. *His* people.

She told him stories of Noko and the Iroquois. How they had once flourished here, living off this great land, before the Europeans came. How they were betrayed, persecuted, and forced to give up their lands. They fought long and hard, but lost. Yet they stayed strong, their culture survived, and they remained tied to the place they loved.

Her stories about the Sky Woman and the Eagle who came to the people soothed his thoughts. Legends of fire and earth, and how this world and its people were all connected filled his mind and soul.

He listened and healed, Seneca's whispers keeping him anchored in the sea of darkness and light that he drifted through. When he felt his worst, her healing touch would stop the pain. When he lost his way, her voice would lead him back. When he wanted to give up, she reminded him of all he had to live for.

◆ ◆ ◆

Seneca clutched Noko's diary to her chest, feeling the strength it always gave her. The night was cold and clear, and the moon had relinquished its station to the stars. Bright and twinkling in the sky, they danced as they had for millions of years, even before there were people to see them.

Here in the northernmost tip of New York State, the night was hers once again, just like it had been when she grew up here. It was quiet beside the frozen Deer River behind her aunt and uncle's house. Fresh snow blanketed the ground and clung to the tree branches. The tall pine trees swayed gracefully. The air was clean and crisp as she drew it into her lungs. And in the silence, everything made sense.

She closed her eyes and prayed that her love would be enough to heal Max. She believed it, but did he? After all he'd been through, could he believe in anything?

The past few weeks had both drained and tempered her. Bringing Max here to recover was a gut decision that she didn't regret. He seemed to improve every day, but he had been awake only long enough to eat and drink. He could be like that forever. And if he was, she'd be here with him. Nothing was going to take her away, not XCEL, not the madness or fear that gripped the country.

Noko was here along with her relatives. Family ties, unconditional love. This was her home now. They'd have to drag her cold, dead body from this place.

A crunch of snow startled her, and she dropped the book, spun around, and pulled her gun from her coat in one swift movement. Max stood behind her, smiling. His Shifter shadow was whole and strong.

The relief and shock was so powerful, her thoughts jumbled over one another. He was awake. He was walking. He was in human form for the first time since Hager's death. He'd shifted himself.

She holstered the gun. "You're lucky I didn't shoot you."

"That would be a shame, considering how much time you spent healing me," he replied.

His voice sounded good, and she was suddenly on the brink of tears. All the emotions she'd kept deep inside while she tended to him began to surface, one after another in powerful waves.

Max walked up to her, limping a little, and retrieved Noko's book from the snow. He opened it up and paged through it. Then he looked up to meet her gaze, his silver eyes the most beautiful thing she'd ever seen.

"You read this to me," he said softly.

"Yes," she whispered. "You remember?"

"I remember everything," he said. There was so much understanding and tenderness in his expression. "Every word you said, everything you did."

Tears were streaming down her face, and she couldn't stop them. "I love you."

Max reached out and gently touched her cheek with his fingertips, tracing the trail of tears, looking awestruck. "I know."

"Is it enough?" she asked, her voice cracking. "I need to know if my love is enough."

Time froze as Seneca watched Max. She'd put it out there, her heart and her soul.

Max moved closer and put one warm palm around her neck as he kissed her tenderly. Her fear fell away with each brush of his lips. Finally, he put his forehead against hers. "It was always enough. More than I deserved. I should have told you, but I just couldn't accept it then."

"And now?" she asked.

His eyes shone iridescent in the night as he peered into hers. "Now I'm all yours. For good or bad. This won't be easy."

"Oh please," she said with a little laugh, and wrapped her arms around his neck. "I live for danger."

He smiled and bent to kiss her. "Then you've come to the right man."

Turn the page for a preview of
C. J. Barry's next novel in the series . . .

The Body Thief

Coming soon from Berkley Sensation!

"Next time, I use the valet service," Cam muttered to herself as she dragged her suitcase to her car on the fourth level of the self-parking garage. The Atlantic City morning sun gleamed across car hoods and smooth concrete in the open garage. It was bright and quiet, and a long freakin' way from the hotel and casino.

It was her own fault. She should have opted for valet parking, but then again, she was trying to be a normal human being. Blending in with the locals was an important part of her modus operandi. Swoop in, make tons of money off the casinos, and sneak out quietly. It'd worked for the past year, and unless proven otherwise, she was sticking with it.

She finally reached her Honda Accord and opened the trunk. As she threw her suitcase in the back, a prickle of foreboding spread across her body. In a split second, her senses heightened.

Footsteps shuffled behind her—three, maybe four, humans. Pant legs of men's suits brushed together. No talking, moving fast. Her nose picked up aftershave and sweat, definitely male.

Maybe they were looking for her, maybe not. She wasn't taking any chances. Slowly, she bent over her suitcase and reached inside the outer pocket for her Glock 17 9 mm. It was small, but a gun was a gun in close quarters. She kept her hand and the gun out of sight inside the trunk and turned her head just enough to pick the men up in her peripheral vision.

Three humans, one in front in a gray suit, two behind wearing military street clothes and carrying assault rifles. Yup, they were definitely here for her.

She had one second to weigh her options—make a run for it or stand and fight. Cam smiled. She'd never been one to run. After all, there were only three of them. She'd bet on those odds any day.

She stood up, keeping the gun out of their line of sight and slipping it into the back of her jeans as she turned around to face them, then tried to look as innocent and naïve as possible.

The suit stopped ten feet away, and she inhaled a quick breath when she met his eyes for the first time in bright daylight. Deep brown, confident, and focused. Nice, aside from the predatory gleam. The other two men regarded her with dutiful intensity. She could handle them. This one was different from your run-of-the-mill human, which intrigued her.

He said, "I'm special agent Griffin Mercer, working for the local extraterrestrial law enforcement agency."

Her pulse jumped. XCEL agents. Shapeshifter hunters. That explained all the guns.

"You're under arrest," he added smoothly.

"I'm sorry, I think you have the wrong person," she blurted, her eyes widening in horror. It was a damn fine acting job, if she did say so herself.

While she talked, she glanced around the parking garage for security or any guests. She noticed the black van parked two spots down. That was how they'd snuck up on her. They'd planned this, and probably shut down the entire garage. Plus she was alone, and it was daytime. Daytime was a problem for a shapeshifter.

Mercer said, "Today, you're Camille Solomon. Alien shapeshifter, twenty-eight years old, five foot five inches tall, no permanent residence, fake identity, you make your money by cheating casinos, and there's a gun tucked against the small of your back." Then he smiled. "How am I doing?"

Not bad, she conceded. "I'm five-six."

"I'll note that in your file," he said, and his smile vanished. "Throw the gun in the trunk, please."

The van pulled up behind him, and every molecule in her body aligned for battle. She could see a driver, and a passenger who jumped out and opened the back doors. That made five. The odds were stacking against her fast.

"What am I under arrest for?" she said. "Being different?"

A hint of anger crossed his features, ever so lightly. But she saw it.

"Cheating the casino. Federal offense."

She laughed at the irony. "Right, like the casino doesn't cheat anyone."

"They tell you the odds. It's all legal and everything," he said, just a little too smugly. "Gun in the trunk."

Damn, how had she tipped them off? She was very good at cheating. Like, the best. She mentally shook her head. It didn't matter how they knew, and she needed to focus. It was time to get this show on the road. She had a dinner date in Soho tonight.

"Of course," she said. "Anything for XCEL."

Mercer's eyebrows rose a fraction, but he didn't respond to her acknowledgment of his agency. She knew all about XCEL and their weapons against Shifters—disrupters with localized effects, UVC grenades that mimicked the sun's rays to prevent shapeshifter transformations, and tranquilizers that no one ever woke up from.

Fortunately, she didn't see any of those weapons, just assault rifles. Not that that wasn't bad enough.

And then every rifle was pointed at her as she reached around and tugged the Glock out of her jeans. She held it out in front of her with two fingers on the gun butt.

"You want it," she said to Mercer. "Come and get it."

His eyes narrowed dangerously. "Trunk. Please."

"Here," she said. "*Please*."

"Trunk," he repeated, more firmly this time.

She smiled. "Have it your way."

Cam turned and hurled the gun against the open trunk top with all her might, which, considering she was a shapeshifter, was pretty mighty. It bounced off the metal and fired indiscriminately.

Every man ducked, which gave her the split second she needed to shift into Primary form. A collective gasp arose once she'd transformed.

Surprise, she thought at the looks of disbelief on their faces.

And then everything moved really fast. Someone shot at her. She thinned her molecular structure, and the bullets passed through harmlessly. Her form remained vaporous but whole, prepared for anything else they might throw at her.

"Don't fire!" Mercer yelled. "We want her alive!"

She thinned her structure even more and "popped" through the thick air, re-forming in front of the men with the rifles. She grabbed both their rifles and jammed the butts to their heads, knocking them out in unison.

Someone screamed, "Get the disrupter!"

She popped to the van and wrenched an agent out of the back by his belt, tossing him across the garage's concrete floor. He rolled a few times, bounced off a support column, and didn't move. The driver came around the corner with a disrupter, and she kicked it out of his hands. It hit the ceiling and broke into pieces.

Then he had the nerve to get all pissy and reach into his jacket for a gun. She grabbed his forearm and broke it with a loud snap. He yelled, dropped to his knees, and cradled his arm with his other arm as she kicked him in the face. He flipped backward and landed ten feet away.

Then Cam turned to find Mercer holding the disrupter. Everyone else was down, and she didn't see or hear reinforcements. Too bad for them.

"That's quite a trick you have," he said. "Shifting in daylight."

She took a step toward him, wary of the disrupter. It wouldn't slow her down for long, but it *would* hurt like hell. "I find it comes in handy, especially since Shifters aren't supposed to do that. Keeps you guys on your toes."

"We just want to talk to you."

She laughed. "Right. And the rifles and disrupter are, what, conversation pieces?"

He pursed his lips. "I know you don't trust us—"

"Why would I?" she snapped. "XCEL has spent the last two years hunting us, freezing us, killing us, and moving the lucky ones to prisons."

"They aren't prisons," he said. "They're safe zones."

Now she was getting mad. The disrupter would hurt for a moment, but it would totally be worth it to kick his ass. "When you lock someone up and don't let them leave, that's a prison. Even for humans."

"You're not human," he said, challenge in his eyes.

That did it. Cam popped a split second before he dropped the rifle. When she re-formed beside him, he gripped her arm. Shocked by his speed and strength, she froze. How did he know where she was going to re-form?

She tried to strike him, but her arms wouldn't move. In fact, nothing would move. She stared at him in disbelief and panic. What was happening to her?

"I have a few tricks of my own," he said softly.

Then he jabbed a tranquilizer dart into her arm. The tranquilizer swamped her senses, and she couldn't do anything to fight it. Her body simply wouldn't respond, and it occurred to her that he was the reason.

Just before she blacked out, she heard him say, "Sorry about this."

◆ ◆ ◆

Griffin stood on the safe side of a bulletproof, shatterproof, Shifter-proof glass wall and watched his captive sleep. She hadn't moved since they'd dumped her on the bed in the holding cell two hours ago.

Her Primary form was a charcoal black humanoid-like body that was just female enough to be interesting. Her face was more delicately featured than the male Shifters he'd seen, her body leaner, and her frame tall and leggy. In Primary form, shifters looked like blank canvases, and they were. All they needed was a little bit of DNA to replicate any human they wanted.

The door behind him flung open.

"For Christ's sake, what were you thinking?" Griffin's boss yelled, loud enough to shake the long glass. "You think that tranquilizing her is going to help our cause? Did you not understand your orders?"

Griffin didn't look at Roger Harding. "I understood them."

His boss stood next to him, his cologne sucking up all the good oxygen. He wore a black suit, as always, along with a black tie and black shoes to go with his black personality.

"Those orders came from the President. Do you want to be the one who tells him that our one chance of protecting this country was blown because you couldn't apprehend one shapeshifter without incident?"

Griffin responded calmly, "No sir, I wouldn't."

"Then what was the fucking problem?" Harding said, his voice getting higher by the minute. If Griffin was at all lucky, Harding would have a heart attack right then and there. He waited, but it didn't happen. Maybe next time.

"We didn't have a choice. She shifted."

Harding frowned. "You were supposed to prevent that from happening. You blew the operation—"

"She shifted in broad daylight," Griffin amended.

Then Harding put his hands on his hips. "Bullshit. Shifters can't do that."

"She can. Ask the team. I don't know how, but she converted completely in a millisecond. All her abilities were full-strength. It didn't slow her down at all."

"Christ, what next with these damn things?" Harding said, running his hand through his hair. He stared at her through the glass. "Has anyone else reported that ability?"

"No," Griffin said. "Obviously, she's more special than we originally thought. It will certainly work to our advantage."

Harding sighed. "Well, that's just ducky. But we can't force her to work with us, and this was not a good takedown."

Griffin took offense to that but didn't say so. The fact was, the takedown had gone as well as it could have. Everyone survived. Camille Solomon had been captured unharmed and was recovering nicely. And no one outside of XCEL even knew it had happened. It couldn't have gone better. Except the part where he tranquilized her.

Harding asked, "So how do you intend to guarantee her co-operation now?"

"We have plenty of motivation for her."

"Those motivations better be bulletproof, Mercer," Harding muttered.

They were. Griffin hadn't spent the last month tracking her for nothing. Hadn't spent hours going over her file, watching her on video, and tracking her movements and every single one of her identities. He knew more about her than she probably knew about herself.

Harding asked, "You're positive that you can handle her? If she gets off your leash and does something stupid, it's my head that will roll."

Griffin could always count on Harding to cover his own ass. "I'm positive."

For a moment, Harding just stood there staring at him, and Griffin knew he was considering putting another agent on this case. Someone who didn't drink too much, who followed orders to the letter, and who would kiss his uptight ass. Well, screw that. Griffin wasn't the perfect agent, but he was for this case. And that was why Harding hated him.

"Let me know when she wakes up," Harding said as he turned to leave.

Griffin smiled. Right. "Yes, sir."